THE BRAES OF HUNTLY

THE THIRD BOOK IN THE HIGHLAND BALLAD SERIES

KRISTIN GLEESON

Published by An Tig Beag Press

Cover design by JD Smith Designs

ISBN:
978-0-9956281-2-0

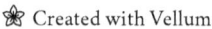 Created with Vellum

CHAPTER 1

The arrow whizzed by Abby's ear and lifted a curl that had dried tightly after the morning's rain. Before she could open her mouth to shout a warning, her father, Calum, had dismounted and pulled her from her horse, his sword drawn and his eyes scanning the landscape around him.

"I thought this was your family's land," said Abby in a soft whisper.

"It is," he said darkly.

He frowned at Jeannette, the sturdy French woman who might have been excellent at scything grass, scrubbing floors and passable as Abby's maid, but was not a horsewoman. She'd promptly fallen from her little highland pony in fright and now lay moaning on the track, complaining of an injured leg.

Abby made a move to go to Jeannette, but her father stopped her, his eyes narrowed. He drew a dagger and handed it to her. Surprised, she took it. It was the first time he'd acknowledged that she might have some idea how to use it since she and Iain had rescued him over a month ago. She shoved the thought of Iain from her mind. It was too painful right now. A month and more gone by and no word. Nothing.

Calum scanned the area again. The track bordered a woodland. It was from there the arrow had come. At least she thought so, and judging from her father's careful scrutiny, he did as well. He had the horses and pony in between them and the woodland. A moment later, several horsemen emerged from the wood and headed in their direction.

Calum studied the figures, tightened his jaw and pressed his lips into a smile. She gave him a quizzical look and turned to look at the men. Some were dressed in unfamiliar livery and carried a variety of weapons including bows, spears, daggers and swords. The two not wearing a livery were richly dressed, and as they drew closer, Abby noted they were also young and extremely handsome.

"Do you know them?" she asked. She went over to Jeannette and knelt beside her. Other than a bruised dignity and possibly a bruised thigh, Jeannette seemed unharmed.

"Nay, but I can hazard a guess as to their identity." Calum walked from behind his horse and slowly sheathed his sword.

"Who do you think they are?" she asked, losing patience.

"The two richly dressed boys are my nephews. Or my great nephews, to be precise."

She stared at the two young men, surprised. She knew she shouldn't be, but after years of thinking she had no family at all other than her father, here she was, confronted with two—what were they? Cousins.

She stood up slowly, helping Jeannette who clung to her arm, a dead weight. Abby glanced down at Jeannette and realised she still had the dagger in her hand. With Jeannette safely on two feet, she handed the dagger back to her father and he replaced it at his side.

She took a moment then to smooth her travel stained riding gown and check that her hair wasn't too wild after the hasty dismount. Except for the usual stray curls that always seemed to escape, the bulk of her hair was safely tucked in the dark velvet hood she wore.

She studied the approaching men. Her cousins. It seemed strange to think of them in that way, if indeed they were her cousins. But as they approached she could find no cause to doubt it. She could see the hair on both, glinting red gold in the sun. Her hair. The shape of the face and something in their bearing reminded Abby of her father.

They drew up in front of her and her father. The taller and broader of the two swept off his hat and bowed slightly from his horse.

"Greetings," he said in English. "May I offer you welcome to the Gordon lands." He spoke in clipped tones, with only a little trace of any accent.

Calum swept off his bonnet and bowed. "I thought the 'welcome' had already been given. My daughter's ear nearly found itself reshaped," he said.

The young man turned to eye Abby with interest, his expression only faintly curious. Beside him, his slimmer and presumably younger, brother stared at her with remarkable large blue eyes, unlike his companion's striking hazel eyes. His hand rested on his sword, poised and ready.

"Forbye, there's little need for alarm," said Calum said to the younger of the two. "Your cousin wilna harm ye. Unless ye give her cause."

The younger of the young men stiffened, his eyes taking on a deadlier look. "Cousin? What is this? We know naught of such a cousin."

"John, leave this to me," said the older one. He gave a slow smile and turned it full force on Abby. "Forgive my younger brother. He can be overly eager at times. And I cannot think for the life of me why he would object to any claim of relationship to one as lovely as you." He gave another bow, slight this time and directed at Abby. "I am George Gordon, the eldest son of the Earl."

"Well, nephew," said Calum. "I'm glad tae see ye're mending your manners. I am Calum Gordon and this is my daughter, Abby, and her servant. Though by rights ye should be escorting us tae a proper welcome and leave the questions for later."

George gave him an amused look that didn't reach his eyes. "Of course…uncle? My apologies again. And for the unfortunate incident with the arrow. We were out hunting and arrows were loosed. One was sent mistakenly in your direction."

"Oh aye," said Calum. "I would omit that fella from your hunt in future since he obviously suffers from poor eyesight. Either that, or he doesna ken the difference between a horse and a boar. I presume that's what ye were hunting in the woods?"

"Yes," said John, his voice stiff. "One of the men was over eager. There was no harm intended, I assure you."

"Yes, well. Maybe we'll save that for another day. For now, I would trouble ye for an escort tae the castle and a word with your mother, or your father if he is at home."

"Father is at court, of course," said George.

"Of course," said Calum.

"But we will happily escort you to the castle and offer you hospitality. Any hope for the charming company of your daughter is enough inducement to accompany you anywhere."

"Indeed?" said Abby. "You speak very prettily, my lord."

Abby had viewed the whole exchange with growing puzzlement and alarm, too stunned to say much. Her father had called George "nephew" and he, in turn, had referred to him as "uncle", albeit with a great amount of scepticism. But George had mentioned his father was an earl. Did that mean her father was also related to an earl? There were so many unanswered questions.

George studied her anew. "You inspire such speech, cousin.

And your own speech, do I hear trace of an accent? Have you been abroad?"

"You have a good ear," she said, resisting his probing. She tried for a different subject. "Are you a musician?"

He tilted his head. "I am, but nothing compared to John here. I only dabble in it. My time is taken up so much with my duties that I find l can only enjoy others playing on occasion."

"Perhaps I will hear you play." Abby tried to maintain a casual manner, but her words came out stiff amid the underlying tension in the air.

"We'll no be playing much if we dinna bestir ourselves," said Calum, with studied good humour. "Darkness is falling and there's every chance that that boar ye were hunting will show his face and gore us all tae death."

George and John gave a polite laugh, but the point was made. Their story about the boar was not believed.

They rode on mostly in silence, except for George dispatching one of the men ahead to alert the castle to their arrival. Abby considered her new relatives. Where did her father figure in all this? She tried to remember what she knew of titled members of the Gordon clan. Her knowledge wasn't large, but there were few candidates. She added to it the numerous times people had asked her if she was related to the Earl of Huntly since her arrival in Scotland and it didn't take long to confirm what she'd just heard.

She looked over at her father, studying his face and those of her newly met "cousins". There was no doubt, the resemblance was there. But with her recent knowledge that her father's light-hearted lothario attitude was merely a ruse to cover a deadly acuity that served him in his years spying for Queen Mary, anything was possible. Was her father exploiting a likeness and a distant connection to gain some end? Something beside his spoken desire to find her a home safe from the tentacles of those that wished to entangle her in the plots at the French court?

It was when they drew in sight of Huntly Castle that it became clear to Abby that the Earl of Huntly was every bit as powerful as she'd suspected. She knew he was close to Marie of Guise, the Dowager Queen and current regent along with some of the noblemen. Was he one of the noblemen? Looking at the impressive castle clearly built for comfort as well as defence, she had little doubt the Earl was one of those noblemen. What was her father's real reason for coming here? He'd never had an interest in his relatives in all the years she'd known him. Not even when her mother left them, when she was five. So why the sudden desire to see them now?

THERE WAS no shortage of servants. From the time they arrived through the gate into the courtyard amid servants unloading carts, dogs barking from the kennels, the ringing of the smith's hammer, scent of new baked bread from the bakery house and the clanging from the weaving shed, it was clear that the household was large.

Servants took their horses and George barked a few orders. There was no doubt that he was used to command and he carried it easily. John seemed the more gallant as he led her over to the mounting block and helped her down from her horse and then turned to do the same for Jeannette. By the time they were ushered through to the hall Abby was prepared to be impressed. There was no doubting the wealth of this household.

The hall was lined with highly polished linenfold panelling. Faces with severe expressions stared out of the cluster of portraits on one wall and several tapestries depicting hunting scenes hung on the remaining walls. A great table, chairs, kists and cupboards filled the room, all made with skill that would rival anything she'd seen in the homes she'd seen in France.

Standing in the front of the room was an elegantly dressed fair haired woman of no great height and past the first flush of youth. If Abby thought her size made her easy to handle, the steely grey eyes that turned to her and her father told a different story. Two women, less elegantly dressed, but no less fashionable, stood at either side of her.

George approached the woman, swept a bow and then kissed her briefly. "Mother," he said. "I thank you for welcoming our guests so handily." He turned to Calum and Abby. "May I present my mother, Elizabeth Keith Gordon, the Countess of Huntly." He looked at his mother. "This man, or so he informs me, is my uncle. And the young lady is his daughter…my cousin?"

The Countess raised her brows. "Uncle?"

Calum bowed deeply. "Your pardon, my lady. I am Calum Gordon, son of Alexander Gordon and Elizabeth Gray. And may I present my daughter, Gabrielle."

The Countess studied Calum carefully, barely giving Abby a glance. "Yes," she said finally in a careful voice. "I see. Elizabeth Gray's son. We haven't seen you…in some time. I understood the family connection had been…."

"Severed?" said Calum, his voice bland. "Aye."

"And yet here you are," said the Countess, matching his tone.

"I have a matter to discuss with your husband," said Calum.

"I'm afraid my husband isn't here. He's at court."

"Aye, so your son told me." Calum glanced over at George, who eyed him suspiciously. "Will he be detained there long?"

Elizabeth stiffened slightly. "My husband is a man of high rank. An adviser to the Dowager Queen. His presence at the court is required for as long as she needs his services."

"Of course," said Calum. "Perhaps I might discuss the matter with ye, then. Can I impose on your hospitality in the meantime?"

"The hospitality at Huntly Castle is unrivalled," said the

Countess. "You will of course be accommodated. The orders have been given already." She gestured to the table. "Please, join John and George and have a seat. Some refreshments should be here shortly for you to enjoy while your rooms are readied. I'm afraid I must leave you for now, but rest assured I will speak with you about this matter of yours, later."

The Countess swept from the room, her ladies in tow. Abby followed her father's lead and took a seat at the long, heavy carved table. The mullioned windows gave the room an airy feel and a newly lit fire blazed in the hearth opposite.

Moments later, a plate of meat, bread and a flagon of French wine were laid on the table by two male servants. George and John sat down with her and her father, obviously hungry after their ride. John glanced across at Abby and Calum while they all ate, clearly sizing up Abby and her father. He caught her eye and smiled a little. It was genuine.

The meat was deliciously seasoned and the wine expensive and smooth. It was evident that the tastes of this household had been shaped by the Earl's time at the Paris court. Abby noted this only briefly, her mind consumed with recent events. Her father had never mentioned his father's name, or his mother's – at least not in context to his relationship to the Earl of Huntly. She still found the relationship difficult to believe.

She glanced at her father quizzically. How much more had he kept from her all these years? And why? When anyone with the slightest connection to noble blood would flaunt it widely, why had her father kept this relationship secret? Illegitimacy? Though many wore such relationships lightly, perhaps there was something unsavoury about this one.

"You've not been in these parts for some years, I take it, uncle?" said George.

Calum gave a polite smile. "That is so. It was before ye were born. Your parents were young and newlywed, I believe."

John nodded. "Much has changed since then."

"Aye. It has," said Calum. "How many of ye are there now, besides ye and your brother?"

"Too many," said John with a laugh. "There are ten of us since Thomas died four years ago. But Elizabeth doesn't live here, now. She's married to the Earl of Atholl."

"And neither of ye are married yet?" asked Calum.

George shrugged. "I've been busy. I was appointed Sheriff of Inverness this year and I've been carrying letters for the Dowager Queen."

"Following in your father's footsteps," said Calum. "Commendable."

"Have you come far?" asked George.

"Aye," said Calum. "From France."

"France? Is that where you've been biding?"

"Aye," said Calum.

Abby cast him a glance. He was giving little away and she didn't wonder at it. She wasn't certain she trusted them either.

"Have you been to court there?" asked John. "Father was there, with the Dowager Queen."

"Aye, I've been," said Calum.

John turned to Abby. "And were you there too?"

Abby gave a small smile. "Yes."

"So you're familiar with the Queen," said John.

"Aye," said Calum.

"And were you in France a while?" asked John. "I've heard nothing of any uncle biding in France."

The unspoken additional question hung in the air. Why hadn't they heard about him from their parents? Abby was interested in the answer too.

Calum regarded John carefully. "Your father and I haven't met for some time, as ye might have gathered. And we were never on the best of terms."

"And you're here seeking to mend things?" asked George politely. "I'm certain my father would be happy to receive you if he was here."

Calum gave a wry smile. "Many thanks. Your mother has been most kind."

"Father may be here in a fortnight's time. Or perhaps sooner. He has some business to attend to here," said George. "You'll stay until then?"

A liveried servant entered and bowed. "The rooms are ready for the guests, my lord," he said in a thick lowland Scots.

Calum rose and gestured to Abby to rise. "If I may beg your pardon, my daughter and I will refresh ourselves a moment in our rooms. I'm the sure the servants will have our chests there now. Would ye be so kind and tell your lady mother that if she has a moment to spare later I would be pleased tae speak with her?"

George and John rose and gave a curt bow to both Abby and Calum. "Of course," said George.

Abby and Calum followed the servant along to the winding stairs and up to the floor above. They travelled the corridor to the end, until the servant stopped in front of a door. "Your room, my lord," he said. "And your room, my lady is next door. The kists have been placed inside and your servant should be unpacking them now." He bowed again and left them.

Abby nodded and looked at her father. "I'll join you in a moment."

"There's nae need," said Calum quietly. "I'll speak with Lady Elizabeth and come to ye later."

"No, there's every need. I intend to acquaint myself with Lady Elizabeth as soon as possible. I want to determine the sort of welcome to expect." She kept her voice firm, her eyes directed on her father. She wouldn't take no. "You owe me that much."

"I'm trying to protect ye, lass, that's all."

"You'll forgive me if I question your ideas of protection," she said. "What I do appreciate is that all you're doing is your level best to keep me from Iain. And the only reason I've complied is that you promised to ensure his name is cleared of treason."

Calum gave her a tired smile. "'Tis done, lass."

"What? When?"

"I wrote the letter before we left France," he said. "I keep my promises."

Her face softened. It was most likely true. She knew that he had secret messengers and it was possible that he'd arranged for a message to be sent without her noticing it.

"So he's pardoned? Is it certain?"

"I've no had confirmation yet, but I'm sure it will be soon if it hasn't happened yet."

She allowed herself to believe it and her temper cooled. It was only for her to honour her side of the bargain and keep away from Iain. "Thank you."

She walked on towards her room and turned just before she entered. "I won't be long."

A soft sigh was all she heard from her father. She entered the room and saw Jeanette there by a large four poster bed, Abby's gowns and other items strewn across it and her chests on the floor.

Jeannette gave her a tight smile when she entered. "Well, madame," she said in rapid French. "I can only say I was giving up hope that we might stay in surroundings that are some way close to civilisation in this godforsaken country." She fingered the rich brocade coverlet. "At least they understand some luxuries." She gave a nod to the small brazier filled with coals. "Though they still have strange notions about what it means to warm a room. It is like ice in here."

Abby laughed. "Ah, you just haven't acquired the hardiness for this climate."

Jeannette sniffed. "I hope that I will never have to remain here long enough to do so, madame. I shall pray every night to the holy mother that your father will see fit to send you back to the French court soon."

"But, Jeannette, I will have no need for you if he sends me back to court," said Abby. "There are plenty of servants there. So I'm afraid if you want to remain with me you must pray that I like it here well enough to stay."

If her first few hours were any indication, except for her promise to her father, she knew that she would have done all she could to get away. She gave a deep sigh. Could she keep away from Iain when all she wanted to do was get on a horse and ride all the way to Glen Strae? Was she a woman to keep her word? A word she'd given solemnly to her father? In her heart she knew the answer.

CHAPTER 2

*A*bby entered the drawing room next to the great hall in her father's wake, steeling herself against Lady Elizabeth's manner. A large fire crackled brightly in the hearth and there was a lit brazier situated near the countess. Fresh herbs scented the air and a large array of candles gave the room a cheerful outlook. Outfitted with plenty of chairs and benches, all comfortably cushioned, the panelled room gave off an air of welcome and refinement that Abby couldn't help but appreciate.

The Countess was seated in the middle of the room with several women gathered near, chatting softly or intent on needlework. On the other side of the room some boys were gathered around a table containing a chess board, two of them seated and studying the board carefully. A young woman embroidered half-heartedly nearby in the light of a candle, while a girl, no more than eleven, read a small book intently.

Abby regarded the group with open curiosity. She could only guess that they were the large Gordon brood and the Countess's ladies assembled to greet the new guests. Or perhaps intimidate them. Abby placed a smile on her face, determined to remain unruffled by this encounter.

Calum bowed and gave Lady Elizabeth a brief greeting and Abby quickly followed suit, curtseying deeply. "My lady cousin, I thank you for this kind welcome."

Lady Elizabeth acknowledged both greetings with a nod of her head. Her jewelled hooded cap caught the light from the group of candles placed on the table near her. She had embroidery in a framed hoop on her lap. The light was softer, creating a warmer expression on her otherwise stern features. Her light hair and thin nose were reflected in the children that surrounded her.

She gestured briefly to each child, starting with the oldest to the youngest, and introduced them. "My married daughter, Elizabeth, is currently with her husband, Lord Atholl. These are my other girls, Margaret and Frances."

She pointed first to the fair haired young woman who was seated with her needlework near the chess players. She was somewhere in her mid-teens, with grey eyes and a full, sensual mouth. Presumably that was Margaret. Frances, then, must be the slim girl seated with her book. The eyes that held Abby's were a lively blue. Each Gordon girl rose and gave a quick curtsey when their names were mentioned. Abby noted the appraising looks the older daughter gave her. The younger daughter seemed happy enough to meet her new cousin and gave Abby a beaming smile. Abby returned it.

Lady Elizabeth indicated the boys gathered around the chessboard. "This is James, William and Adam, my middle boys, and here beside me are the youngest boys, Patrick and Robert."

James, William and Adam already had the family resemblance punctuated on their face along with the fair hair, though in varying shades. They studied Abby and Calum, the oldest boy, James, fingering his chess piece idly. Mischief lurked in the two youngest boys, and with only a half a head between them Abby was certain they were more allies in high jinks than enemies in this household. The middle boys held themselves with varying degrees of correctness that their years of training in the tiltyard and the care of their tutor most likely had much to do with. And of course a heavy dose from the parents, or at least Lady Elizabeth. Abby had no doubt that Lady Elizabeth was conscious of every bit of consequence she was entitled to.

Abby and her father made all the appropriate greetings and words of appreciation, though there was no discernible softening or increased warmth in Lady Elizabeth's manner. The children themselves spoke to Abby and her father with courtesy and marked interest, though no inappropriate word was said.

"George said you wished to have a word with me," said Lady Elizabeth eventually.

"Aye," said Calum. "If ye wouldna mind, I would prefer to have the conversation a bit more private." His tone was neutral, but Abby could see a trace of tension in his jaw.

Lady Elizabeth raised a brow. "Ah, indeed? And this cannot wait until tomorrow, when I would have a private moment for you in my own rooms? Now is the time I enjoy the company of my family."

"I beg your pardon for intruding on an hour that I'm certain ye hold of great importance, but it is a matter I would wish to have resolved soon. If ye will have it otherwise, I can only bow to your wishes."

"I understand there are matters about the family to resolve that you can only be anxious to deal with quickly. But you must remember...cousin," she said with an edge to her voice, "You're the supplicant here. And I am not at all certain my lord husband would even approve of your presence."

Abby glanced at her father. His expression was unreadable, but the tension in his jaw increased.

"I apologise, my lady. I will of course await your pleasure. Tomorrow it shall be." He bowed. "My daughter and I will take our leave of ye, then, so that ye may enjoy the company of your family and your companions."

Calum placed his hand along Abby's back and after a quick curtsey, she allowed him to usher her from the room. Lady Elizabeth had made no protest over their departure, but Abby was full of questions.

The questions barely waited until they were outside her father's chamber door. They'd been silent as they proceeded up the staircase and along the corridor. When her father opened his door she followed him in and closed the door behind him.

She looked at him expectantly. "Well?"

He gave her a surprised look. "I think it's time for ye to seek your rest."

"Rest can wait. Are you going to tell me what the countess meant about matters to resolve between you and the Gordon family? Why are you the supplicant?"

"Och it's too late for stories of that nature," said Calum in an amicable tone. "We'll save it for another time."

"No, you'll tell me now." Abby kept her tone forceful. "You've kept this from me for too long already. I'm tired of your evasions. What did you do that caused them to discount you?"

Calum gave a mild snort. "I'd say my biggest offence was being born. George and the others were nae too fond of my mother, or me. I was born just before my father died. So ye could say that I never knew him. The family bundled us off tae one of the remote houses and if my mother had been the lying down sort, there we would have lingered."

"So, it's true. The Earl is your brother?" asked Abby.

"Nay, lass. He's my nephew. His father, John was my brother, but he died long before I was born."

Abby blinked, trying to make sense of this. "But George, being the oldest son of John, the Earl at that time, inherited the title?"

"Aye, more or less."

"But he could have been no more than a young boy when he became Earl. How is it he had you and your mother banished?"

Calum gave a wry smile. "Well we werena banished, more like provided with alternative living quarters in the Highlands. It was comfortable and befitting my mother's station, but far enough away from court. But George's mother was a daughter of the King. From the wrong side of the blanket, but royal nonetheless. He and the rest of the family have great influence and power. I was too lowly for them."

"I gathered that," Abby said with an acerbic tone. "So, did you grow up in this remote place?"

"I was there for some years." He gave her a wry look. "Hence my speech. Eventually, though, my mother negotiated with her family tae arrange for another marriage that would be advantageous. And marry she did, tae a man that had no liking for me, nor I for him. My mother didna seem tae mind his disdain for me. She was safe and that was all that mattered." Calum shrugged. "I left as soon as I could."

"But you were at court, you said, when you met my mother. You were a musician."

"Aye, it was the music that drew me there. Cormag Kerr. I'd seen him the rare time I'd been tae court when I was young." He shook his head. "When I first heard his music I kent only that it was pure, without taint and it reached out tae me. It cared not who I was or wasn't."

Abby nodded. She knew the feeling and could appreciate what it must have been for her father, disregarded and for the most part unwanted. And she knew Cormag Kerr's undeniable talent from her own experience of him at Kilchurn Castle.

"But didn't they know you were related to the Earl? Surely he was there?"

"Aye, he was there. But he gave me nae countenance and I was happy tae keep it that way. There were a few rumours initially, but George quashed them."

"But there is enough of a resemblance…" Abby said.

Calum laughed. "Och we're all related among the nobles, one way or another. They just took me for someone's byblow. And my mother was dead by then so there was nae person willing tae deny it."

"But why now, then? Why are you choosing to renew the connection now? It's not just that you want me to stay somewhere safe is it? Surely we can find somewhere else among your connections, that network of spies you've been running for how many years?"

Suddenly Abby's frustration at the number of secrets he'd kept, the lies he'd told her welled up in her and gave heat to her words. All of her understanding of who he was and who she was formed over years had crumbled in just a matter of months, so that she was no longer sure of him, or of anything.

Her father put his hand on her shoulder and cupped her chin. "Abby, lass. Ye must believe I want only what is best for ye. Everything I've ever done, or said, has been tae protect ye. Always." He kissed her forehead. "Ye're my daughter. I'd never harm ye in any way."

Abby allowed him to take her into his arms in a comforting manner. But though his arms around her might give him some assurance, it did nothing to allay the turmoil and suspicion in her heart.

ABBY PAUSED QUIETLY OUTSIDE the door to the drawing room. The door was slightly ajar so she could hear her father's voice and Lady Elizabeth's answering murmur. She held her breath, suppressing the anger that arose. That he should discuss her with

Lady Elizabeth without her knowledge! Even though she'd suspected it was the case when she'd found his chamber empty a few moments ago, it still angered and disappointed her that her suspicions had been confirmed.

"I owe ye a great debt," said Calum.

"The understanding, of course, is that I'll undertake this only if my husband agrees," said Lady Elizabeth.

"Aye, of course. But ye say he will be here soon?"

"He will. Perhaps in a fortnight's time, maybe longer. He's meeting someone here."

"A fortnight?" Calum sucked in his breath. "I dinna think I can wait that long. Would ye be happy if the lass remained here for the time? If your husband doesna agree then I'll return as soon as I may. Ye can leave word with my man at Edinburgh."

"So you would leave your daughter here, regardless?"

"If ye permit. I must away today. Tomorrow at the latest."

"Very well," said Lady Elizabeth. "You'll explain this to your daughter before you leave." There was no question in the tone, it was an order. "I expect no problems with this, whatever the choice may be."

"I'll talk tae her," said Calum. "And there should be nae resistance if ye go with what I've outlined."

"Again, it will be as my husband sees fit, Calum. He will probably agree to your wishes, though. After all, if it is as you say, and overtures have already been made, I imagine he'll want to exert himself as little as possible."

"Good," said Calum. "I'll take my leave of ye, then."

Abby backed away from the door and looked around her. The corridor was empty but there was nowhere to hide. She quickly headed down the corridor and bore right, looking for a door other than that which led to the Hall. She located one, opened it and slipped inside. She paused on the threshold, listening for sounds of any presence and was relieved to find none. She moved forward quietly and realised it was a bedroom. The bed was draped in a rich deep velvet and brocade, the wood finely carved. Large kists and chairs were placed around the room, but there was no sign that anyone had been here recently. It was too tidy.

Suddenly, the door opened and she turned to see George, a serving girl in tow, giggling excitedly. George pulled the woman inside and kissed her roundly, not noticing Abby at first. He began to raise her skirts, biting her neck and shoulder lightly. The servant spotted Abby and her eyes widened. She pushed George off and he looked up at her, puzzled. It was then he noticed Abby. Annoyance crossed his face for a brief moment, but then his face relaxed into a grin.

"Cousin," he said easily, releasing the serving maid. "I must say I didn't think to find you in my father's bedchamber."

"Oh, I am sorry," Abby said feebly. "It's only that I seem to have lost my way."

"Easily done," said George. "It can be confusing which floor you're on, I'm sure. Your chamber you might recall, is on the floor above. You have stairs to climb, first."

Abby flushed. "Yes. I remember. I've come from there. I was looking for the kitchens. In search of breakfast." She eyed the servant. "It appears you have your own breakfast got," she couldn't help but add.

George laughed and patted the servant girl's bottom. "Thank you, Fenella That will be all."

Meg bobbed a curtsey and took her leave. When the door shut behind the servant, George moved close to Abby, took her hand and kissed it. "Perhaps we might breakfast together. It isn't often I have the pleasure of one as lovely as you to keep me company here at Huntly." His tone was playful and friendly.

Abby forced a smile and kept her own tone light. "I'm certain you could have any of the court ladies you chose."

"Ah, but this isn't the court, and the women are either too

young, or too old." He raised a hand to tweak a lock of hair that had escaped the French hood she'd hastily thrust on earlier. "And even at court you'd rival the ladies, I've no doubt."

"I thank you for the compliment...cousin."

"It more the truth than any courtly compliment," George said. He took her hand and drew her close. "Come. Will you not give your cousin a proper greeting and grant me pardon for its lack yesterday? I plead only that I was ignorant of our connection and now I would like to rectify that."

Before she could reply George leaned down and kissed her fully and deeply, his hand supporting the back of her head. Startled, she felt her mouth give way and then she pulled back, stunned and breathless.

"I-I had no idea kin greeted each other in that manner here," she said, confused. "I confess I have no great experience of family, other than my father."

George brushed her face with his hand. "I will happily acquaint you with all the ins and outs of it."

She gave a small smile. "That's very kind of you, I'm sure."

"It's my pleasure," said George. He took her hand. "I'll start by showing you where to get a bite to eat. We generally do that in the dining hall." He gave her a sly smile and raised a brow. "You know the place?"

Abby nodded and allowed him to take her out of the chamber and down along the corridor from whence she came not so long before, trying to fathom her cousin. She had little success except to note that she mustn't take him for a fool.

CHAPTER 3

*H*er father looked up when she entered the dining room. He had a plate of cheese and bread at the table in front of him and was talking with John and two of the middle boys, James and William. Margaret, the oldest daughter was seated at the table as well, but she was gazing thoughtfully out of the window, a small lump of bread in her hand.

Calum glanced behind her at George and his eyes narrowed slightly.

"I've discovered a lost sheep and have shepherded her home," said George.

John rose abruptly, greeted her. James and William followed suit, though James reddened visibly and William gave her a curious look.

"Were ye lost?" asked Calum rising slowly.

"Ah, I only lost direction temporarily," said Abby. "George was good enough to set me right."

George, still holding her hand, drew her to an empty chair and guided her to sit, his hand lingering on her back. He gestured to the table centre which was filled with plates of fowl, meat pies, bread and cheese. "What would you like, Gabrielle?"

She winced at her very French sounding name. "Please, call me Abby," she said. She caught her father's lifted brow. "All of you. It's what my father calls me."

"Abby," said John. "I like it. Are ye named for your mother then?"

Abby glanced at her father. "Er, no."

"It could only be because you looked like an angel as a babe," said George light-heartedly. "And so you remain," he added softly so only she could hear.

She felt herself blush. "I'll just have a bit of bread and cheese, if you please."

George piled her selection on a plate and set it before her. He filled a plate for himself with a meat pie and a slice of cheese and took the chair beside her.

"So uncle, are we to have the pleasure of the company of you and your daughter for a while?"

Calum gave him a tight smile. "Ye'll have my daughter's company for some while. As for me, I'm no able to tarry long."

"'Tis a pity, then," said George. "It seems we only discover an uncle then we have to lose him again. You'll return soon?"

Calum looked at Abby. "Soon. Aye."

"Fear not," said George. "She'll have my protection while you're away."

"And mine," said John. He smiled at Abby, his eyes alight.

"I hope all of ye will keep an eye on my daughter," said Calum, his tone pleasant.

Abby frowned at her father. "I'll be fine. There's no need to be minding me like I was a young child in danger of falling into a stream, or the fire in the hearth."

"Of course not," said Calum. "But there are other dangers just as threatening to a young woman." He gave George a direct look. "Some not necessarily evident, and others not physical. I just want to ensure that every care is taken for my daughter's well-being."

"Och, mother makes certain of that," said Margaret, coming out of her trance. "You've no need to worry yourself. She's a keen eye and a quick enough tongue that can keep even George in line if she wants to." She gave her brother a sweet smile which elicited a dark look from him.

Calum laughed briefly. "I am glad to hear your mother takes such an active role with all of ye."

Abby gave Margaret a grateful look. All the tension that had built since she entered the room had been dispelled with Margaret's remark. Though said in an offhand manner, Abby had no doubt as to its truth.

The rest of the meal was filled with more mundane topics and Calum seemed content to make no issue out of George's marked regard for her. It was decidedly different in tone from James's attentions which were more of an adoring puppy dog, or even John's which were gallant and heartfelt, but missing the polish of his older brother's manner. George's seemingly innocent touches of his hand resting on her shoulder or her back were charged with a sensuality that was unmistakable. Was he like this with every young woman who came his way? She hoped it might be true. She wouldn't contemplate that his attentions were other than frivolous flirting.

"Abby, Lady Elizabeth tells me there's a braw garden behind the stable. Will we walk there a while?" asked her father when he'd finished his plate.

She glanced down at the few remaining bits of cheese and opened her mouth to protest when she felt a hand brush her leg. "Yes, of course. I would love to."

She rose without looking at George, gave a small curtsey to the group and followed her father through the castle and outside. When they reached the garden he led her to a stone bench and they sat. She drew her skirts closer against the cold mist that clung to the plants. Around her were box hedges enclosing shrubs, and rows of raised beds containing a variety of flowers and herbs. The roses were long past their bloom, the gilly-flowers disappeared and only stalks remained of the carnations. Despite the wintery nature of the garden, the tang of rosemary and thyme filled the early morning air.

"Ye must have a care for George," said Calum.

Though she knew he was right it didn't help her to accept his words easily. She shrugged. "He likes women. Any women."

"Aye, and that's all the more reason tae take care."

"He's my cousin. He'd hardly do anything untoward."

"I wouldna count on it. It's best not tae trust that."

She frowned. "Then why do you leave me here, if you can see already that there are potential dangers?"

Calum took her hands and looked at them. "Ye're my daughter, I love ye and I will protect ye, whatever it takes. Even though it may no be necessarily what ye want," he added softly.

She stiffened. "What do you mean?" she said, her tone insistent.

"Abby, lass. Promise ye'll hear me out?"

"Hear you out? Why? What have you to say?"

"Just promise me ye'll do that and then ye can say tae me what ye like." He squeezed her hands.

She relaxed a little and then nodded.

Calum took a deep breath. "When ye were little, your mother and I discussed who might be a suitable match for ye." He gave a wry smile. "Even then, we could see ye'd be a handful. But we wanted someone who would be kind and understanding. Be a friend and companion as well as a husband. That's why Henri de Villiers was chosen. Your mother knew his grandfather and his father. They were both kindly men."

"Henri's mother more than made up for that," said Abby tartly.

"Aye, well. I kent only the father. And we couldna foresee that the father would die in the meantime. But Henri was kindly. And a friend."

"Yes," Abby said quietly. "Yes, he was."

"And would have made a good husband to ye if he hadn't died sae soon."

"For the few short days of our marriage he was as good a husband as he could be."

"Aye. But he's gone and it falls tae me tae uphold your mother's wish and marry ye accordingly."

"Accordingly?"

He worried his lip. "I've a few likely men in mind. Ones that are good and kind and befitting your status."

"My status?" Abby felt like an echo, but she found it difficult to believe what her father was saying. "What status is that?"

"The granddaughter of an Earl," Calum said flatly. "As such I can find a man who will have the power and influence tae protect ye as ye need."

"But I can stay here. Until it's safe."

Calum gave a sigh. "Aye and when will that be? There are dangerous men after ye. Men that have power and influence of their own. The Comte de Damville, for one."

"But they're after you, not me."

Calum shook his head. "Nay. For some reason it's ye they want as well. I mean tae put a stop to it."

"Can't I wait until then?"

"I don't know when that will be. In the meantime ye're still in danger unless I can see tae it that ye're safely wed. Lady Elizabeth has agreed to help."

Abby started to protest but Calum held up his hand. "I asked ye to let me finish." He waited a moment and she nodded. He gave a heavy sigh. "It wasna easy, the thought of giving ye up tae someone and me not here tae see that it comes out aright. So I've only two that would be a choice that I would have nae doubts about. Two kindly men who'll treat ye well. William Douglas and James Hamilton."

Abby stared at him blankly. "And just who are they?"

Calum looked down. "Two men of honour who I've known for some time."

She narrowed her eyes. "Are they part of your network?"

He looked up, startled. "Good God, no!" He calmed himself. "No. They are men I knew from court. We all served together at the battles of Haddon Rig and Pinkie Cleugh."

Abby's eyes widened. "You fought in those battles? I thought you were a musician."

Calum laughed. "Musicians can take up swords."

She stared at him hard. There it was again, something she didn't know about her father. He fought in battles with two men she'd never met or heard about. "These men are your age?"

He nodded. "Level headed and experienced. I couldn't wish any better man for your husband."

Tears filled Abby's eyes suddenly. She could think of one man. Only one man and no other. "So you would marry me off to one of these men. I get to choose?"

He nodded. "It seemed best tae gi' ye a choice if I could. They're both fine. I have no preference which one ye choose."

"How nice," said Abby caustically.

"Lady Elizabeth has consented to contact them and set up meetings with both of them," said Calum in a reasonable tone. "Once Huntly has agreed, of course. With their influence and connections the wedding can be arranged quickly and irrevocably."

"Of course." She remembered the conversation she'd over-heard and had no doubt this was the same matter. "And if he doesn't agree?" she asked, curious if he would repeat what Lady Elizabeth said.

"She will notify a designated contact. That contact will make arrangements with Douglas and Hamilton directly. The process will take longer and the wedding may not be as public or as undeniably supported by the powerful noble families at court."

Abby had a sudden hopeful thought. "And you're certain these men aren't married?"

He grinned, seemingly encouraged by the more or less compliant reaction. "I checked and made tentative overtures. They're nae married at all. Though Hamilton is a widower of some years. His wife died in childbirth. They are both from minor branches of the Hamiltons and Douglasses, but the kinship is close enough tae matter."

She was stunned that he'd put so much thought and effort into arranging her marriage without any word to her. Was he really concerned about her welfare or was it more that he wanted her safely away from Iain? She tried to think of what she could say that would make him understand how she felt, but abandoned it almost immediately. All the words had already been spoken and had made no impact. But she forced herself anyway. She had to try.

"Release Iain from his obligation to work for you and the network," she said.

Calum lifted his head and stared deeply into her eyes. His eyes filled with sadness, concern and a trace of pity. Abby stiffened, waiting for his words.

"I canna," he said. "It's no for me tae release him. Only he can do that."

"You can," she said, choking on the lump in her throat. She breathed deeply. "You can make him."

Calum shook his head. "Nay. Nor would I. It's between him

and his queen. Ye can no release a man from protecting his queen."

"Damn the queen," Abby said. "Damn her and all her stupid Scotsmen."

"Whist now," said Calum stroking her hair. "I greet for ye, lass. I do. But ye must accept it and promise me ye'll nae try tae change it. It's for the best. Trust me, I ken that well."

She looked up at his face, a tear spilling over onto her cheeks. "You put the queen before all others."

"She's the queen." Calum spoke softly. "It's an honour and duty tae serve."

"You put her above my mother." Abby said it as a statement and no denial came. She nodded heavily. "Aye. I see it now."

He drew Abby in his arms. "Ye're my child. And I will protect ye wi' my heart and my body. None can touch the love I have for ye. Even the queen." He pulled away and chucked her under her chin. "I'm leaving my best lute for ye. Ye canna measure the love I have for ye more than such a gesture as that. I'd never part wi' that for anyone."

She gave him a weak smile. "My thanks to you for that, Father. You needn't worry. I'll keep it safe."

He took her hand and squeezed it. "Come, now. Let's get in away from this cold. It's enough tae chill the dead out here, garden or no."

Abby followed him in, this man who was all that he'd just described. A queen's man and also her father who bore her great love, and desired above all to protect her. He seemed to forget though, that she was just as much her mother's daughter as her father's. And from what she knew of her mother, she had followed her own mind. Abby would do the same.

CHAPTER 4

*A*bby sat on the bed, her hand resting on the lute beside her. As promised, her father had given her his most prized lute before he'd left the day before, only hours after her conversation with him in the garden. She'd spent most of the remaining day in her chamber, pleading fatigue. Jeanette meanwhile was about her own work, restoring Abby's wardrobe to some semblance of decency, washing and mending somewhere in the depths of the castle.

It was when her father had come to say goodbye that she woke from her torpor long enough to force a smile and say her farewells as though little had changed between them. His gift of the lute she had taken with good grace and had even picked out a short tune on it for him before he left.

She took the lute up now and plucked a few strings, listening for the deep, rich resonance she knew it possessed. It was a handsome gesture, but it made up for nothing. She was still confined to this castle and the plans and designs of both her father and Lady Elizabeth. She must take care of her words and her actions, that much was clear. Not just for Lady Elizabeth but George and John. She gave a grimace. George's charm was undeniable and he knew it. But perhaps it could be used to her advantage. Perhaps she could charm him as much as he thought to charm her.

She mulled over these thoughts and continued to pick out a few tunes on the lute. The action soothed her eventually, and in time she found herself ready to face the world below. She'd sent Jeannette down to find her some food yesterday evening and this morning to avoid encountering anyone, but now she was prepared. Or at least she hoped so.

She put the lute back in its leather sack and began to stow it in the kist at the foot of the bed, but thought better of it. It might serve as a distraction for her and the others, as well as give comfort. It was better than needlework in any case.

Downstairs, she made her way to the large drawing room where Abby and her father had met the bulk of the family on the night of their arrival. Inside she found the room warm and welcoming with a healthy fire in the hearth and the sun pouring through the windows. Seated on a cushioned chair, Margaret poked idly at her needlework and in another chair Frances sat reading a book. They looked up when Abby entered.

Frances smiled and put her book down and gestured Abby to a seat. "Oh good. A perfect excuse to abandon the most boring Greek passage I have yet to read."

"Greek?" Abby asked, taking a chair next to Frances.

Frances grimaced. "Yes. Mother insists we follow the same programme of study as Queen Mary."

Abby glanced at Margaret who gave her a thin smile. "I'm not the scholar my sister is, I'm afraid. Our tutor has long since given up on me. My Latin and Greek are very limited."

"And your Spanish and Italian are appalling," said Frances with a laugh. "Though you speak French with a sauciness I can't match."

"Saucy?" asked Abby.

"Oh yes," said Frances. "You ken what I mean. She has a way

she emphasises certain words. The tone she uses, her manner. It seems so very...suggestive?"

Abby gave Frances an amused look. The child was extremely precocious for her age, there was no doubting it. She eyed Margaret's swelling bosom, more revealing than confining in her square cut bodice edged with fine seed pearls. And the full pouting lips. Abby could picture the saucy delivery of French without any effort.

"That's only because you think more on the words and getting them correct, rather than how you say them," said Margaret. She lifted her head. "You have the languages and the philosophy and all the other subjects that Mother insists upon, but you're a terrible dancer and you have the manner and grace of a bullock. I don't see that you have any hopes of becoming a skilled courtier." Her tone was matter-of-fact, though it possessed a slight air of condescension.

Frances laughed again. "And nor would I want to be. I have no desire to go to court."

"Just as well," said Margaret. She sighed. "Though why I should be forced to remain home, I cannot say. I certainly will get little enough practice refining my skills around you." She looked at Abby. "Have you been to court?"

"Yes. Briefly," said Abby.

Margaret's eyes lit up. "When? I was there years ago, before my sister Elizabeth was married, but I was barely twelve. Were you there then? I don't remember you."

"No, I was there only recently."

"Father's been to France, to the French court. With the Dowager Queen," said Frances. "We didn't get to go, though. It would have been nice to see the Queen."

"It's possible I'll be going soon," said Margaret, a pleased expression on her face. "Father said that he would ask the Dowager Queen. I'm skilled enough in courtly ways."

Abby smiled at her words and her unshakeable self-confidence. Her manner was stylish, but she was outspoken which wouldn't serve her well and though she showed bravado and a certain sense, her other qualities, that her sister called "saucy" would likely get her into trouble.

"Is that a lute in the bag? Do you play, then?" asked Margaret.

"Yes. Do you play at all?"

"Yes. My tutor instructed us. He said I have a keen ear. Frances, though, is hopeless."

"I'm not," said Frances, huffily. "It's just not something I particularly enjoy."

Abby looked down at her bag containing the lute for a moment. "Would you like to play it?" she asked Margaret.

"Yes, all right. Then you'll play a piece."

Abby withdrew the lute slowly and gave it carefully to Margaret. Margaret took it from her and handled it with confidence, settling it on her lap.

"Where's the quill?"

"I manage without one. I find the sound is different, more subtle."

Margaret raised a brow. "Really? Frances, fetch John's over there on thon table."

Frances frowned but did as she was told, placing the quill in Margaret's hand. She took up the quill, strummed it carelessly, then twiddled a peg to fine tune it and Abby tried not to wince at her action. Margaret plucked a few notes with the quill and began a short piece.

Margaret played with some skill, Abby was glad to note, so she relaxed a little and listened with interest. It was a lively piece requiring some proficiency and she managed the intricacies well enough, though with a little impatience at times. She ended the piece with a flourish, looked up and smiled, pleased.

Abby nodded. "Lovely. Would you play another?"

Margaret lifted her brow. "Of course. Do you have a preference? I know some of the songs from court. Perhaps you'd like one of those."

"Yes, I would love to hear one," said Abby.

"Not the naughty one," said Frances. "Mother wouldn't approve."

Margaret gave a slight toss of her head. "I'll play what I choose. And they're all sung at court, so there can be no objection."

"Not everywhere in the court, I'll wager," said Frances primly. "Despite what Master Cameron says."

Margaret's nostrils flared slightly, but she made no further remark, only plucked a few notes and then began the song. It was a song Abby knew only faintly, possibly from her visit to court a few months ago, or perhaps something she came across at the French court. There was a slightly impertinent tone to it. A song her father would have thought amusing. The thought of her father made her frown and she made an effort to put it aside. There was time enough to consider how to handle the situation he'd created.

"You also find the song naughty then, Abby?" asked Margaret when she finished a few moments later.

"What?" said Abby. "Oh, no, not really. I'm certain they sing worse songs at court. No it was fine. And you have a very pleasant voice."

"Thank you," said Margaret. "I've been told that as well by Master Cameron." She gave a sigh. "Pity he is only the younger son of a most unremarkable knight."

Abby looked at her, suddenly amused. "Master Cameron taught you to play and sing?"

Margaret nodded. "Father says he's one of the best instructors. Mother would have no one else."

"I see. Well you certainly show great skill."

Margaret gave her a thoughtful look. "Here. You'll play now, won't you." It was a statement rather than a request. She handed the lute and the quill to Abby.

Abby took the lute from her and placed it in position, but refused the quill.

Margaret frowned. "But your fingers. Won't you lose the softness?"

Abby glanced at the calluses that had formed on the tips and shrugged. "It just means that the fingers on my right hand match the fingers on my left hand, for they already are hardened from depressing the strings."

"But, you play that often?" asked Margaret. She narrowed her eyes.

"Enough that it gives me no pain to play. I feel nothing of it, in fact."

"Oh, I see," said Margaret her tone containing no trace of admiration or approval.

"Now, what will you have me play? A song? An air, a dance piece?"

"Oh, a song," Frances said eagerly. "Something with a story."

"A Highland tale?" said Abby. "I've recently learned a few there."

"You were in the Highlands?" asked Frances.

"Only for a little while."

"Was it wild and full of murdering barbarians like Mother says?"

Abby laughed. "No, not really. Some of it was quite beautiful and the people cultured enough. Some of them," she added as an afterthought, thinking of Glenorchy and his treacherous ways. Though she knew others would probably call him exceedingly cultured.

"Oh, play us something you learned there," said Frances. She looked across at Margaret mischievously. "Something sad and romantic for my sister. She's always dreaming of a handsome knight or some such."

Margaret shrugged. "Aye, that's as good as any."

Abby plucked a few notes, deciding what to play and before she knew what she was about the air slipped out, forming into its familiar pattern, doleful and moving, reaching her deep inside. She began to sing the words, learned in Gaelic recently enough, but so ingrained in her mind, and in her heart. *Iain Glinn Cuach*, the air that Iain had taught her, at Lady Arbella's insistence. She hadn't sung it since she was in the Highlands, at Glenstrae. At her handfasting to Iain. A handfasting that was half farce. But so very real to her. Even now. A handfasting that all thought easily nullified, to leave her to marry as she pleased, because they hadn't bedded. But she knew differently. To protect him, to give him his pardon from the crown for killing Campbell kin, she had chosen not to say anything, so her father would arrange it. But now? Should she go back on her word and say that they were man and wife truly?

The words of the song caught her up, and though she wasn't fluent in Gaelic, she knew them well and their meaning. Oh Iain, Iain. His name repeated in the song, at the last verse and they echoed in her head, almost as if she was summoning him. Iain the man of the song, Iain the breaker of hearts who put his queen above all. Her answer was there. He would deny anything she might say about their relationship.

She finished the song, lost in its sorrow and her own sorrow. The notes lingered in the room and it took her a moment to realise where she was. She looked up and saw Margaret, an uncertain look on her face.

"Oh, that was lovely, lovely," said Frances. Her face was alight, the enjoyment written in full. "But tell us what it means. It sounds like it was a sad, though."

"Aye," said Margaret. "Very lovely indeed. It's in that awful Highland tongue, isn't it? We know nothing of that language."

"Nor did I when I learned it. But the air was so beautiful." Abby explained the song and its meaning as best as she could, trying to remember the translation that Lady Arbella had told her, and the few fragments that Iain had added later.

"Oh, but that is sad," said Margaret, won over now. She sighed dramatically. "And romantic. Such a man he must have been, for a woman to forgive him for forsaking her and to wish him well." She paused, her eyes taking on a dreamy, longing look. "What it would be like to know such a man?" She frowned. "There are none such here. Nor are there likely to be in the near future." She sighed again. "Perhaps when I go to the French court."

Abby hid a smile, thinking of the type of men at the French court. There were plenty in number ready to forsake a woman, and more than one, if need be.

"Teach me," said Margaret. "I'd like to learn this air. You must teach me."

Startled, Abby merely looked at her for a moment. "It's not an easy air to learn."

Margaret shrugged. "I'm sure I can manage it."

Abby suppressed a sigh. "Of course. I'd be happy to do that." She couldn't have been less happy, but it was too late now.

The door at the other end of the room opened and John appeared. At the sight of Abby his face brightened.

"You're here," he said.

"You missed it," said Frances. "She just played a lovely piece on the lute. She's very good."

John smiled at Abby. "I heard a little and wondered if it was you. Aye, it was lovely."

"Thank you," said Abby. "Do you play at all?"

"He plays very well," said Frances. "Even better than Margaret."

Margaret flushed. "He plays in a different manner, is all. It isn't better. That's what Master Cameron said."

"Och, he just said that so as not to offend you," said John, his tone teasing. "You know I'm better, really."

"Shall I?" He picked up the lute from Abby, giving her a tentative smile.

"Yes, of course. I'd love to hear you play."

She relinquished the lute and he took a seat on the bench nearby. Abby handed him the quill and he thanked her. He plucked a few notes, testing the instrument.

"A handsome lute," he said, envy in his voice. "Is it yours?"

"My father's really. He's given it into my care while he's away."

John nodded and plucked a few more notes, then eased himself into a galliard. His playing was skilful, intuitive and containing an ease that Margaret's playing lacked. Abby smiled at him and nodded her approval when he finished.

"You have great skill. That was delightful," she said. "Did you learn from Master Cameron, too?"

"Aye," said John. "He's a good musician as well as a tutor. He has a love of the music."

She was suddenly struck by a thought. "And who was his teacher, do you know?"

John frowned. "I think he learned at court. It was someone there."

"A Master Kerr, perhaps?"

"I don't know," said John.

"Yes, it was someone named Kerr," said Margaret. She looked at John. "He told me when I asked him."

John shrugged. "Do you know Master Kerr?"

Abby smiled slightly. "Yes, a little. I know that he's a very good musician and tutor." She would leave it at that. She'd rather avoid any questions that would certainly arise if she'd told them that Kerr had not only taught her father, but she'd also recently played music with him, posing as a boy musician at Kilchurn Castle in Glenorchy's household.

"Did you want anything in particular?" asked Margaret, her manner haughty.

John eyed Abby, reddening only slightly. "I came to ask Abby if she'd like to go for a ride. I can show her the area."

"With you?" asked Margaret. "She might prefer to wait for George."

John shrugged. "George is busy. Besides, I'm a better rider."

"Hah!" said Frances "You'd better not let George hear you say that."

John gave France's sleeve a tweak and turned to Abby. "We'll let Abby decide. Are you interested in a ride?"

Abby had watched the interplay with interest. John's manner was different now that he was out of earshot of his mother and his older brother. A manner that was at ease, even teasing at times. Given this observation the offer was tempting. It would give her an opportunity to see the area and perhaps also find some solution to her current situation. She would ask John what he knew about the prospective suitors and anything else she could think of.

"Oh, yes. It would be wonderful to get to see something of the area," said Abby.

John's eyes shone at her reply as he gave her instructions on where she should meet him after she had changed for riding. A slight uneasy feeling swept through her briefly as she passed him, the leather bag containing her lute clutched in her hand.

CHAPTER 5

*J*ohn was waiting for her at the entrance to the stables, stamping his leather boots against the cold. The frigid temperature created puffs of air from his breath. He wore a leather jerkin and dark breeches, all plain, but elegantly made. The only fancy touch was the pair of light-coloured embroidered leather gloves that covered his hands. He bounced a riding crop against his leg, the only sign of nerves she could detect.

He smiled when he saw her approach, reached out tentatively for her hand and took her towards the mounting block nearby. There, a stable boy led a dappled mare.

"She's sweet natured, is Milly," said John. "Mother rides her on occasion, when she has to, so you can be certain there is no temper in her."

Abby didn't know if that was a recommendation or a warning. Surely no mount would be beyond the formidable Lady Elizabeth? She eyed Milly carefully but could detect no outward signs of wayward behaviour or temperament. A moment later she was mounted and testing the reins. She was satisfied to proceed onward where John waited for her on his own horse.

That his horse as well as hers were expensive mounts was obvious, even to her eyes.

The pair made their way through the courtyard and out to the road that led to the castle. From the rise she could see an array of hills in the distance, beyond the small expanse of woodland on the left. Not far along, John veered off the main track onto a smaller one. It was a different direction from their journey to the castle days before and one that took them through the woodland and then across fields and up a small rise. John halted his horse and dismounted. She drew up alongside of him and he helped her down.

"I thought you might like the view from here," he said.

Her cheek burned from the cold wind that blew across her face and lifted the strands of hair that had escaped from the bonnet she wore. It was a soft green velvet that matched her riding gown. She was riding side saddle, but the skirt was roomy and she longed to sit astride and have the comfort of a secure seat. The days when she'd rode in breeches had taught her that much.

"What are you thinking?" asked John.

Abby caught herself. "Oh, just reflecting on the view. It is lovely."

She gazed out in earnest, noting the rolling countryside covered with hills, fields and scrub lands and small pockets of woodland. "Is this all Huntly's land?"

"Aye, well most of it," said John.

"All to go to George, eventually," she mused softly. An arrogant amount of land for an arrogant young man. She turned to John. "What will you do, then?"

John's eyes darkened. "Father's promised me that he will find a place for me at court. And a title to go with it, so I can command soldiers and raise a militia, should they be needed in defence of the Queen."

"Do you expect to need to do that? Defend the Queen?"

John shrugged. "Aye, perhaps. There's trouble afoot."

"Trouble?"

"Aye. You may have heard. John Knox and his cronies, stirring up people. Calling for an end to the Catholic faith in Scotland and muttering against the Queen."

"And you think this John Knox will likely raise an army against the Queen?"

"Perhaps not John Knox, but some of his sympathisers, from England for instance."

"England? But Queen Mary of England is a Catholic."

"Aye, but many powerful men would see her downfall. Or so Father says. He would prefer to be prepared. And the Dowager Queen supports that, too."

John took her hand and lifted it to his lips. "Abby," he said. "As you've asked me the question regarding my future plans, may I hope that you have some regard for me?"

Abby forced a smile, her hand still trapped in his. "Of course I have some regard for you, John. Are you not my cousin?" A reminder of their relationship could do no harm.

"Aye, but more than that." He drew her into his arms and began kissing her mouth, her eyes, her cheeks and making his way down to her neck, declaring himself all the while. "Since I first saw you, you've enchanted me, Abby. You're so beautiful, so graceful and your love and understanding of music has capti-vated me. You're beyond compare. Can I hope that you might return such feelings for me?"

Abby tried to push him away but he held her firmly. "Please, John. I'm flattered by your compliments, but you hardly know me."

John frowned and released her. "I know my mind and my heart." He paused a moment staring at her and his face cleared. "It's too soon, isn't it? I'm sorry, though I may be quick to know what I want, it's not to say that you do. I must give you time."

"I'm certain your parents must have a match planned for you already."

John waved his hand, dismissing her concerns. "They've changed their minds three times since the first match was proposed when I was small. One more won't matter, especially when I tell them how much I want you."

"But I'm not well connected, I have no prospects, other than what my father may give me, which I assure you is not much. And we're cousins."

"Our blood relationship is easily dealt with. And the rest doesn't matter, you'll see." He pecked her lightly on the cheek. "But I see it's too soon for all that. You must have some time." His face darkened again. "My brother hasn't been after you, has he? You mustn't pay any heed to him. A marriage has already been arranged for him. One that can't be set aside."

"No, you mustn't think that I would welcome George's attentions," said Abby.

"Good," he said in a relieved tone. "George enjoys various flirtations with women. They are never serious. He even has a reputation at court. That's why Father sent him here to cool his heels."

Abby had no doubt that his words were true. Her calm had been restored to some degree, but though she suspected John was more sincere in his interest than George, it made the situation no less problematic. She'd bought herself some time to decide how best to put him off, but she knew it wouldn't be for long.

"We should return," said Abby, stepping towards her horse. "The air is getting fresher and I think that rain might not be too far behind."

"Aye," said John. "A goodly amount, too. We'll take the shorter route, so you don't get your lovely gown and bonnet drenched."

He helped her mount the horse and once he was astride his,

they turned and made their way back to the castle. The ride was somewhat briefer, but still the rain caught them just as they approached the castle, so by the time Abby dismounted, her gown and bonnet were wet through. John grabbed her hand and the pair made a dash across the courtyard for the door. They entered the castle, laughing. John released her hand once they were inside and brushed off some droplets that clung to her hair.

"Wait here and I'll get a cloth," he said.

She nodded, seeing the wisdom in towelling off her garments here instead of trailing drops of water all the way to her chamber. He returned after a short while, cloth in hand, blotting his face with it. He lifted it to her face and proceeded to tenderly wipe it.

"May I ask what you're doing?"

Abby turned to see Lady Elizabeth standing there, her expression full of disapproval.

"We've just returned from a ride and were caught in the rain," said John. "We're drying off the worst of the water."

"I see," said Lady Elizabeth. Her tone made it clear that she saw a great deal more than two people drying themselves with a cloth. "I think you've done enough here, the pair of you. It's best if you both go and put on a change of clothes."

"Of course," Abby said hastily, glad to remove herself from the situation. She made her way towards the door.

"When you're finished," said Lady Elizabeth, "I'd be pleased if you would attend me in my private drawing room."

"I'd be happy to do that, Lady Elizabeth," said Abby.

She bobbed a brief curtsey and left the room, even less easy than when she entered it. She could think of a few reasons that Lady Elizabeth would want to see her, and none of them good. But perhaps she was wrong. Perhaps it was just an innocent request. She could only hope so.

~

SHE PATTED the damp curls that she'd missed when she'd tucked her hair in the net snood she'd pinned on her head in her haste to change, and attempted to slip them in with the rest. She smoothed the simple gown of plain dark wool jersey and dark sleeves, worn over a white linen blouse that revealed a pale blue kirtle underneath. It was a gown that didn't call for attention. A gown she thought best for what she had to face. She took a deep breath and knocked on the door.

At Lady Elizabeth's bidding she entered and saw that the interview would indeed be private, for Lady Elizabeth was alone. Abby made a small curtsey.

"Pray be seated," said Lady Elizabeth.

Abby took the chair indicated. The light from the window cast half of Lady Elizabeth's face in shadow, but there was no mistaking the frown that was still present.

"As you know, your father left you in our care. The care of my husband more specifically and since he's not here, I am acting on his behalf."

"And I do appreciate your kindness for taking me in," said Abby.

"You also may be aware that your father left me with some… matters to arrange on your behalf. The matter most principally of your marriage."

Abby stiffened. "He spoke something of it, yes," she said cautiously.

"I must say that I'm surprised that you haven't wed again yet. How long is it since your bereavement?"

Abby frowned. "Barely a year."

"Indeed? But it was a brief marriage, wasn't it?

Abby nodded.

"As to whether your widowhood puts your situation in a

different light, it's hard to say. Your father gave me to understand that yours would be a small dowry, but that's all he said. Is that correct?"

"It is."

"There is nothing left of your dowry to your first husband. Being a brief marriage, as you describe it, I would have thought that you could have reclaimed your dowry. I don't suppose you have anything from your husband? Jewels, for instance?"

"Nothing of significance."

Lady Elizabeth sighed. "Well it is how it is and there's little to be done about it. Still, given your youth and your health, it might be possible to contract a good match. What accomplishments have you? Do you play the lute well, like your father?"

"I do," said Abby. "As to other skills, I'm afraid I cannot boast of any talent at needlework."

"But you can run a household, surely? With your mother gone so long?"

Abby suppressed a flinch at the mention of her mother. "Yes, I'm well versed in that."

"Good. Then we have some possibilities."

"Has my father made any suggestions?" she asked casually.

"Not anyone specific. I will consult with my husband of course, but it can do no harm to make some inquiries."

"The Earl won't mind, then?" Abby thought of the conversation she'd overheard and wondered at what the sudden rush to arrange her marriage was. And why wouldn't Lady Elizabeth mention the names her father had given? This wasn't the slow process she'd imagined. Anxiety rose up in her, taking her breath for a moment.

Lady Elizabeth raised a brow. "No. I'll act on his behalf. He'll have no objection." She gave Abby a long, piercing look. "There are one or two men who live not so very far from here that would be suitable candidates. I'll invite them to visit."

"That soon? Is there some hurry? Did my father ask you to arrange this quickly? I would think he would want to have some idea who you have in mind?"

"It's not necessary to involve him to that degree. He assured me he had every confidence in us. In me." She narrowed her eyes. "You can rest assured that I will take every care with your well-being."

Abby forced a smile. She had no doubt what kind of care Lady Elizabeth would take. "May I ask who these suitable men they are? What they are like?" Abby said, trying to keep her tone reasonable.

"No, I think it's too early for that. I wouldn't want to get your hopes up. There's time enough to have a reply. In the meantime it would do ye no harm to practice your needlework and perhaps your dancing. Ask Margaret. She'll let you know when the dance instruction takes place with the children."

Abby bit back the biting retort that came to her mind. Lady Elizabeth nodded to her and took up her needlework. A clear dismissal. Abby rose, gave a quick curtsey and left the room.

Back in her chamber, she sat down on the bed and forced herself to be calm. She would not have it, that much was clear. Her father had pleaded that she listen, but Lady Elizabeth's manner had made it clear she wasn't thinking in Abby's best interest. No, she must act for herself. The question was what to do. Glen Strae seemed out of the question given Iain's rejection. She wouldn't humiliate herself there. No, she must go to the Scottish court and throw herself on the Dowager's Queen sympathetic ear and ask for a place as a musician. The Dowager Queen knew her father and his talent, after all. Surely she'd be safe under the protection of the Dowager Queen?

CHAPTER 6

*A*bby stared out of the window, bleary-eyed as the weather while Jeannette helped her dress. A wintery mizzle had settled on the land, obscuring the surrounding countryside so that all Abby could see was the few trees and track that led to the castle grounds. She'd spent a sleepless night planning her next steps and now she had little energy to face the likes of George, John and Margaret. She couldn't be certain, even at this late hour, that those three would have eaten. After a wishful thought she brightened.

"Jeannette," she said on impulse. "Would you mind going down and getting me something to eat? I don't think I'm quite ready to face the others."

Jeannette frowned. "Are you sickening for something my lady?"

"No, I'm fine, really. Just tired. I didn't sleep well."

"I thought I heard you tossing, though if you are as uncomfortable as I am in my little trundle bed, it's no wonder. How is a person expected to sleep with the draughts and the noise?"

"Noise? I didn't hear any noise."

"*Exactement*! The life, the reassuring sounds of your neighbours, they are all missing. And the servants—bah, they know nothing of the ways of civilised living."

Abby recalled the pots and waste thrown in the streets of the French towns from windows and the rotting, spoiled vegetables trodden to filth. She suppressed a laugh at that and Jeannette's reference to her little trundle bed. A sturdy woman, she no doubt found the small bed a bit lacking in support.

"Now, what shall I bring you, my lady? A small slice of venison, or I think I saw some partridge in the kitchen, though whether the cook will deign to give it to me is another thing again."

Abby laughed, suddenly a little better. "No, just a cup of ale and some bread and cheese will do fine."

Jeannette nodded and after a brief curtsey took her leave. Abby sat on the bed and looked outside for something to distract her from her situation. Below her, in the courtyard, she saw a young couple, a man clasping tight the hands of the woman, both in earnest conversation. Abby strained to see them and realised that the woman was one of the countess's ladies, Jane. The man, she didn't recognise, but his dress marked him as someone other than one of the household servants.

The door opened and Jeannette entered with a tray in hand, the food and ale on it. She set it down on the small table in the room with a thud.

"One of the young ladies of the house, Margaret, I think, asked that you attend her as soon as possible in the drawing room."

"Margaret?"

"Yes, the one with the figure that blooms out of her gown. Is that not Margaret?"

Abby smiled at the description. "Yes, I believe that's Margaret. Can you tell her I will be with her soon?"

Jeannette nodded and withdrew to take the message. Abby

went over to the table and surveyed the food set there. She picked up a chunk of bread and began to eat. She would put something in her stomach, regardless of how urgent Margaret's request was.

A while later she opened the door to the drawing room and was relieved to see Margaret was there on her own, seated on a bench by the window.

"Oh, it's about time," said Margaret. "I was wondering if your silly maid had told you that it was urgent."

"I'm sorry for the delay, Margaret. What's the problem?"

"There's no real problem as such. I wanted you to teach me that song. You did promise and now I'm ready."

Abby suppressed a sigh. "I haven't my lute with me. I'll have to go and get it."

Margaret gestured to her feet, where a lute rested carelessly on the floor. "There's no need. We can use this one. It belongs to John, but he won't mind."

Abby wondered if that was really the case. She also wondered how kindly he would look on the casual treatment of his lute. Margaret leaned over, grabbed the lute by its neck and handed it to Abby. She reluctantly took the instrument and sat beside her. She settled the lute in place and began to explain the melody structure so that Margaret would remember it more easily. She hummed the tune and encouraged Margaret to do the same to fix it in her head.

After a while Abby handed her the lute and had her try it. It took several tries, but eventually Margaret had the piece, though again, her impatience hindered her from learning it quicker. Abby wanted to end the lesson at that point, but Margaret insisted that she teach her the words. Margaret's hasty nature got in the way again as Abby tried to coach her pronunciation as well as the correct sequence.

"The first verse," said Margaret, eventually. "That will do, for now, I think. I've had enough."

Abby, who could not agree more with the sentiment, sat back, easing her shoulders. They'd been at the lesson for over an hour, perhaps two, Abby was certain. She was just about to rise when the door burst open and the younger Gordon boys ran in, a man in tow.

"Margaret, Margaret, you'll never guess!" said Patrick.

He ran over to her and thrust himself into Margaret's lap.

"Ssshh. Must you be so loud?" said Margaret sharply. "Careful now. I don't want you getting my skirts mucky. Where are your manners. Have you been outside?"

Patrick pulled away, his eyes dancing. "Master Cameron took us outside for exercise to calm us down."

Margaret looked over at Master Cameron. "I'd say the exercise had no effect."

Master Cameron bowed. "I did my best, Lady Margaret."

Margaret laughed and tilted her head in a coquettish manner. "I'm sure you did." She gestured to Abby. "Have you met my cousin, Master Cameron?"

Margaret completed the introductions and Abby smiled at the man. He bowed at the introduction and when he rose from his bow Abby realised that this was the man she'd seen in the courtyard earlier with one of Lady Elizabeth's attendants. He was thin and wiry with dark hair and eyes. Some might consider him handsome, but not Abby. There was a barely detectable insolence about him that she found irritating.

"Master Cameron," she said. "I've heard much of your skill and knowledge and seen evidence of your musical ability in your pupils' skilful playing."

Master Cameron smiled, a faint curl to his lip. "You're too kind."

Patrick tugged on Margaret's skirts. "You're not listening."

"What, what is it?" asked Margaret impatiently.

"You didn't guess," Patrick said, his tone petulant.

"I've no time for guesses, what is it?"

"Father's coming!"

"Father? What? When?" asked Margaret. She looked over at the man. "Is this true, Master Cameron?"

"Yes," said Master Cameron. "A messenger just arrived to say that his lordship is expected here this evening."

"This evening?" said Margaret. "Oh, this will put Mother in a tear. You best get the boys cleaned and at their studies or she'll have a fit."

"Of course," said Master Cameron. "If you and Mistress Gordon will excuse me, I'll take the boys now."

He bowed, and gathering up Patrick and the others, took his leave. Margaret rose and tossed the lute in a nearby chair. Abby frowned at such an action and rose quietly to retrieve the leather case and put the lute inside it.

Margaret gave her an amused look. "Well I think I'll retreat for now, and I advise you to do the same or my mother will find some unpleasant task for us to do to prepare for my father's arrival." She looked outside and frowned. "If the weather was better I might have contemplated a ride, but I'll just go to my chamber and read." She nodded to Abby and left.

Abby stared after her, still holding the bag with the lute tucked safely inside it. The news of the Earl's imminent arrival meant nothing good for her, she knew. Her marriage prospects would undoubtedly be on the top of Lady Elizabeth's list. George and John's attentions to Abby had apparently not gone unnoticed and had figured in Lady Elizabeth's decision to commit to arranging a marriage for her promptly.

Well, it mattered little in the long view. She would be quitting this place, and now, with the Earl coming she would leave as soon as she could find an opportunity. She glanced around. What better opportunity than the present? She rose. There was much to do to make ready. With any luck Jeannette would be elsewhere.

~

ABBY HEARD the clatter of horses from her bedchamber. She ran to the window and looked out to see The Earl of Huntly and his retinue.

As she suspected, the retinue was large, evidence of a powerful man with significant influence who would attract many retainers as well as soldiers and servants. No Highland gillies for him, running barefoot ahead scouting the way, or behind, to defend the rear. Retainers, attendants, these men were all mounted, and mounted well. A flash of crimson, blue and gold skirts made Abby amend her thought. Women as well as men. Enough for a court. Powerful indeed. The clatter and shouts grew loud as the people gathered in the courtyard, looking for assistance to help dismount, to take their horses, or to give them direction for the baggage. Wagons piled high with baggage and stores lumbered in at a slower pace.

The disarray below convinced her even more that it was an opportune time for her. She looked across the room and surveyed the bed. She'd laid out a change of gown and some underclothes to take with her on her journey, in addition to the set of servant's clothes she had taken from the washing house. The gown was a good one, but it was barely suitable for court. It would have to do, there was nothing else. She hadn't much time, she knew. Jeannette, thankfully, was downstairs, presumably involved in the confusion below. She would change into them later, once she'd put distance between Huntly and herself.

She placed the clothes in a sack. When that was completed she donned her dark cloak and slipped out of the room, giving the lute, resting on the floor in its leather bag, one last look of farewell. She knew better than to try to take it with her.

There were plenty of servants and strangers milling in the corridor and stairs, but they took little notice of her. With her sack well hidden under her cloak, she slipped out through the door to the courtyard and made her way towards the stable, ploughing her way through the servants unloading carts and the soldiers milling around until their billets in the Tower House were arranged. She was nearly at the stable door when a familiar laugh caught her attention.

She turned, unbelieving, and searched the faces of the soldiers gathered in the group. At first glance she could recognise none of the men there. The laugh came again, this time softer. She looked at him carefully. His bonnet was pulled down low over his head. He also sported a thick dark beard and he wore a patch over one eye. There was no sign of the long, dark locks that she'd known so well. But the shape of the nose and mouth were unmistakeable. Iain.

Her heart stopped and briefly, joy filled her and a quick rush it left. He couldn't be here for her. Impossible.

Just then he looked across at her, the one uncovered eye focused on her and for a moment a look of complete shock filled his face. A moment later it was gone and his gaze passed over her. Abby blinked and forced herself to continue into the stable.

She stopped a passing stable boy, still half numb, and stared at him, trying to collect her thoughts.

"Do ye want something, my lady?"

"Is Lady Margaret here? She mentioned something about going riding,"

"No, my lady," said the lad. "She's no been here at all."

"Thank you," she said. "I'll check inside then."

She turned around, her sack still hidden under her cloak and threaded her way back across the courtyard to the castle door, acutely aware of Iain's eyes following her. Once inside, she made her way along quickly, praying no one would notice her. The corridors, hall and drawing rooms were still filled with people either milling around, or walking purposefully, clearly on some errand. It wasn't until she reached the safety of her chamber that she allowed herself a small sigh of relief.

What was he doing here? Clearly he didn't expect her here. The words cycled through her head, but she knew in her heart. What else could it be, but what he'd been doing for the past several years under her father's direction. He was a spy here. For some reason her father had placed him here to spy on someone specific. Could it be the Earl of Huntly? Or was it someone else? She shook her head. What did it matter to her, after all. She was still where she was, here in the castle under the protection of the Earl of Huntly and his wife, to be directed towards any particular man they chose to select as a husband. Iain had made his choice.

She threw a gown across the bed in frustration and then a thought struck her. She had no need to promise her father that she would keep away from Iain in return for securing a pardon for him from the crown. Her father would have done it anyway. He wouldn't be without his best spy. But then why would he place Iain here, where she was? Could he be that confident that his plan to marry her to one of his cronies would happen even with Iain living in the Huntly household? Or was it something else?

CHAPTER 7

The noise was nearly deafening in the dining hall when Abby entered. The large table had been moved to the front to make room for trestle tables that lined the walls in a 'U' shape, leaving the centre open. Each table was covered in a rich cloth and held expensive silver and pewter plateware. At the far end of the hall, Abby was surprised to see musicians, playing two lutes, a rebec, a tambour and a recorder.

Finely dressed men and women gathered in the room. Men in silks, brocades, velvets in all hues adorned with beading, jewels and embroidery rubbed shoulders with each other and women in elaborately trimmed gowns, framed with farthingales, crowded together. It was sumptuous enough for the Scottish court. She realised, that for all intents and purposes, this was something of an extension of the Scottish court. The Dowager Queen had little interest lately in entertaining. There were too many factions, and for some, too many French people at court. But here, she picked up phrases in French as well as English and Scots. She gave a grim smile. No Gaelic, though. She glanced around the room for Iain. No sign of him, but then he would most likely be with the other soldiers.

She smoothed her own gown, suddenly conscious that though it was one she'd worn at court, it wasn't her best gown. This, the saffron silk, with the heavily embroidered underdress, she'd chosen not to wear with a farthingale, which she found sometimes confining, especially when she danced. The sleeves were puffed at the top and slashed to reveal more of the embroidery. Her hair was pulled back into a stiff, beaded cap. She had pearls at her ears and had nearly worn the pearls that Iain had given her, but something had made her take them off in the end. Now, she wished she'd worn them. Her neck seemed bare compared to the bejeweled ladies and men. Unlike everyone else, her fingers lacked jewels too, as she clasped them tightly for a moment, they seemed positively naked.

She brushed the thought aside and took the seat next to Margaret, who turned to her and eyed her carefully before giving her a thin smile.

"You're looking well, tonight, Abby," she said.

"As do you, cousin," said Abby.

Margaret wore a mulberry coloured gown over a small farthingale which gave her a soft innocent appearance at odds with her fulsome breasts. Breasts that left too little to the imagination to anyone viewing them from above. A ruby and pearl necklace encircled her throat, matching the ruby earrings and rubies and pearls on the cap adorning her blond hair. Rings lined her fingers and Abby wondered at their weight.

George, seated on Margaret's other side, leaned forward. "You look enchanting tonight, cousin. A true angel come down from heaven."

Margaret forced a laugh. "Oh, George, your compliments exceed necessity all the time."

"Nay, sister. I only speak the truth in this case."

"My thanks," said Abby. She gave a quick bow of her head.

"The compliment is much appreciated. Especially among all this grand company."

George looked out at the people assembling along the tables and gave a toss of his head. "You are a unique rarity among the commonplace. Don't compare yourself to them."

Margaret pointed. "Who's the new soldier in Father's employ?"

Abby looked in the direction indicated. Just at the entrance a small group of soldiers stood, their dusty jerkins and hose shed for clean doublets and hose in the Huntly colours. At their centre was Iain, his eye patch still in place, his beard trimmed and neat. She looked away quickly before he caught her glance.

"That's Duncan Kerr. He's some man Father acquired in Edinburgh. He's been fighting abroad and has only just returned. Apparently he's good with a sword."

"Oh, I have no doubt," said Margaret, tilting her head. "I would dearly like to see him wield it."

Abby stared at Margaret. The remark could be taken innocently, but Abby knew enough about Margaret to be clear there was nothing innocent about it.

"Hold there, sister," said George. "You're asking for trouble if you go sniffing around one of Father's men."

"Father doesn't have to know," said Margaret. She gave George a coy look. "I shan't do anything silly, don't worry. He might be worth a light flirtation."

George frowned "He isn't someone ye want to toy with, so leave him be."

Margaret grunted and turned towards Abby. "Do you dance much at all?"

"I've danced on occasion."

"Which dances?"

"The galliard, the pavane, the gavotte, the branle." Abby added a few others, all the while watching Margaret's eyes narrow.

"Well, I can see you have experience," she said, barely concealing a sniff. "Where did you have such opportunity? At court?"

Abby nodded. "Mostly at court."

"Abby, you look lovely," said John in her ear.

He took the seat beside her and Abby nearly groaned. It was the last thing she needed, John paying court to her on the one side and George close by, adding his own brand of flirtation. She would have to manage the situation carefully. There was no advantage to having John presume to guard her jealously from George's attentions. She looked at Margaret briefly for assistance but her eyes just twinkled mischievously.

"George just remarked on it too," said Margaret. "Said she was like a veritable angel."

John frowned. "Hardly original. Did I not hear you say something of the sort before? Or perhaps it was to someone else."

"Ah no, brother," said George smoothly. "There is only one angel in this household."

"Margaret is no less the shining beauty," said Abby hastily. She glanced around for some distraction. "Is that your father arrived?"

They all glanced over to the door, much to Abby's relief. Lady Elizabeth was at the Earl's side with a few of her ladies clustered behind her.

"Oh, it is," said Margaret languidly. "And I see Frances trailing behind Father as usual. She's ever anxious to gain his attention about some trivial piece or other she's learned."

The Earl and his retinue moved towards their table. Abby could see he was an imposing man, not so much in height, but in manner. His long face and nose had an imperious air and his brown eyes gazed keenly over the room. The resemblance to her father was there in the nose and the mouth, but her father's manner was less severe, even with the underlying air of menace that he chose to show on occasion. Huntly's eyes lit on her and she gave a brief smile. He nodded and spoke a few words to his wife. When they arrived at the table they stopped in front of Abby.

"My lord, this is Gabrielle Gordon, Calum's daughter," said Lady Elizabeth. "As I mentioned briefly before, Calum asked that we take her under our care for a time while he settles some affairs of his."

Abby rose and curtseyed. "My lord, I hope you don't mind the intrusion on your household."

He acknowledged her curtsey with a brief bow. "No intrusion, I assure you. I understand that there are some matters to discuss later. For now, I bid you welcome, and ask that you enjoy yourself tonight and for the rest of your stay with us."

"Thank you, my lord," said Abby.

The Earl and Lady Elizabeth moved on to their seats some way down, at the table's centre. Frances dashed into the seat beside John. A moment later the middle boys, William and James came in and took seats at the other end of the table. Patrick and Robert, it seemed, were deemed too young for such a gathering.

The food was served. Plate upon plate of fish, fowl, and every other kind of meat Abby could imagine came in several courses and was laid upon the table under the keen eye of the steward. He was a wiry young man, fashionably dressed, with beard and hair curled to perfection. She could imagine him overseeing the kitchen, yet just as easily managing the gatehouse billeting and armoury. There was a shrewdness in manner and an underlying strength that told Abby she shouldn't underestimate him.

There was a reasonable calm over the small group as they ate and drank their way through the courses. George definitely liked his wine and drank with an expertise that left Abby in no doubt that this wasn't an unusual occurrence. John was even more attentive to his wine, though he seemed to carry it with less aplomb. It was almost as if he was determined to find the bottom of his cup and the servants were ensuring he wouldn't. Margaret was a little more circumspect, but nevertheless Abby increasingly worried that such deep drinking would bring trouble later on. Abby refused to look in Iain's direction, seated as he was at the end of one of the far tables among the soldiers.

The music from the end of the room was difficult to hear at times and Abby longed to go there to listen. It would be a welcome distraction and provide her with an opportunity to hear other skilled musicians. It was therefore something of a relief when the meal ended and she could rise.

"I'm just going over to listen to the musicians," she said to Margaret and John.

John rose quickly. "I'll go with you."

Abby sighed inwardly but gave a nod. She made her way carefully past the tables, John at her elbow, guiding her. Abby was still careful not to look in Iain's direction.

They reached the other end of the hall and she studied the musicians appreciatively. All of them were relatively young and seemingly abreast of the most recent tunes from both the Scottish and French courts. Unsurprising, given the Dowager Queen's French background and Huntly's position as Chancellor for Scotland and member of the Council of Regents. One of the musicians was a Frenchman, judging by the cut of his clothes. She examined him closely for a moment, suddenly anxious that he might know her. There was something familiar about him, but it could have been her anxiety producing it. Did she want the household to know exactly what she'd been doing in France? But then again, what did it really matter? Surely they must know that her father had been a musician there. She sighed.

"They are good, don't you agree?" asked John.

She turned to him blankly and then realised that he'd interpreted her sigh as a positive comment on the musician's skill.

"Yes," she said.

"It's Father. He will have the best of everything. I wonder that the Dowager Queen doesn't take issue with it, for he rivals the court when he's here. But then at the moment he can do no wrong."

Abby gave him a curious glance. His comment could be seen to contain no criticism, but she couldn't help but detect an underlying disapproval, if only a hint.

"He certainly demonstrates great taste in all of it," said Abby.

The music paused a moment and then changed its pace as a lively galliard dance tune commenced. As if on cue, various people rose from their seats and made their way to the centre, taking the appropriate positions.

"Come, let's dance," said John, taking her hand with a smile. "I have no doubt that your skill will more than match my own."

She gave a small laugh, caught up by the music, the rhythm of the tambour setting her foot tapping. She did enjoy a galliard with its intricate energetic steps and she was pleased to see John was an intuitive dancer. She found herself comparing him to Iain and though he wasn't as athletic, he was as graceful and light on his feet. The dance engaged her, and for a moment she forgot herself and her problems, until John lifted her in the air that last time, towards the end of the dance, when she caught his amorous expression. When the dance concluded he lifted her hand to his mouth and planted a lingering kiss on it. She opened her mouth to speak a restraining comment, but was interrupted.

"Well danced, little brother, but now I think it's my turn," George said.

He bowed to Abby and held his hand out to her. The musicians had begun another dance, a branle. While not as elaborate as the galliard, it was still had lilting rhythms and required some fine footwork. Abby took George's hand with a little misgiving but comforted herself with the thought that dancing with George would at least halt John's ardent attentions.

What George lacked in skill at dancing he made up for in finesse, his gestures with head and hands adding that little bit of courtliness to the steps. It was a polished and confident approach, one that no doubt was well received with the ladies as his smile and manner conveyed so convincingly. He flirted outrageously, lifting her fingers for little kisses when their hands were joined, or tweaking a stray curl on her head when he passed her by in a movement. It was light hearted enough, and initially she responded with a smile, until his eyes met hers and she could see the sensual message there and in the curve of his mouth. She dropped his hand and looked away, completing the steps automatically and executed the remainder of the dance with most minimal contact possible, her eyes avoiding his.

As soon as the dance ended she curtseyed quickly and moved into the cluster of people before he could say anything. Intent on her purpose, she bumped into a passing dancer who steadied her with a hand on her arm.

"Careful, my lady," said a familiar voice. "I would have expected better grace from a dancer like yourself." He leaned down as if to steady her further and hissed in her ear, "what are ye doing here?"

She looked up into Iain's face, the uncovered eye filled with a mixture of amusement and anger. She had a deep urge to rip off his patch and fling it on the floor. She frowned instead.

"I'm a Gordon, you ninny, what do you think I'm doing here," she hissed back. "I do apologise sir," she said loudly. "But even with all the grace in the world, it's difficult to manoeuvre around oafs."

She shifted her position, ensuring that she stepped on his feet with all her weight, though she knew her dance slippers were no match for the boots he wore. With a few quick moves on his part he had removed his foot and planted it on her shoe so that it came half off her foot.

"An oaf I am, my lady, for I fear ye've half lost your slipper. Allow me." He moved her to the side of a room, to an empty section of one of the tables and leaned down to help her put the slipper back securely on her foot. "I must meet wi' ye soon," he whispered to her. "By the privy, in a quarter of an hour."

She opened her mouth to protest but he stood, bowed and left before she could say anything. She glanced around, hoping that no one had seen the exchange. She met Margaret's speculative eyes across the room. Abby shrugged and shook her head as if to say that she found Iain completely uninteresting. She walked casually towards Frances who was talking with James. He would be a good choice of partner and hopefully convey to the rest of the Gordons that she had no particular interest in either of the two older Gordon brothers. It would also ensure that those two Gordons wouldn't be able to seek her out while she waited until she was to meet Iain. It was a meeting she both desired and dreaded, and was cross with herself that she felt either. One thing was certain, she would make it clear that she was not the woman in the ballad. She would sing no praises of this Iain who was protecting his queen above all else, if that was what he was doing.

ABBY WRINKLED her nose as she neared the privy by the back hall. She was glad to see there was no one in view, though nothing could be read into her desire to visit it after such a meal that had been served that evening. Even if she hovered outside, any observer would only conclude she awaited her turn. Nevertheless she was glad when she saw Iain waiting for her. He nodded and made his way towards her.

"Come," he said.

He took her arm, moved further down the corridor and slipped behind the arras of a hunt scene that covered a small windowed alcove. Though leaded glass covered the window, it was ill-fitting and draughty. She shivered slightly and looked up at Iain. His uncovered eye glittered in the dim light.

"I know ye're a Gordon," said Iain through clenched teeth. "There are Gordons enough. But these Gordons? Ye mean tae tell me ye're one of these Gordons? Why did ye no say before?"

"I didn't know," she hissed back at him. "And more importantly, why ask me, why not ask my father? It seems he's kept this entirely to himself."

"Ye didna ken that your father is related to one of the most important families in the whole of Scotland?"

"No," she said sharply. Tears unexpectedly came to her eyes. She looked away. All the anger and hurt rose up that she'd suppressed since she'd first discovered she was related to the Earl and his family. All the years she'd thought she had no other family but her father. To find that she not only had connections, but noble connection. Suddenly, it was all too much.

"Your father didna think to tell ye," said Iain, his tone soft and sympathetic. "I'm sorry lass. I'm sure he had his reasons. He'd no think tae hurt ye deliberately."

She forced away her emotions. "Yes," she said with studied calm. "Very complicated reasons, I'm sure."

"What is the Earl tae ye, then?"

She gave a wry smile. "My father is his uncle."

His eyes opened wide with surprise. "Uncle?"

"Half uncle, really."

Iain sighed. "And ye're here under the Earl's protection."

"Yes. Until my father returns from whatever business it is that takes him away. Would you happen to know what is?"

Iain frowned and shook his head. "I've nae idea."

"And why are you here?" she said.

"I canna tell ye that. I only ask that ye keep my identity a secret."

She gave a soft snort. "It's no concern of mine. I will say nothing. Though it's not difficult to guess what you're doing."

His face eased and then became blank. "I ken that ye must be angry wi' me and I can only wish it would be different, but I made a promise."

"A promise," she said tartly. "You made a few of those, but I see that some promises take precedence over others."

She couldn't help her bitter words. She'd sworn to herself she wouldn't allow him to see how much she cared, how much it hurt her that she wouldn't be his first choice, or that his love wasn't enough to make her his first choice.

He cupped her chin. "Lass, I can only tell ye I'm sorry."

She pushed his hand aside carefully. "I have no need for your apologies Iain. It is done. Things have changed. I'm to be wed." She gave a small laugh. "Wed properly this time."

He stiffened. "Wed? Tae one of those Gordon lads? Tae that jumped up dandy who slobbered all over ye during the branle, or is it his little brother who may be handy with his dance steps but I would wager his sword skills are nae better than a wooden post."

Abby blinked at his tirade. "No. Well, it might be their wish, but I don't see Lady Elizabeth approving of such a match."

"Then ye would marry one of them, given the chance," said Iain, frowning. He gave a snort. "Well if ye must have one of them, at least pick the elder one. He'll get the title and then ye can be a grand lady."

"You think I want to be a grand lady? Do you think I care for a title?" She gave him a shove. It was childish, she knew, but she couldn't help herself. "There is no plan for me to marry either one. I may be related, but I have nothing to tempt them to a stronger connection."

"But ye say there is a plan to marry ye off." His words were curt, sharp even.

"Yes. My father asked them to secure a match between either one of two men he named. Friends of his, apparently. A Douglas and a Hamilton. I don't know them."

"Ye canna marry either one of them. Ye dinna even ken the men, who they are, what they are."

Abby gave a mirthless laugh. "I think you gave up your right to say anything in the matter."

Iain pulled back and straightened. "Aye, ye're right. 'Tis no my concern."

"No, it isn't." The words, spoken with all the tartness she could muster, still cost her. "Now we've established that I shall keep your secret, there's no more to be said. I bid you goodnight Mister Kerr."

She slipped from behind the arras and made her way back down the corridor towards the dining hall, erect and graceful. She didn't look back.

CHAPTER 8

"Where are you off to, madame?" said Jeannette, entering Abby's chamber, newly washed linens in hand. She gave Abby a disapproving look. "You're surely not going anywhere looking as you do. Come, you have a smudge on your face."

She moved towards Abby with determination, a linen cloth in her hand. Abby backed away slightly, but then relented. She had no doubt who would win this battle. In the need to prove herself above these Scots barbarians, as she liked to call them, Jeannette had mentally risen above her own background as a spinster daughter of an innkeeper and taken on the airs of a French courtier's personal attendant. Or what she imagined them to be, because Abby knew she had no better idea than any of the servants here at the castle. Or perhaps a few of them had a better idea than Jeannette, because they had attended the Earl when he'd visited Paris.

"I thought I'd go for a ride," said Abby, while Jeannette scrubbed at her cheek.

"A ride? But you cannot go out like that."

"In the woodland, or along the road a little."

She wanted to be alone so she could think, without any danger of anyone coming upon her. No servants, no courtiers, no family. There were too many people eager to interrupt and exchange social pleasantries. A hunt was organised for tomorrow, so she'd have no chance then to ride on her own. Seeing Iain yesterday had thrown her plans awry so dramatically it wasn't until now that she thought herself ready to lay new ones.

"Let me help you dress in your riding gown, at least," said Jeannette. "It will be easier for you."

Abby sighed. In truth she'd hoped to ride astride and had donned her oldest gown with its wide skirts to allow it. A good gallop out of sight of everyone would surely help. Before she could open her mouth to object, Jeannette was searching through the kist at the end of the bed for her riding gown.

"Don't bother with it, Jeannette, I'm fine as I am."

"Not at all. How can you say such a thing, madame?"

Jeannette bustled the gown over to Abby and began removing the other one. Abby realised she would escape the room much quicker if she just gave into Jeannette. But once the gown was on, it seemed her hair was unsatisfactory as well. Much brushing, braiding and pinning was required to achieve the desired effect before Abby was finally allowed out of her room. Sullen and tired from Jeannette's exhortations and ministrations, she descended the stairs. A few servants passed her by, but no one else. She was just at the head of the stairs when she heard voices drifting upwards. She crept down the stairs enough to see Margaret resting her hand on Iain's arm.

"I hear you like music, Mister Kerr," Margaret was saying.

"Ye heard that?" Iain's tone was neutral.

"Oh, yes. And I know that you love the dancing, too. Did you admire my dancing last night?"

"Ye're a fine dancer, Lady Margaret."

"Come, now, Mister Kerr, you can do better than that. Forbye, I'll wager you've a fine tongue on you."

"Ye ken that do ye?" His tone was amused now, a trace of his soft Highland lilt evident.

"Aye, I know all that. And do you ken how I know?" she said, emphasising the word 'ken'.

"I'm certain it's not my concern."

"Oh, but it is, Mister Kerr. You see, despite your affliction," she said touching his patch, "your eyes are that of a poet's…and your hands, well, they are shaped like a fine musician's. I can see that, because I too am a musician. Can you tell from my hands?" She took up his hand and matched it palm to palm with her own. "Wouldn't you say I have the eyes of a poet, too?"

"I'm sure ye possess all the talents ye say, my lady."

Margaret pouted. "You doubt it?"

"Not at all, my lady." He bowed and kissed her hand. "You clearly have all the accomplishments of a lady of your station. Now if ye'll excuse me…"

Margaret tilted her head in a coquettish manner. "Oh, but I don't excuse you, Mister Kerr. Not until you accept my challenge."

"Challenge?"

"Aye. I challenge you to describe the beauty and skill with which I play the lute. This evening, before the meal. I shall see you in the small drawing room."

She held onto his hand, keeping it raised under his chin, her eyes sparkling with her daring. Iain smiled at her and nodded, kissing her hand once more.

"Very well, my lady," he said.

Margaret dropped his hand and walked off towards the large drawing room, her hips swaying slightly. Above, Abby watched her retreat, suppressing at the same time the urge to laugh and to slap the impudent young woman across her face. She must have made a noise because Iain looked up and caught her staring down. He frowned.

"You should have a care with Lady Margaret," she said. "She aims to get what she's after."

Iain raised a brow. "There's nothing tae get."

Abby gave a careless smile and continued down the stairs towards him. "But she thinks so. She's already admired you. Perhaps it's the patch. So mysterious, intriguing."

"She's bored. She'll find another plaything soon enough."

"In the meantime, laddie, ye should have a care," she said, giving her best bid to imitate his highland accent. He'd warned her enough with just those words, it was his turn now.

"Are you going for a ride?" came a voice from behind.

Abby turned to see George join Iain at the bottom of the stair. He gave a small bow.

"Yes, I'm just off now."

"You're not going alone, surely? I'll go with you. Just let me put on my boots."

"Nay. There's no need. I'm not going alone." She gestured to Iain. "I've just asked your father's man to accompany me."

George narrowed his hazel eyes and studied Iain. "Kerr, isn't it?"

"Aye, my lord."

He gave Iain a stern look. "See that you don't allow her out of your sight. I'll have no harm come to her. Is that understood?"

"Are ye expecting something, my lord?"

George frowned and Abby bit her lip. If she could detect the small hint of insolence in Iain's tone, she was certain George could too. She wanted to pinch Iain.

"Just do as I say," George said curtly.

"Of course, my lord."

George turned to Abby, lifted her hand and kissed it. "Ordinarily I would insist on accompanying you regardless, dear cousin, but Father does require my assistance today. I hope you understand."

Abby smiled. "I do, George."

George gave a small bow and left the hall. Abby felt her breath release as he disappeared.

"Cousin George is verra attentive to your needs," said Iain softly.

"Yes, well he's more attentive to his father's wishes at the moment," she said. She added a silent prayer of thanks for it. "Now, if you'll excuse me, I'll go for my ride."

"Oh, but ye've asked me to go with ye," he said, his lowland accent back in place.

"No, I haven't. That was just for George's sake, as you well know. I'd rather be on my own, if you don't mind."

"But I do mind. Your dear cousin has asked me to accompany ye and see ye come to no harm."

"There's no need," she said sharply.

"There's every need. I've had my orders and I must obey. He made that very clear." His voice was firm, brooking no argument.

Abby sighed, resigned to losing her much desired solitude. It seemed she wasn't going to be able to find a way out of this mess right now. She would make the ride as short as possible, though. The less time she spent in Iain's company, the better. It only distracted her and made her lose sight of the need to leave this place.

THEY CLEARED the castle and headed for the woodland. The earthy odours of wet, mossy trees and decayed leaves filled her nostrils. Abby had chosen the woodland so that Iain would have to ride behind her, instead of at her side, making it more difficult to have a conversation. She was still too hurt and angry to want much speech with him.

Iain followed, ducking the low branches quietly as the pair cantered carefully along Abby's chosen path. Abby listened to the clop of the horses' hooves, trying to find something soothing in their rhythm, but in the end it only agitated her further.

"Will ye no slow down and stop a minute so I can talk tae ye?"

Abby frowned and did as he said, drawing the horse to a stop at a small rise. It was the same one to which John had brought her. Iain pulled up behind her and dismounted. He came over to her and held out his hand to assist her down. She hesitated a moment and then complied. She wouldn't put it off any longer. She would make it clear he had no claim on her any more, so any concern was misplaced.

Iain paused beside her and pointed to the distant hills. "The braes here are no so vast or stunning in their beauty as home, but there is a certain quiet elegance tae them."

Abby looked where he pointed. She could hear the homesickness underlying his voice. "Elegant, yes. They are that," she said, neutrally.

"As elegant as Huntly Castle, as elegant as the Earl and his sons?"

She stiffened and looked at him, stony-faced. "What is it you need to say?"

He took her hand but she shook it off. "Nay, lass, I'm sorry I said that. Dinna be this way toward me."

"What way would you have me be?"

"Civil, at least."

"I beg your pardon if I was rude, sir. I assure you I will endeavour to treat you with the utmost civility."

Iain sucked in his breath between his teeth. "Wheest, lass, if this is civil I wouldna want tae see uncivil. Polite, then, if you canna be friendly."

"Friendly? Why would I need to be friendly? We'll return to the castle and we can agree now that we'll stay out of each other's way. Once I am quit of this place there's no need for us ever to meet again."

Iain placed a firm hand on her shoulder. "Nay, I willna let it be like that between us."

"You have no say in the matter, Iain."

He smiled wryly. "So ye can say my name, at least, then. I suppose that's some progress."

"Progress? Progress to what? Have you not heard what I just said? I am not and never will be your concern."

"It won't always be like this, *Francach*. The time will come when my obligations will be done."

She raised a brow. "Really and when will that be? When we're both old and grey? Or perhaps when you are buried beneath the ground?" She snorted. "No, there's no future for the two of us, not in my view. My mind is made up. I'm quitting this place," she said impulsively.

Iain gripped her shoulder tighter. "What do ye mean?"

She pursed her lips, hoping that she hadn't said too much. "Just that. I don't intend to stay at Huntly Castle longer than necessary."

Iain eyed her warily. "Promise me ye willna do anything stupid."

"I have no need to promise you anything."

Iain shook his head. "Remember *Francach*, I ken ye well, and I see it in your face. You're up tae something."

"I assure you I am not," she said in a firm voice.

Iain frowned. "And I ken when ye're lying." He gave her a direct look. "I'll be watching ye like a hawk, Abby Gordon. So anything ye might be thinking of, ye can just put it out of your mind."

She lifted her chin. "You have nothing to concern yourself

with. You are not my keeper and I would be obliged if you confine yourself to your own business. I'm certain that's enough to keep you occupied in the time you're here at Huntly Castle."

Iain stared at her a minute, shook his head and released her from his grip. "As ye wish." He gestured to the horses. "Shall I assist ye tae your horse, my lady?"

Abby gave a slight nod and waited while he linked his palms to allow her to mount. Once seated, she turned her horse and urged it forward. Iain mounted quickly and was soon close behind her, following her movements now, just as she knew he would follow every subsequent movement of hers from now on.

CHAPTER 9

The ride back was silent and for that Abby was grateful. She kept her eyes focused on the trees, careful of the branches, determined to think of nothing else. When they arrived at the castle, Iain silently took the horse from her after she dismounted at the block. She left him there, at the stables. Inside the castle, her hope to retreat to her room without any encounters was dashed when she met Frances.

"Oh, good. I was just going to your chamber to see you," said Frances. Her hair shone brightly with vigorous grooming, her burgundy gown freshly brushed and the linen and lace pressed to a crispness. "Mother says you're to come to the drawing room as soon as possible. We've more guests come and she wants you there." She grimaced and gestured to her gown. "You can see she means to impress. She's made me put this on."

Abby gave her a tight smile. "I'll be there as soon as I've changed. I've been riding."

"You're lucky. I've been stuck inside while Mother primps me and everyone else she can get her hands on."

"You look lovely, Frances." She turned and made her way up the stairs.

Inside her chamber she was faced with a distracted Jeannette. All her gowns and kirtles were on the bed, her sleeves tossed on top, and her linens and underskirts draped across the chair.

"Ah, madame, at last," said Jeannette. "You must hurry and change. The Countess is waiting for you."

"I heard. But she can wait. There is no rush. I'm sure I'm not really required so immediately."

"Most definitely you are, madame. She made that very clear."

Abby dismissed her comment and looked at the mess of clothes. "Have you selected something then?"

Jeannette held up a brocade gown of deep blue with silver thread running through it. It was her best and had too many memories attached to it.

"No," she said. "Not that one. The gold."

"But you wore that the other night."

Abby shrugged. "It's fine enough for whatever has been planned. I wore it at the Paris court and if it's good enough for there, it's good enough for Lady Elizabeth's drawing room."

Jeannette pressed her lips together but refrained from further word. She helped Abby remove her riding gown, gloves, hat and boots. Jeannette emitted a few tsks and sniffs as she smoothed the rumpled cloth, the tattered feather on her hat and rubbed the stains on Abby's gloves. She remained silent while she helped Abby into her farthingale, white brocade kirtle and gold gown, but insisted that Abby sit properly while she arranged her hair in a suitable fashion. Abby had conceded to the farthingale reluctantly and just as reluctantly allowed Jeannette to contrive something with her hair. At least it wouldn't be as elaborate as some of the fashion for intricate curls she'd seen at the French court, worn by those who still aspired to Diane de Poitiers's clever hairstyles.

Finally, with pearls woven into her hair and a large pearl pendant hanging from her bodice, Abby was freed and allowed to go to the drawing room. She halted at the door, listening to the chatter and music that came from within. The tune was familiar. All too familiar. Slowly she opened the door, hoping she'd been mistaken. She was not.

On a large cushion amid other of her mother's ladies, Margaret sat draped, her farthingale and skirts arranged carefully, John's lute in her lap. Her eyes sparkled and her lips and cheeks, reddened either by nature or artifice, looked becoming. Margaret continued to pluck out the familiar tune, a little hesitant in places, but there was no mistaking it. *Iain Glinn Cuach.* For a moment Abby felt a flash of anger. That she would dare. But of course she would. Margaret had requested Abby teach her for this specific purpose. To charm a gathering. To charm one person in particular, by her steady look. Abby followed its direction and saw Iain leaning against the wall, his arms crossed, regarding Margaret. His eyes gave away nothing and his beard covered any hint of tension she might have noticed in his jaw.

The room was crowded with retainers, attendants, family members and a few guests. She recognised many from the Earl's retinue and those from the household, but there were a few new faces. Subconsciously, she registered their fashionable attire until she realised the style was French in a most definite manner. Were they lately from the Scottish court where Marie of Guise, the Dowager Queen, still favoured her French tastes from her home country? A faint no echoed from her mind. These people were directly from the French court. A curious thing, though with the Earl's role as Chancellor and member of the Council of Regents, he would of course have some interaction with French diplomats and friends of the Dowager Queen.

She slipped in behind a man standing near the door. She would prefer to attract as little notice as possible. Margaret began to sing, startling Abby. Her voice was steady enough, but the words, so clear in Abby's mind, came out a little jumbled and uncertain in Margaret's. Still she sang with assurance, as if her pronunciation and wording was the correct way.

Iain looked at her. It was barely a glance, but she saw it all the same. She knew the question it held and she gave a mental shrug. It couldn't be helped. She was thankful, though, when Margaret ended the song after the first verse. Everyone clapped politely and Margaret gave a little nod of acknowledgment.

"Thank you," she said in French. "That was one of our quaint little songs from the Highlands. I hope you enjoyed it."

"But it is charming," said a woman from the corner. "And so prettily played," she added in heavily accented Scots.

The woman was seated in a heavy oak chair, her black skirts spilling out the sides. She was large in both height and width, though her beringed hands were elegant and her heavily painted face showed no trace of fat. She wore a black hood that matched the severe gown, with only a white starched linen border and a white pearl pendant at her breast to relieve the sombre colour. In one hand she held a feather fan and waved it slowly in front of her face. But most striking of all was the pair of tinted spectacles perched on her nose, little straps keeping them in place. Abby had only seen spectacles once before, worn by a foreign diplomat at the French court. But those had been clear and used to help the person read the many documents he had to handle in the course of his work.

Margaret smiled at the woman. "Thank you, Madame d'Eauville. You're very kind. Do you play the lute?"

Madame d'Eauville waved her hand. "*Oui*, it is the one pastime I can still enjoy without straining my eyes. But I am no match for you."

"Oh, but please do," said Margaret.

She rose gracefully with the lute and placed it on Madame d'Eauville's lap and then wandered to the other side of the room, all attention on Madame d'Eauville now. Madame d'Eauville gave a little *moue*, tucked her fan at her side and took up the lute. Holding it against her large stomach, she began to play.

She began simply with an Italian piece, one that Abby vaguely knew, but then she began to ornament it, adding complexities that only a skilled musician could achieve. Abby stole a glance at Iain, but he was engaged in a conversation with Margaret. She frowned. She could easily imagine Margaret's words. She turned her attention back to Madame d'Eauville, determined not to be distracted. There was a definite grace to her hands and her whole manner of playing. One could nearly imagine how she must have appeared in her youth, for the charm was still there, despite the glasses, the painted face and her size. She finished the piece with a flair, looked up and smiled. She caught Abby's eye and her smile widened. Abby returned the gesture and clapped, extending true appreciation.

While the clapping continued Lady Elizabeth came to her side and took her hand "Ah, you've come. Finally. I want you to meet someone."

She drew Abby across the room, weaving among the people seated, standing and sitting on cushions, negotiating her farthingale as if it was part of her. Abby followed suit, scanning the room carefully, trying to identify who it might be that she was supposed to meet. It didn't take her long to locate a middle aged man, his eyes carefully appraising her. He was dark haired, bearded and wore a brown velvet bonnet and matching doublet and breeches, the doublet trimmed with gold edging. His eyes gave nothing away and as she approached with Lady Elizabeth he smiled at them blandly.

Lady Elizabeth made the introductions, her tone conversational. "Sir Robert Hamilton, may I present my husband's cousin, Gabrielle Gordon."

Abby regarded him then, remembering herself, held out her hand. He took it, kissed it and bowed low.

"Madame," he said. "I've heard much about you and may I say it's a pleasure to meet you and see that you are everything and more than I imagined."

The words were courtly, his manner graceful and practised, but it was as though he'd rehearsed it carefully. Abby curtseyed. "Thank you, sir. But it seems you have the better of me, for I cannot say that I know much about you beyond your name."

"Sir Robert has been lately at his home, near Linlithgow, attending to some family matters," said Lady Elizabeth. "He has only now been able to join us here at Huntly."

"Linlithgow?" said Abby, searching her mind for a connection. Was he one of the men her father had mentioned to Lady Elizabeth? She tried to find a connection. "You're related to the Earl of Arran?"

He forced a laugh. "Not directly. There is a connection, but it's distant."

"Sir Robert is a man of learning," said Lady Elizabeth. "His interests are fascinating. I believe he makes a study of the stars. Isn't that so, Sir Robert?"

"Plants, my lady. I find the study of plant life interesting."

"Of course it is," said Lady Elizabeth. She patted Abby's arm. "I'll let you two get better acquainted." She gave a nod to Sir Robert and moved off.

Sir Robert smiled tightly. "I hope you find plant life as fascinating as Lady Elizabeth finds the stars?"

"I'm afraid I know next to nothing about both. Though I know a little about herbs. For healing and such."

He nodded. "Yes, there is much to understand in that area, too. Too many old women think they can make magic out of what is really very clearly part of nature. My interest is broader. I do have a large collection of specimens, though, that would fall into what you might call the category of healing plants."

He continued to explain the different areas of his plant interests and Abby felt her mind wandering. She stole a glance in Iain's direction and saw that he'd moved away from Margaret and was talking with one of the ladies of the Earl's retinue.

"Monsieur, you must excuse my impertinence, but I wonder if I might steal this lady away from you so that I could put to her a particular question."

Abby turned to see it was Madame d'Eauville who spoke.

Sir Robert frowned a moment but bowed graciously. "Of course." He smiled at Abby. "I hope that we may talk further later. I look forward to continuing our acquaintance."

Abby nodded and he took his leave of both women. She turned to Madame d'Eauville, who smiled and gave a little snort.

"Ah, such a little prig," Madame d'Eauville murmured in French, waving her fan. "I hope you will forgive me for intruding on you like that, and with no proper introduction, but the man was clearly boring you to death and I decided to take pity on you."

Abby suppressed a little giggle and decided she liked Madame d'Eauville. She was a refreshing change after the stuffy manner of most of the people in the Earl's retinue. "Not at all madame. You arrived at a most opportune time."

"Please, you must call me Claudine." She gave Abby's arm a squeeze. "I feel we will become friends. We are of like minds, *n'est-ce pas?*"

"That's very kind of you to think that," said Abby.

"Shall we sit down? It's just that my leg aches so if I stand for more than a little while."

"Oh, of course, madame. Claudine. Shall I take you back to the oak chair?"

"If you would. Though I feel like an old queen on her throne, too ancient for her subjects." She gave a youthful trill of laughter, belying her words.

Abby laughed too and put her hand under Claudine's arm.

The two made their way over to the chair, Claudine leaning heavily on Abby. Her limp was pronounced and it was evident it caused her pain. She sank into the oak chair in relief.

"There," she said. "So much better." She looked at Abby. "But child, you must fetch one of those cushions they seem to perch on so daintily and sit beside me. I want to know all about you."

Abby smiled and nodded. Quickly she retrieved a cushion just recently vacated by one of Lady Elizabeth's women and placed it beside Claudine. Carefully, she lowered herself as she'd seen one of the other women do earlier, to allow the farthingale room. She was lower down than Claudine, but it was comfortable enough.

"There, now," said Claudine, patting Abby's shoulder and waving her feather fan. "We can have a cosy tête-à-tête. Now tell me, how is it you are here? You're not one of the Earl's children, I know."

"No," said Abby. "A cousin, of a sort."

"*Cousine? Vraiment?*" Her mouth opened to say something but she closed it. She studied Abby. "Ah *oui*, I suppose there is a resemblance. Though you are much prettier than the Earl." Claudine gave a tinkly laugh. "And I'm certain you can sing and play the lute better than he can."

"Can he play the lute?"

"Bah, he is nothing remarkable."

"You play very well, Claudine. There are few who could excel such playing."

"Why thank you *ma cherie*." Her mouth gave a mischievous twitch. "You know someone who plays better?"

Abby reddened. "My father. But he's a trained musician who's been in the employ of high ranking nobles. An unfair comparison, I suppose."

"Not at all. I am flattered that I should be ranked with such a skilled player. Even though it is a ranking just below."

"What made you think I played the lute?" Abby asked.

Claudine gave another tinkling laugh. "Ah, it was your eyes. The way you studied me as I played. The way your foot peeked out from your skirt, tapping away. But I am not wrong, am I?"

"No. You're not wrong. I play."

"And I suppose your father taught you and honed your discerning ear?"

"He taught me, yes."

"Ah, *bon*! I shall have to hear you sometime." Claudine gave her fan a vigorous wave, sending a stray dark curl awry. "And now you must tell me who some of these people are. I'm afraid I they are mostly strangers to me."

"You are newly arrived in Scotland?"

"I am, for my sins. *Mon cousin*, he is in the employ of the Dowager Queen and since my poor Francois died and I was full of such sorrow, he thought to invite me to stay with him. A change of scene, you understand. Such a bore, *mon cousin*, I'm afraid to say. Always worried about the draughts, so that of course he takes cold and I must nurse him. He is afraid to go anywhere. But then the Earl, such a kind man. He said when I was free of the nursing I must join him here at his home. So, *voila*, I am here, another addition to this little party."

"A welcome addition," said Abby and she meant it.

"You are too kind, *ma cherie*. Now, continue." With her fan she indicated to a group over at the far side where John, Frances and James were talking. "We can begin with those fine looking children. They are the Earl's children, *n'est-ce pas*? Also your cousins, I think."

"Yes," said Abby.

She told Claudine their names and began to identify a few others nearby. Some she knew little or not at all, but Claudine just waved her fan and declared them not worth knowing. She stopped when she came to Iain, who once again was engaged in conversation with Margaret.

"And that is the Earl's lovely daughter, too, I think, talking to that young man." said Claudine. She looked at Abby. "Such a handsome man. The eye patch, it adds something, don't you agree?" She sighed. "If I was only younger. But never mind, it seems our Earl's young daughter has her eye on him."

"It's unsuitable. She should cast her eyes elsewhere," said Abby, trying hard to keep her tone even. Claudine studied her, the tinted glasses glinting from the light from the window.

"Ah but surely not. He is perfect for the flirtation. A soldier, so romantic, *non*? What harm?"

"I'm sure I don't know."

Abby looked away, searching for a distraction. The door opened and the Earl entered, two men behind him. The first man she didn't know. The second one was all too familiar. The blood drained from her face.

"My dear," said the Earl, addressing his wife. "I'm sorry we're so late, but we had matters to discuss."

He made his way forward, the two men in tow, and stopped before Lady Elizabeth. "May I present the Comte de Damville, lately come from the French court, and his aide."

Before she could stop herself she looked at Iain, knowing that the fear was written plain on her face. But he was gone. Had he seen Damville? Abby lowered her head, desperate to remain invisible. The Comte, here. She'd thought she'd escaped him after he'd tried to abduct her in France several weeks before. Back then, it had only been Iain's quick action and protective instincts combined with her own efforts that had enabled her to foil Damville's kidnap attempt. Though other problems had loomed large here at Huntly, she thought she would at least have escaped Damville's schemes.

"*Ma cherie*," said Claudine lightly. "I fear I have dropped my fan behind my chair. Would you be so kind as to look for it?"

Abby looked at Claudine blankly. "Yes, of course."

She leaned over and searched behind the chair, taking her time. There was no fan evident. In that time the Earl and his two guests had left with Lady Elizabeth and several other of the Earl's retinue, bent on some private discussion. It was with relief then that Abby could sit up and declare her failure to find the fan.

"But how stupid of me," said Claudine. She pulled the fan from under her skirts. "I have been sitting on it the whole time. You must excuse such a fat old woman who can feel nothing at all underneath her. It is fortunate that there is no lap dog in this house, for I would fear for him with my backside looking for any convenient seat." She laughed heartily this time and Abby joined her, more from relief than anything.

CHAPTER 10

*A*bby stared out of her chamber window to the courtyard below, searching for Iain's figure. The irony of her situation now didn't escape her. Searching for Iain rather than avoiding him. It nearly made her laugh. Just as her presumption that her biggest problem was to escape from here in order to avoid Lady Elizabeth and Huntly from pushing her into unwanted marriage. Now Damville was here, she knew that a real danger had arrived, not just for her, but for Iain. Despite what she'd said to him, she had to warn him, just in case he didn't know about Damville.

There was no sign of him by the stables. She glanced over at the entrance to the Tower House, where the soldiers were housed, looking to see if he was standing outside there. She immediately dismissed the idea of getting Jeannette to take a message to him. It was no use, she must risk seeking him out on some ruse. After a moment of consideration she decided that pretending to carry a message from Margaret to request he dance with her this evening would serve. The thought nearly made her laugh.

Before she could change her mind, she donned her dark cloak

to cover her hair and her gown to avoid undue notice, and made her way downstairs and out to the courtyard, avoiding any glances from servants or guests. She crossed the courtyard, avoiding the muddy puddles and the stray hunting dog that seemed to have escaped its kennel. She pulled herself up short when a cart nearly collided with her because she was so caught up in looking where she stepped. The carter let off a loud complaint, until he saw her face and the quality of her cloak and ended with a shake of his head.

She hesitated outside the entrance to the Tower House only a moment and pushed her way through a small group of men that were gathered just inside talking.

She turned to them. "Could you give me the direction of one the soldiers? I believe his name is Mister Kerr. Duncan Kerr, I think."

"Kerr?" said one of the men, dark-haired and clean shaven, with a scar running across his left brow. He studied Abby carefully, examining every inch of her.

"Aye, ye know him," said another man, blond, burly and ruddy cheeked. "The new lad. Joined us only a fortnight ago." He turned to Abby. "He'll be upstairs, my lady. In one of the rooms. Second or third. I forget which. Do ye want me to fetch him for ye?"

She debated her virtue versus standing here with the scarred man and decided virtue was overrated in this case. Besides, she might have a better chance of speaking to Iain in private.

"No, though I thank you, kindly. It's just a quick message I've been asked to deliver."

"Do ye want me to deliver it for ye?"

She gave him a sweet smile and sighed in a resigned manner. "That's very good of you, but, alas, I promised someone I would make certain that he got the message personally."

The man nodded and pointed the way for her. "Just up thon stairs, my lady."

She gave him a nod of thanks and made her way as directed. The staircase wasn't especially well lit and she concentrated on her footing to avoid any mishap. She was near to the top when two hands took hold of her shoulders.

"What are ye doing here?" a voice hissed in her ear. "Have ye taken leave of your senses?"

She looked up into Iain's face. "I needed to talk to you," she said in a low voice. She glanced around and decided to be cautious. "I was asked to deliver a message."

He took her arm and led her part way down the small corridor and opened a door. Inside were several pallets strewn across the floor with discarded bits of clothes and other paraphernalia, a small table with a few candle stubs, and two chairs.

"In here," said Iain.

She slid past him and he closed the door softly and turned to her. "Now what's this about a message?"

She waved her hand. "There's no message. I only said that for the benefit of others. I came to warn you. The Comte de Damville is here."

He nodded. "I saw him. That's why I left the drawing room. I plan to keep out of his way as much as possible."

She studied him. "Is that your only concern? That your disguise might not be sufficiently convincing?" Her tone was steely. "I came to warn you and you have no other thought but that?"

He raised a brow. "Nay, that's not my only concern. I aim tae find his reason for coming here. They say he's some kind of envoy for France."

"A very easy and convenient guise, I'm sure." She paled. "You don't think he's after me, still?" She shook her head. She knew the answer. Her father wouldn't have placed her here, thinking her safe if he hadn't thought Damville would still be after her.

His brow darkened. "I dinna ken, perhaps there is something

tae his diplomatic commissions, on the surface. I want tae be certain before I take any steps. Rash action willna do anyone any good. In the meantime, I think ye should be careful to be in company at all times. Keep Jeannette wi' ye in your room." He searched her eyes, holding them. "Promise me?"

She opened her mouth to object, paused and then nodded. "I promise," she said.

"Good," he said, satisfied. "I'll do my best tae keep an eye out for ye too, until I ken exactly what his business is here. Since we ken he's a French spy working for the Guise family, the chances are there's something other than diplomacy that brings him here." He eyed her anxious face. "Something that has nae connection wi' ye at all."

She nodded again and allowed herself to take some comfort from his words. "I hope that's so."

He squeezed her hand. "It'll be all right, lass. Ye'll see. Now go, before anyone wonders where ye are."

He opened the door and gave her a little push out into the corridor. She hastened down the steps and out into the yard. Thankfully, the little group had gone. She was left to pass to other side of the courtyard and the entrance to the main palace without hindrance.

THE DINING HALL had grown hot with the press of the people dancing and the numerous candles and torches that lit the room. Abby waved her hand in front of her face as George bowed before her. She realised she was giddy. Damville hadn't appeared this evening. Her relief was such that her head felt light and she had an urgent need to laugh. She smiled instead and made the curtsey required at the beginning of the contra courante, the light-hearted and easy dance in which George had asked her to join him.

She skipped past George and performed the required twirl, passing the other women who made up the circle. The need to scan the room had receded now that dinner was finished. She had only to dance a little while more and then she could retire safely to her room. Secure for one night more. And then she would leave, no matter what Iain said or tried to do, before Damville discovered her. It seemed unlikely at this point that Damville would make an appearance. The Earl had been absent from dinner and Abby could only suppose that the two of them had important matters to discuss elsewhere.

Iain, apparently feeling the same, had danced his way through a few partners, including Margaret, much to Margaret's delight. Now, in a different formation to hers, he danced with one of the countess's ladies. She recognised her as the same woman she'd seen with Master Cameron, the tutor.

"May I compliment you on your dancing, cousin," said George as he completed one of the figures and faced her once more.

"Ah, but it's such a simple dance. And my skill is no less than your own, George."

She moved out of range, still smiling and caught sight of John. He was dancing with Margaret and she breathed a little sigh of relief. If she could only move away quickly after this dance completed, John might not catch her for the next dance.

Thankfully, the dance was not a long one and the concluding bars were soon playing. One more curtsey and she was free. She made her way across the room, careful to avoid John. The press of people was enough to obscure his view of her and she slipped behind another cluster of people nearer the door, edging her way along the wall. She stopped a moment, halted by the movement of the group.

"You are not leaving now, surely, Madame Villier," said a familiar voice in her ear. "Or is it Madamoiselle Gordon, now?"

Abby whirled around to face Damville, his expression a bland smile of politeness. She stiffened and stared at him, trying to collect herself.

"Monsieur le Comte, what brings you to Huntly Castle?" she said.

She looked at him carefully, while at the same time she scanned the room quickly for signs of Iain. He was nowhere in sight and for that she was thankful.

"The Earl and I have matters to discuss. A fortunate occurrence, for what do I find? A little bird who has flown the cage."

"I'm here under the Earl's protection," she said as calmly as she could. "He is my cousin."

Damville raised a brow. "Is that the connection? You? His *cousine*? Well that's an interesting twist." He put a hand on her arm. "Do not think that changes anything. In fact it might assist matters."

"Oh, I don't think your influence is that great," said Abby, bluffing. Would he convince the Earl that she should be handed over?

He opened his mouth to retort but his aide came to his side and spoke into his ear. He frowned a moment and looked over at her again, recalling himself.

"We'll leave this for a later time. For now I must go." He bowed and made his way out through the entrance, his aide in his wake.

Abby found herself trembling slightly, taken aback by the surprise of the encounter and the words he'd uttered. Vaguely, she heard music for another dance strike up and she started to make her way to the doorway, but paused. She really didn't want to follow so closely behind Damville in case he should meet her.

She looked blindly out into the assembling group of dancers and someone bumped into her side.

"My lady, ye'll pardon me, I wasn't paying attention."

Abby looked up into Iain's face and he bowed. She forced a smile. "It's quite all right. No harm was done."

"I thank you. Will you assure me of your forgiveness and have this dance with me?" He held out his hand.

She gave a slight nod and took his hand. "It is kind of you to ask and I accept."

He led her to the floor just as the dance was beginning. A volta. It was one of her favourites, but it made her hesitate. A dance whose steps required the man at certain points put his arm around her and lift her several times, among other steps.

They began their skipping steps, holding hands facing each other and processing forward with the rest of the group. Then his arm slid around her waist and he lifted her up, swirling her around, processing back. It was then the question came.

"What did he want?" Iain said in her ear, as she hung next to his side during the lift.

She knew what he meant, there was no need to explain. She waited until the next lift to answer. "He says the fact that I'm under the Earl's protection means nothing, that it might assist matters."

Again it was the next lift that brought his comment. "He's bluffing. Ye've nae cause for concern."

She tried to find his words reassuring and looked for further comfort in his next words, but when the time came in the round of lifts, his comments took her by surprise.

"Ye must do as I said and take care never tae be alone," he told her.

"You think there's danger," she said, at the earliest opportunity. Her tone was almost accusing.

The next time she waited for his words, but there was nothing. The lift was shorter and then they were skipping lightly again, all agility and grace.

The dance ended, he bowed over her hand and murmured so low she hardly heard him. "It does nae harm tae be safe, *Francach*." He kissed her hand and left, making his way towards some fellow soldiers. She stared after him, thinking on his words. What comfort was that? There was no word of a plan, no action or direction outlined. Nothing. Just hope for the best and instructions to always be in company. Did that mean she must find her own solution? It seemed so. She sighed.

"What was it you talked about while you were dancing?"

Abby turned to see Margaret at her elbow. "Do you mean Mister Kerr?"

"Yes, who else?" said Margaret impatiently.

A mischievous thought flashed across her mind. "Nothing so much. He was curious about you."

Margaret brightened. "Me? Really? What did he say?"

"Oh, he wondered what your interests were. Whether you were going hunting, things of that nature."

"And what did you reply?"

For a moment Abby nearly felt pity for Margaret. She was so eager for male attention. "I told him that I didn't know you well but I was certain you liked music. As for the hunting, I told him that I thought you liked it and so it was probable that you would be participating in the hunt. Was that sufficient enough? I felt my answers would give him some direction."

Margaret gave her a wide smile. "Yes, that's sufficient. My thanks to you, cousin. I appreciate your assistance."

A sudden bit of guilt made her add some further comment. "Have a care with the soldiers, though, Margaret. They're used to little harmless flirtations, but you wouldn't want to take it further than that. Your father wouldn't take it kindly and he could show his disapproval towards the soldier, rather than you."

Annoyance filled Margaret's face. "I will thank you to keep your advice to yourself. When I need it, I will ask for it."

She turned around and walked off, leaving Abby to wonder if she'd done Iain a real disservice. She bit her lip. Perhaps it would be best to warn him. She glanced around the room, but he'd gone. She frowned. It seemed it would have to wait. She wouldn't go searching for him in his quarters. Not twice in one day, and certainly not this time of the night.

A hand touched her shoulder. She turned. Sir Robert Hamilton bowed before her and smiled. "Would you spare a dance for me?"

She arranged her face into a pleasant smile. "I confess I'm tired. Perhaps another evening?"

"Surely not too tired for a pavane? And another evening I may not be here."

"No? Your visit is a short one?"

"Alas, yes. But worth it, I assure you." He held out his hand. "So, may I persuade you?"

"Yes, of course. How can I refuse such a plea as that? "

She took hand and he led her out to the dancers, the stately music already begun. It wasn't difficult to take up the steps, the pace slow and deliberate.

"Your father is away, I understand?" asked Sir Robert.

"Yes, do you know him?"

"We are acquainted. But it was some time ago. Your mother, I understand is …dead?"

She gave him a level look. "Gone. But perhaps dead as well." She shrugged. "I haven't seen her since I was a small child."

"Ah, I'm sorry. I hadn't meant to bring up something uncomfortable."

"No, I assure you. It happened many years ago. I just wanted to be accurate."

He nodded. "You have lived all these years since with your father?"

"Yes." She gave him a vague smile.

"And now you're under the Earl's protection."

"At my father's wish. Just for the time. When he completes his business elsewhere, we will return home."

"And home is? The last time I saw your father, he was at court."

"Yes, it might be court."

Her evasiveness frustrated him, she knew, but she couldn't bring herself to trust anyone, especially him, a stranger, for all he claimed to know her father and her father had named a Hamilton as a possible suitor.

"And you, Sir Robert, were you at court long?"

He laughed. "No. I am a man of the land. Country affairs, mostly. Cattle. Hunting." He caught himself a moment. "But my household is large enough. Alas, at the moment I rely on a house-keeper to look after the domestic side of things. Not completely satisfactory, especially for my poor young daughter, Anne."

He gave her a meaningful look and it was all Abby could do not to snort. She reminded herself he was a kind man. There seemed no malice in him, as well as no subtlety. His intent was clear. She could do worse. For a brief moment she wondered what Iain would say if she told him that Sir Robert Hamilton was considering her as a candidate to be his wife.

She sighed. It mattered little how kind he might be. She must direct her mind to the business at hand. She had preparations to make tonight, for tomorrow, during the hunt, she would slip away and make her escape.

CHAPTER 11

*T*he courtyard was thronged with barking dogs, milling horses and people, all restless at the knowledge of the coming hunt. Mist hung in wispy clusters and the threat of snow permeated the air. Laughter rang out occasionally, as courtly manners prompted witty banter. The gowns and doublets were brushed to a shine, the bonnets all at cocky angles, some with feathers, others with jewels. The real game was not the animals to be killed, but the entertaining spectacle of the hunt itself. A boar or a stag, it mattered not. All the bucks in sight at present were mounted on horses, young, virile and ready to prove themselves in a variety of ways.

Abby mounted her horse with bleary eyes, still groggy from a sleepless night filled with decision making and planning. The small purse of coins was hidden on her already, all other baggage abandoned in the interest of necessity. She took up the reins and looked around her for Iain. She had decided that she would warn him about her conversation with Margaret, before she left. Now might be the time, an innocent conversation between two people waiting for the hunt to begin.

She noticed the tutor, Cameron, mounted and ready to ride.

He was talking to the same lady, Jane, she'd seen him with the other day. Jane passed him a folded bit of paper. He took it quickly and slipped it inside his doublet, speaking quickly, his face a warning. A love note passed too indiscreetly for his liking?

"Ah. I hoped I might see you beforehand," said Sir Robert.

Abby gave an inward sigh and looked over at him. "Sir Robert, good morning."

He bowed his head slightly. "You are looking very well. The morning air suits you. Brings roses to your cheeks."

She forced a smile at the awkward compliment, taking in the old fashioned cut of his doublet. Fine enough, but still out of date and slightly worn. "Thank you," she said. "Though I confess I am a little tired after the evening before."

"But it shows not at all, for you look as lovely as always." He laid a hand on her arm. "Last night we didn't have a chance to talk as fully as I wished. I neglected to mention that I have a townhouse in Edinburgh. I would be honoured if you would allow me to entertain you and your father there. Should you return to court."

"How pleasant. I'm certain my father would be happy to accept your invitation. When we are next at court."

His attempt at subtlety had improved, but only marginally. A knight's holding and a property in Edinburgh. That was his offer and he seemed eager that she accept it. Did he imagine the Earl would add a sizable dowry, or was it just that her charms that won him over? She suppressed a sardonic smile. There was no doubt in her mind which it was.

"A fine morning, cousin," said John.

"John. Yes, isn't it." She eyed the mist that had formed droplets on the peak of his bonnet. She indicated Sir Robert. "I presume you two are acquainted."

Sir Robert bowed. "Yes, I met young John some years ago. His father introduced me. You were just finished your lessons with your tutor. You and James, I believe. I think George was perhaps elsewhere."

John flushed at the reference to his youth. Perhaps not so bad at subtlety, after all, thought Abby. She looked at Sir Robert with an assessing eye. Or perhaps just a man's instinct for a perceived rival. Cockerels strutting before the hens.

"Many years ago, I think. But time passes and changes us. We all grow older," said John. "You like to hunt, Sir Robert?"

"I'm not sure, it's about liking. I see it more of a necessity than something to enjoy."

"Ah, but perhaps you've not had the opportunity to participate in a hunt with company such as this," said John. "It is more than a matter of chasing after prey."

"My brother is right. There is more to the hunt than chasing animals," said George. He came closer and managed to manoeuvre his horse between John and Abby. He nodded to Abby. "Cousin."

Abby returned the nod. "George."

"There is more than one type of prey," said George. He gave a wicked smile and gestured to Abby. "And the ladies can be so much more rewarding than a bristly ill-tempered boar."

John frowned at George. "That's not what I meant." He gestured to the surrounding countryside. "There is much sport and challenge riding through our lands. It requires agility, even cunning."

"Cunning, yes indeed," said George. He took Abby's gloved hand and kissed it. "But when the lady eludes capture, applying such cunning can be reward in itself."

Abby withdrew her hand. "I think you have to be careful what prey you choose to chase. Some simply aren't worth the effort."

The trumpets sounded. Abby looked over to the two heralds, seated on their horses. The Earl strode across the courtyard and mounted his horse in one majestic athletic movement, a commander ready for battle. Lady Elizabeth nodded to the servants from her own horse and one moved forward, a large cup of ale in his hand. The Earl took it, drank deeply and handed it back. Another nod to the trumpeters and they sounded the call to hunt.

The hunting party moved out through the gate on to the track at a steady trot, the trumpeter and the dogs at the head, ready to take the lead. Soon they veered off the track and picked their way across the rough ground, gaining pace. Abby held herself at the back. She was more than happy to appear less able and less interested than the others, as it would serve her plan to escape. Not so George, who nodded to her genially and took off after the hounds with the rest of the group, once they left the track. Much to Abby's dismay, John made an effort to stay with her, as did Sir Robert.

The group headed towards the woods and Abby spent her time concentrating on ducking branches and searching for an opportunity to slip away from John and Sir Robert. Everyone had spread out by this time, making their own pace and negotiating the obstacles in their own time and manner. Abby thought she caught a glimpse of Iain not far off, in the Huntly livery, but she couldn't be certain. She saw Sir Robert, his seat easy and confident, his face determined, avoiding branches as a matter of course. Ahead she could hear the dogs baying, more insistent this time. The riders just ahead of her increased their pace, disappearing as they followed the hounds. John shouted at her to come. Sir Robert flashed by her, caught up in the hunt now, the scent fixed.

There were a few stragglers besides herself, she could hear them behind her. Not everyone thought riding under the threat of breaking your neck was a sport, she thought. She continued at her same pace, the sounds of the dogs receding.

She slowed even more and made the pretence of checking her

saddle and adjusting her position. When the others had gone ahead she urged her horse forward and veered off the track slightly, heading towards another track that she was certain would take her to the road. She was just negotiating a fallen log when a man came out from the side and attempted to grab her. Perched as she was, sidesaddle, with little grip, it was an easy task and she was soon on the ground, the breath knocked from her. The man snatched her up and dragged her away. Abby looked over to the perpetrator and saw Damville's aide. Fear rose up and she struggled against his grip.

"Steady, madame," he said in French. "If you just comply, you will come to no harm."

"What do you want?" she demanded.

"Ah, such a question, but I'm sorry I cannot say anything. I will leave that to my master."

"Le Comte de Damville?" she said scornfully. "Aren't you one of his errand boys?"

"Exactly so, madame. And I have my errand to complete."

She looked around and saw no one. Before she could say more, he dragged her further into the trees, where he had a horse secured. He withdrew a small dagger from his side and pressed it to her throat.

"You will struggle no more, madame, for rest assured that I will not hesitate to use this on your pretty face. And perhaps your throat as well, should the need arise."

"Damville wouldn't thank you for that."

The aide shrugged. "Perhaps not the throat, but the face, I think he would not care." He pressed the knife deeper, to emphasise his seriousness.

Resigned, Abby did as she was told and allowed him to assist her up on the horse. A moment later he mounted behind her.

"Where are you taking me?" she said, forcing herself to be calm.

The dagger pricked her again. "Silence, madame."

They rode on for a little while and she wildly considered various courses of action. He was more firmly seated on the horse than she, with his stirrups, saddle and legs astride, so she had little hope of knocking him off. Wresting the knife from him was out of the question, it was too uncertain in its outcome.

Behind her, she heard the dogs barking, coming closer. The aide cursed in a low voice and tried to urge the horse onward.

Horses crashed through undergrowth not far away. Out of the woodland a rider emerged, and then another. More and more emerged from different places, all heading towards Abby's right. The hounds rushed out from another direction. Another group of riders emerged and made their way towards Abby and the aide, careening at a mad pace, among them Claudine, the French widow. The aide tried to sidestep the oncoming horses. Abby, seizing her chance, shifted her weight to jump off, but he held her tight.

"Oh, monsieur," shouted Claudine. "Help, I cannot stop."

She pulled on the reins ineffectually and before the aide could pull his horse aside Claudine tumbled from her mount, knocking off both Abby and the aide. The three of them fell to the ground, Claudine landing on top of the aide with a hearty thud. Abby rose, and before she could assist Claudine, another rider was beside her, extending his hand. The tutor, Master Cameron, seeing their distress, had ridden over. Behind him were more riders, Iain among them, trailing her own horse behind him.

Claudine took Master Cameron's hand and allowed him to help her up. She rose, fell against him a moment, unsteady on her feet. Abby saw something flutter from Cameron's doublet, unnoticed. A folded note. Abby shifted on top of it and, when no one was looking, secreted it in her gloved hand.

"*Merci*, monsieur, you are too kind," said Claudine. She turned and addressed Damville's aide. "You must excuse my actions. I am a most terrible rider. The hunt, I think, is too much for me now. You see I am very weighty for the poor horse, for a start. And it has been many years." She gestured to her horse that had stopped a little way off. .

"No need to apologise," said the aide smoothly.

Claudine looked at Abby. "And you, *ma cherie*, you are not hurt, I hope?" She looked around. "Your horse. It seems to have taken fright in all the excitement."

Abby pointed to Iain. "Mister Kerr has it."

"Ah, I see," said Claudine. She cocked her head at Damville's aide. "Another mishap and rescue?"

"Something like that," Abby said. "You are unharmed yourself, madame?"

"Bah." She patted her stomach. "With all this padding, I am unharmed, of course."

Though most of the people had left to continue the pursuit, Abby was reluctant to accuse the aide or demand explanations. There was too much unknown. The only person to whom she could talk about this was Iain. She glanced over at him. He was staring at Claudine, his eyes speculative, until he caught her look. He gave a courtly smile, dismounted and led both horses towards her.

"Can I assist you to mount, my lady?" he asked.

"Thank you," she said.

He leaned over and cupped his hands together. She put her foot in, he lifted her up and she mounted securely.

"Did you want to continue with the hunt? Or shall I accompany you back?" asked Iain.

"I think I would prefer to return," said Abby, eyeing Damville's aide. "Your escort would be appreciated."

"I am finished with the hunt, too," said Claudine. She gave a giggle. "Or rather, the hunt is finished with me. I am such a poor participant." She looked at Iain. "You would not mind an addition to your company?"

Iain bowed, an amused smile on his face. "Of course, madame. It would be a pleasure to have you too."

"Oh, such a charming man," said Claudine. She looked at Abby. "*N'est-ce pas?*"

"*Oui*, madame," Abby murmured in reply.

With Claudine along the journey there was no opportunity for Abby to have a substantial discussion with Iain. But the widow was charming and full of light-hearted banter, so that Abby couldn't find it in herself to resent the unwanted intrusion. In fact she found her mood lightening and the fear and anxiety that had left her nerves frayed after the fall were alleviated to an extent that she felt some semblance of calm by the time they arrived at the courtyard and prepared to dismount. After she stepped down from the mounting block to allow Claudine her turn, Iain came over to her and held out his hand for the reins.

"We'll talk," he said quietly. "I'll find you."

She gave a quick nod and waited while Iain took the reins of Claudine's horse. She watched him lead them both to the stables.

"So helpful. A good soldier, I think, too. A good lover, perhaps?" said Claudine. "But maybe not so much a suitable husband."

"Lover?" asked Abby. She stared at Claudine.

"For Margaret, *ma cherie*."

"Oh," said Abby.

"Too serious. A man who is a lover of his duty. Don't you agree?"

Abby watched Iain remove the saddles one by one. His strong, capable hands patting and calming each horse, the strong, muscular legs. Solid, assuring and more.

"Yes," she said finally. "I'm certain you're right."

Claudine slipped her arm through Abby's. "Come. You and I

are in need of some wine. Good wine. Do you think it is possible here?"

Abby, laughed, her humour returning. She would put aside her worries, if only for a short while. For now, she would enjoy the simple pleasures of Claudine's charming company. She matched her pace with Claudine's limping progress across the courtyard and entered the main part of the castle. The two made their way to the small corridor and the stairs.

"Shall we change, first, *ma cherie?* But then you must come to my room. I will arrange for the wine to be brought there. We can be cosy, just the two of us. If you will help me there now, you will know where it is."

"Yes, of course," said Abby. She gave an inward sigh. As much as she liked the Frenchwoman, meeting with her meant she would lose her opportunity to leave. And something told her that Claudine wouldn't take it lightly if she failed to show. At the very least Claudine would have Jeannette searching for her.

The steps, though circular, were modern and had a wide enough passage for two. It was fortunate for Claudine that she had been housed in a room near the stairs on the floor just above, at the opposite end from Abby's room. Abby left her at the door and went to her chamber, relieved that there was no sign of Jeannette. She closed the door gratefully behind her. Making her way to the bed, she began to peel off her gloves and the folded note popped out, dropping to the floor. She leaned over and picked it up. The folds that had held it in place loosened and a word caught her eye. *Spy.* She stared at it, too paralysed to continue. She forced her fingers to open it further and reveal the remaining words scribbled quickly on the small sheet of paper. *There is a spy. Medici? Guise?*

Abby read the words several times, trying to make sense of their meaning. Trying to determine the note's creator. If she hadn't seen it fall from Cameron's doublet she would have thought it belonged to Damville's aide. Though they were spies for the Guise family, trying to protect their influence in the French court as well as in Scotland. And somehow they thought she was a threat or a tool to use over her father, who clearly must be working against the Guise interests in minds of the Guise family. That much she had concluded since Damville had tried to kidnap her in France. But why would Jane, Lady Elizabeth's attendant pass a note of warning to Cameron? Perhaps this was a different note, though. One passed to Cameron by someone else. Iain? Could Cameron be working with Iain? She frowned. Well there was one way to find out. She folded the note up quickly. She would hide it on her body, next to her skin until she could show it to Iain. He might be able to make sense of it.

CHAPTER 12

*I*n the corner of the room a coal filled brazier glowed hot and the linenfold panelling was covered with tapestries, some French in design, others clearly older and Scottish, giving the room a cosy feeling. The customary kist at the end of the bed was piled with freshly washed bed linens. A discarded farthingale was tossed, collapsed, on the heavy tester bed beside a riding gown and bonnet. Claudine sat in a large oak chair filled with cushions, dressed in a loose overgown of heavy dark brocade, a wool rug over her knees. A simple headdress of matching brocade covered her hair.

Abby, who'd entered at Claudine's summons, was pleased to find that it was, just as Claudine had promised, only the two of them. She felt a little refreshed, having splashed water on her face and exchanged the mud stained gown for a clean one. She could feel the letter, though perched between her breasts under her most modest of gowns. She pushed the thought of it aside and smiled at Claudine.

"Thank you for the invitation. You're very kind," she said.

"Oh, it is nothing." Claudine indicated the stool at the other side of the bed. "Please, bring that over and sit here next to me.

I'm sorry that I can give you nothing more comfortable, but you see my own chair, it takes up so much room." She gave a tinkle of laughter. "But then so does its occupant."

Abby brought the stool over and placed it beside Claudine. A small table was in front of her and on it a tray with a flagon of wine and two glasses. She poured the wine and handed a full glass to Abby.

"You've no need to apologise, madame. I am perfectly fine. There is no draught, and I have the wine and pleasant company. What more could I want?"

Claudine smiled and patted her hand. "You are too kind, *ma cherie*. But please, did I not tell you to call me Claudine?"

"Yes, sorry. Claudine."

Claudine gestured to the tapestries. "You are right. The room is comfortable. I have brought my tapestries for extra warmth and I insist they keep a brazier lit at all times. This country, it is very damp, no? I fear my bones cannot take it and they are kind enough to pander to the complaints of an old woman."

"You're not old," said Abby.

Claudine laughed. "Your manners are pretty. But I know the truth."

She looked at Claudine. They were on the side opposite to the window, away from the draughts and the light was poor, but she could still see the creases at the corner of her mouth, under the white paste of cosmetics.

"Well, you seem very young at heart," amended Abby.

"Now, I will accept that," said Claudine.

She took a sip of her wine and Abby did likewise. "Have you travelled much?"

Claudine considered her question. "Outside of France, you mean?"

"Well, yes. I suppose. Perhaps when your husband was alive you travelled more?"

"Ah, my husband. Yes. We travelled, but not too much. But I have been places, too. Afterwards."

"And you have no children?"

Claudine fixed her gaze on Abby and even with the spectacles and clouded eyes, Abby thought she saw tears gathering there.

"I wish I was so blessed to have a daughter such as you."

"I'm sorry."

"*Merci, ma cherie.*" Claudine sniffed, collected herself and smiled. "But that is the past. Now I have your delightful company, *ma cherie*. A daughter. To laugh with. Do you mind?"

"No, I am flattered you would think of me as your daughter."

Claudine placed a hand on Abby's cheek. "And such a lovely daughter, too. Charming, beautiful and filled with grace in every way. A perfect daughter."

"Oh, no, you flatter me, I fear," said Abby, her tone light-hearted.

"*Pas du tout.*" She withdrew her hand from Abby's cheek, matching her tone.

"Oh, but Claudine, my father could tell you a tale or two to convince you otherwise."

"Ah, but I will not listen to your father." Her tone was momentarily fierce. "Now, you must tell me about your own experiences. Have you travelled much? Have you been to France? To the court, there? Your command of the language is excellent."

"I have been a little. My father taught me French. He's good at languages and he says I have the same talent." She hedged slightly, wanting to trust Claudine, whom she liked very much, but habit made her prevaricate. "I understand the Comte de Damville is from the French court. Would you know him?"

"Damville from the French court? I heard something of that nature. But myself, I do not know him, so I cannot say. But he is a man that makes one feel, how do I put it…uneasy? His manner, yes it is the courtier, so polite, so gallant, but still his eyes tell you that he looks beyond the surface, inside your mind." She tapped her head.

"A man in search of secrets?"

"*Oui*. A man to be wary of."

"But surely only if you have something to hide?"

"Perhaps. Perhaps not. He is someone, I think who will find something even if it is not there."

Abby gave her a quizzical look, nodding eventually. A friendly warning, from a woman of experience. But she had no need of it. She knew it already.

"Thank you for the guidance, Claudine. But you've have only given expression to what I'd already concluded."

"Good. I'm glad," she said. "I would hate for there to be another riding mishap."

The comment made Abby pause a moment. Had Claudine noticed that there was something amiss before she tumbled into her and Damville's aide? That the two of them had been on a single horse had never been questioned in the confusion of the tumble, but perhaps Claudine had noted it. Abby examined the stout, apparently frivolous woman, who perhaps was more acute than she first seemed. There was something motherly about her, though, and it might be Abby's suspicious mind going a little too far.

THE KNOCK WAS soft when it came. She rose from the bed, caught up a shawl and made her way to the door, opening it only just enough to see that it was Iain. She opened the door wider to let him enter, glad that she'd convinced Jeannette that she was going directly to bed, rather than eat with the returning hunters. Jeannette had duly vanished to help to the kitchens then, every hand required, and Abby had told her she need not return, in the hopes that Iain would find a way to see her here while all were engaged in the entertainment below. Relieved at the sight of him, she was glad that she'd been proved right in her decision.

Iain made his way inside, put his hands on her arms, his face full of concern. "I'm verra sorry, *Francach*. I'd have come sooner if I could. Are ye hurt? I'll kill the bastard." He searched her face for signs of distress.

For a moment Abby was taken aback by the strength of his emotion, so used to his studied calm, his acerbic tone or combative words, or any combination of those that had been his manner towards her of late. He took her in his arms and she still mistrusted him, not relaxing, even when he kissed her lightly on the head.

"Ye had me worried, lass. More than I can say. When I saw your horse, saddle empty, I could only imagine the worst." He pulled back and stroked her cheek. "I wasna far wrong, was I? He tried to take ye away."

She nodded, suddenly unable to speak. The experience had unnerved her, she couldn't deny it. And now she felt it even more, with Iain's concern. She tried to put it aside. She mustn't let it distract her from her course. He'd said nothing to change it.

She swallowed hard. "He snatched the reins and pulled me to his horse, holding a knife to me. There was nothing I could do to get away, until Claudine and the others came galloping fast towards us and collided into the horse. If it hadn't been for that..." she took a deep breath and shrugged. "I fear Damville would have me imprisoned somewhere again. This time more securely than the last, I have no doubt."

"As soon as I saw your horse I searched where I could. But with the dogs and the other riders it was difficult. I tried to keep ye in my sights when ye first set off, but ye would lag behind."

He gave her a wry grin, so the protest that rose up died before it was uttered. He stroked her hair, staring into her eyes. "Ah, quean, what am I tae do wi' ye? It's clear ye're no safer here than in France or Kilchurn."

She frowned at him and snorted, suddenly annoyed by the obvious statement. Things could have been different, if he'd not been so honour-bound. She stared at the eye patch and, on impulse, removed it and flung it to the floor. The eye, now uncovered, blinked in the soft light of the candles.

"There," she said. "I can see what you're thinking better now."

He raised his brow. "And just what is it that I'm thinking?"

"Well, your thoughts certainly don't coincide with mine. I'm thinking that you have no need to worry about what you should do with me because it's none of your concern. I'm leaving as soon as possible, so any disposition you might have towards worry can cease.

"Leaving?" said Iain sharply. "Where are you going?"

"To the Scottish court, to ask the Dowager Queen for protection. I wouldn't think Damville would dare to snatch me from there."

"But Damville works for the Guise family and don't forget the Dowager Queen is a Guise."

"Yes, I know," she said impatiently. She forced a smile. "But she knows me and realises that I mean her daughter no harm. If I tell her that Damville is after me because of my father, that I am Huntly's cousin, she would protect me, I'm sure." She tried to put all the certainty she didn't feel into her tone.

Iain stared at her, his face set, unreadable. "And just how do you plan to get there?"

"By horse."

"Alone? No, don't answer that. I can see by your face." He sighed. "Why not stay here and explain the threat to your dear cousin?"

"My father didn't explain it to Lady Elizabeth. He must have had a reason not to trust them that far. Huntly is close to the

Dowager Queen. And besides, it would only make them more determined to marry me off to Sir Robert."

Iain looked away, but before he did she saw the tightness in his face, but still the eyes, even though both were uncovered, gave nothing away.

"I'd advise against it. And your father wouldn't approve of such a step. He placed you here for a reason."

"My father's desires aren't your concern," Abby said firmly.

Iain gave a small sigh. "Regardless of your plans, you won't be going anywhere tonight. Tonight you'll stay here and I'll remain here to make certain you're safe."

"You only want to ensure I don't leave."

Iain ignored her comment. "Would you consider waiting a few days while I finish what I have to do here? Then I promise I'll escort you to the Scottish court myself."

"And you propose to stay here and watch over me every night until then?"

"If that's what it takes."

"And if I don't agree?"

"Please. Just give me time to try to discover what Damville's real purpose is and Claudine's. I promise you it won't take long."

"Claudine?" she asked. "What other purpose could Claudine have?"

Iain shrugged. "I dinna ken for certain she has another purpose. There is just something about her that makes me want to discover what I can about her."

"What do you want to know? I've had several conversations with her and she has told me something of herself. She's a widow, she has a daughter about my age who is most likely married and still living in France, I think. She hasn't seen her for some time."

Iain nodded. "Interesting. I can understand why ye would desire her company, but I caution ye tae have a care until I discover more."

"Funny, she said the same about you."

Iain frowned. "What were her words?"

"Just that I should have a care. That you were fine to flirt with, but not the marrying kind." She took a deep breath, realising she could easily be reduced to hysterical laughter if she wasn't careful.

Iain frowned. "Well, ye can see she isna right about everything."

Abby gave him a blank look. "Really?" Suddenly recalling the note, she withdrew the note from where she'd placed it under a pillow earlier. "Here. I meant to show you this earlier."

He took the note, unfolded it and quickly scanned the contents. "Where did ye get this?"

"It fell from Cameron's doublet after we all collided. I thought it might be the note that I saw Jane, one of Lady Elizabeth's attendants, pass to Cameron, but it's obviously not. That note, I assumed arranged a tryst, because I'm certain the two of them are conducting some sort of liaison."

He studied the note again, tracing his hand along the letters. "It's in English. I ken nothing about Master Cameron, though." He paused thoughtfully. "How long has Master Cameron been here?"

"I don't know exactly, but it has been a while." She smiled wryly. "Long enough to instruct both John and Margaret to a skilful level on the lute."

Iain grimaced. "I suppose too, it was ye who taught her *Iain Glinn Cuach.*"

She gave him a rueful look and nodded. "My apologies for that. I didn't intend it. She heard me play it and insisted I teach her."

"It is of nae matter. Doubtless the lass will forget the words soon enough. And me, for that matter."

"It may be less easy than you think." She gave him an apologetic look. "I may have led her to believe that you were interested in her. That you asked me about her. It was after you danced with me. She wanted to know what we talked about so intently."

Iain sighed. "Well. I suppose there's nae harm done. She'll learn soon enough that she's best off setting her sights in a completely different direction."

"How long do you need?" Abby said suddenly.

"To find out what I need? A few days." He studied her carefully. "So you'll stay?"

She nodded. "A few days only."

CHAPTER 13

*R*ain was long gone when a tap came at the door. Abby stretched a moment and then rose from the bed. Once at the door, a shawl tossed over her night-rail, she opened it and was surprised to see Jeannette standing there.

"I thought it best to knock, madame."

Abby gave her a quizzical look and stepped aside for her to enter. Jeannette carried a tray with a plate of food and a small cup of ale on it. She came inside and set it on the table.

"You are well rested?" asked Jeannette. "Recovered from your tumble?"

Abby studied Jeannette but she could detect no dissembling in her manner. This stolid woman seemed beyond that type of teasing. There was no underlying meaning intended in her query.

"I feel much better, thank you Jeannette."

"You do seem well, if I may say so, madame." Jeannette nodded at the tray. "When you are finished with your meal, I will help you dress, for Madame le Comtesse, she asks that you see her at your earliest opportunity."

"She wants to see me? Did she say why?" asked Abby

"No, madame. Just that I was to instruct you to come to the drawing room."

Abby nodded, but made no further comment. It took no real intelligence to guess what Lady Elizabeth wanted to discuss with her. She sighed and ate some of the bread and slices of meat on the plate and sipped at the ale, deep in thought. A marriage proposal. How would she handle it? Should she come out with a statement that she was already married to Iain? But Iain said he needed time. She could ignore his request. It would be a choice that would compel Iain to fulfil his promise. She considered it carefully, aimlessly eating her food, and was still undecided when Jeannette held up her underclothes in a meaningful manner. Abby gave a sigh and stood, submitting to Jeannette's ministrations.

A short while later, Abby was entering Lady Elizabeth's drawing room, noting that a few of her ladies were seated with her. At the Countess's invitation she took a seat near her. Perhaps it was on some other matter, she thought, given there were others present.

"You have recuperated from your mishap yesterday?" asked Lady Elizabeth. "It seems you're not so well versed in country pursuits as I expected. I suppose it's to your father one must look for the cause of such neglect. Are there any other areas of which I should be aware and seek to address as best as I can?"

"I think not," said Abby. "Though since I'm unaware of which areas or skills you might give weight, I cannot say for certain."

Lady Elizabeth raised her brow, but refrained from any comment. "Well we must make do with what we have, I see." She looked at the woman next to her, Master Cameron's lady of interest. "Jane, can I ask you to observe our guest closely for anything that might require some further...refinement?"

Jane gave a sweet smile. "Of course Lady Elizabeth."

"Just so," said Lady Elizabeth. "Now, my girl, Jane will be your companion. Should you have any questions or feel unable for a task, you have only to ask her. She is my most trusted companion and is a lady of the highest skill and manners."

"It's kind of you to take such an interest, Lady Elizabeth," said Abby, her face carefully composed. She was willing to ignore the barbs and baiting if that's all it was.

"There's a purpose behind it," said Lady Elizabeth. "Yesterday evening the Earl received a most interesting and promising proposal concerning your welfare. It seems Sir Robert Hamilton has not discovered anything lacking in you, even given that you are clearly not at all equipped for a serious day's hunting. As yet. We can remedy that, I'm certain. Sir Robert, in fact, has found you charming and all that he would require in a wife. In short, he has asked for a marriage to be arranged between you and he at the earliest convenience." She gave a pained smile. "A smitten suitor, indeed."

"A proposal of marriage?" said Abby feigning a stunned response. "What made him think of me? Surely there are many among your very talented women who would be just as suitable. In fact, given my shortcomings, I would say they would be even more suitable. What of Lady Jane? Surely the honour should fall on her?"

Abby cast a glance at Jane and saw her pale at Abby's words. A bit of your own back to you, thought Abby.

"He has no idea or regard for Jane. He's not even been introduced," said Lady Elizabeth sharply. "But that's neither here nor there."

"But certainly such a situation can easily be remedied."

"The offer was for you. The Earl, in capacity as your father's appointed protector, has decided that this is a fine and worthy offer for you. He has accepted the proposal and in his great generosity, and given your father's absence, has decided to settle a sum on you as a dowry." She gave a self-satisfied smile. "It would be a neglect of our duty and the Gordon name were we to do otherwise."

Abby stared at Lady Elizabeth, collecting her thoughts. "I am aware of the honour Sir Robert has done me by the proposal of marriage and keenly aware that the Earl is kindness itself to give me a dowry for such a marriage. I would be neglectful of my duty as a daughter, though, if I did not ask that such a decision be deferred until my father returns and meets Sir Robert, so that he too may know the person to whom I would be joined in marriage. I feel it's what he would wish as well."

"You are right and correct to consider your father," said Lady Elizabeth, her tone full of patronising kindness. "But there is no need for such consideration. Your father has instructed me to give the Earl full rein in this matter. In fact he was most concerned that there be as little delay as possible."

"You mean that he left instructions for me to be married?"

"Not in those exact words, but he was concerned for your welfare. He wanted you to have the full protection of a husband."

"Because the Earl's protection wasn't sufficient for him?" The words slipped out and Abby knew they were a mistake before she finished uttering them.

Lady Elizabeth stiffened. "I am not here to bandy words about with you, Abigail. I have taken the time out of my day to do you a kindness and explain to you the nature of the marriage proposal and the identity of the man. Sir Robert is a respectable person and you would do well to marry him. This is not for debate. It is decided."

"My name is Abby. Gabrielle," she said acerbically. "Has any day been named for the wedding?"

"As soon as it can be arranged. Sir Robert is anxious that it occur before he returns home in a few days' time. There are a some details to settle, but that shouldn't take too long. I'm afraid there won't be time for a gown to be made up for you. You'll just have to wear one of your own, or perhaps Margaret might be able to provide one, if none of your own would suit."

"There's no need for Margaret to lend me a gown," said Abby evenly.

"And the subject of Margaret brings me to a final point. I will thank you not to encourage my daughter to spend time in the company of any of the Earl's soldiers. Is that clear? She has been too free with her charms with one in particular. I'm certain you know who I mean, for I understand you have taken up the role of go-between for them. It will cease now."

"I apologise if it seemed that I had done so. It wasn't my intention, Lady Elizabeth."

"See that it doesn't continue. She has a softness and regrettable tendency towards romantic notions that would only do her a disservice. It would be best to nip them in the bud now, though I'm not certain your company does anything to restrain such tendencies. But, since your remaining time with us is short, there is perhaps no need for further measures. On this count. I would emphasise that in addition to a more cautious behaviour around Margaret, you also extend your restraint to my older sons. They have been encouraged, by you, I think, to believe you might have some romantic interest in them. I wish it to stop. Am I understood?"

Abby had listened to the tirade with growing amusement which she was hard pressed to conceal. When it concluded, she blinked hard and nodded before managing to utter, "You are understood, Lady Elizabeth. Clearly."

Lady Elizabeth eyed Abby carefully, obviously uncertain if her meaning would translate to obedience. Abby refrained from further assurances. A petty revenge, but still given her present situation, she wanted to take what comfort she could. She had agreed to give Iain a few days, but if the situation merited it, she would leave earlier, without him, if necessary.

~

ABBY STARED out the window of the small antechamber that looked out onto the courtyard. Through the mullioned windows and the determined mizzle that fell in a soaked mist, she could make out the stables well enough to the right and if she crooked her neck, the entrance to the Tower House. There were several people moving about out there, tramping through the puddles and ruts that covered the cobbled area, but they were servants mostly. A few soldiers huddled in the doorways and hovered around the stables, but none of them was Iain. She sighed.

She wasn't certain how long she could keep vigil here before she was noticed, but a little longer wouldn't hurt, she told herself. Failing that, she would walk outside and glance up at his window in the hopes that Iain might see her and realise she needed to speak with him. She wiped the glass to clear her breath marks. Perhaps he'd gone riding with one of the other men? A foolish notion it might seem, but it was possible, given that soldiers like Iain would detest being cooped up for too long. Dice and cards only went so far.

"Is there something very amusing outside of the window? Please tell me it is so, for I long for some distraction. This weather is too much."

Abby turned and smiled at Claudine who hobbled in, dressed in her usual dark colours, waving her oversized feather fan in front of her face. Her tinted glasses cast shadows on her eyes, creating a hollowed effect. She sat down heavily on the chests near Abby.

"Nothing really," said Abby. "Just people avoiding the mud and puddles."

"Ah, but it is better than staring at the walls, *n'est-ce pas*? At least one can hope for the possibility of amusement. A dropped item, a small slip." Her voice was teasing.

"I know, Claudine. It's very sad that I'm reduced to such pastimes."

"You do not wish to play the lute, or perhaps play cards?"

"Do you play cards?" asked Abby.

Claudine gave a little smile. "I dabble a bit, I confess."

"Somehow I'm persuaded that you are more the expert in cards than one who just dabbles."

Claudine tapped her fan playfully on Abby's arm and gave her tinkly laugh. "You have found me out. So, come, can I not persuade you to abandon your observations here for a game of cards, or, better still, play the lute for me?"

Abby gave an anxious glance out of the window. "I would like to do that, but perhaps a little later."

Claudine pouted. "You are not looking for the handsome soldier are you? The one that has the Lady Margaret so smitten that she must constantly seek him out? Surely you haven't succumbed to such lovelorn mannerisms."

Abby felt herself colour. "No, there is something I must discuss with him."

"*Mon cherie*, can I flatter myself that you might at this point consider me worthy of a confidence? Would you tell me what troubles you and compels you to seek him out?"

"Trouble?"

"*Bien sur*, I think I know you well enough now to see that you are troubled. Perhaps this old woman can give you the benefit of her experience." She patted the space next to her on the chest.

Abby hesitated a moment before sitting down next to Claudine. "It's Lady Elizabeth. She has taken it upon herself, with the Earl's approval of course, to arrange a marriage for me with Sir Robert."

Claudine stiffened slightly. "Sir Robert Hamilton? The little man with the floppy ears who dances like a stuck pig?"

Abby laughed. "Well, it's only now that you have called attention to his ears that I would describe them as 'floppy', but I certainly have no argument with the way you described his dancing, so yes, that's the man."

"And he has agreed to this proposal?"

"In Lady Elizabeth's words, he was the one who made the proposal."

"But surely he has just met you. So quick?"

"Sir Robert would like the matter settled and the marriage completed by the time he's ready to leave."

Claudine waved her fan vigorously. "The *vieux cochon*. Has he no idea of courtship, of the most proper way to woo a woman to be his bride?" She waved her free hand in dismissal. "Bah, he is not a husband and lover, he is merely in search of a housekeeper."

"And child minder," Abby muttered. The sympathetic words soothed her anxiety to a degree.

"But they must consult your Papa. He will not be so unfeeling as to permit this."

"My father asked them to arrange a marriage. He wanted me to have the protection of a husband." The words came out with a hint of the bitterness that had been underlying her thoughts since she'd first overheard the conversation."

"But, *non*! You must marry someone you love, someone who wants you for yourself and nothing more. Is that not what you want too?"

The tears came to Abby's eyes unbidden. She brushed them away. "Yes. It is what I want, but my father didn't approve of my choice."

"Hah! The coward. He fears to lose you to someone who will absorb all your affections, leaving him to manage for himself. It is ever the way. I say let him fend for himself and learn that selfishness is not the way to keep his daughter's love."

Abby smiled wryly. "Your words are very comforting. And I

hope that I might myself resolve my dilemma to my own satisfaction and desire."

"You will not marry Sir Robert?"

Abby shook her head, afraid to say more.

Claudine put her arm around Abby and gave her a warm hug and a kiss on the cheek. "*Ma cherie*, you are a child after my own heart."

The kiss lingered pleasantly on Abby's cheek and her presence was reassuring. "Thank you, Claudine. I feel a very strong connection to you, I must confess."

Claudine laid her head on top of Abby's for a few moments. "And the young soldier, what of him? Surely you don't need him to complete your plan, for my dear, I would advise you against him. I know this type only too well. It is the type *dangereuse*. Very charming and intriguing, yes, but dangerous. Dangerous because danger will always follow him. It is who he is. You must take care and not become too involved with this person." She pulled back from Abby and placed a finger under Abby's chin. "Will you promise me this?"

Abby looked at the clouded eyes behind the tinted glasses. Were Abby's past feelings for Iain so very obvious, or did this lady see much more than her failing eyesight suggested? She was keen witted, there was no doubt. And there was something in her that made Abby trust her, despite the sensible course she should take and be cautious.

"I'm not one given to promises of any kind," said Abby finally. "But don't doubt that I have taken in what you've said and will give your words all the consideration you would have me give them."

Claudine nodded. "I can ask for no more than that."

CHAPTER 14

*A*bby made her way down the quiet corridor, towards the drawing room, lute in hand. As promised, she was going to play for Claudine, but she secretly hoped that though she agreed to play for her in the drawing room, there would only be a few people gathered there. She'd arranged it for early afternoon because she had calculated that some courtiers would be resting and others off riding now that the weather had cleared. At the very worst, those gathered would probably be playing cards or sewing and gossiping in small circles.

She took heart from the emptiness of the corridors on her way there. She really didn't want to call attention to herself, at the moment. It was better if she was unremarkable, a person only a handful could call to mind, so she might move across the court-yard unnoticed, whether it be to the Tower House, or to the stables for a horse to use to slip away.

Abby recalled Claudine's words to her earlier. The widow's indignation and support over Abby's objections to the plans to marry Abby to Sir Robert had only reinforced the impact of the last comments about Iain. Initially, Abby had reacted against Claudine's words, because she felt the older woman had no full understanding of the situation between her and Iain, but later, as the words themselves niggled at Abby and she had to acknowledge their truth in her heart, no matter that she'd been voicing it all along in her mind.

Danger was part of Iain's life, but surely that was only because he was involved with intrigue and spying. She knew though, that even if Iain had offered to take her to Glen Strae and declare their hand fasting irrevocable and sealed like a marriage, he would only leave her there and go off when he was summoned. That would be an arrangement she could never accept. And danger followed Iain, not just because he was involved in spying. Even in the short time they'd been at Glenorchy in the summer, he'd still managed to get himself threatened with banishment after a clash with the Campbells, the MacGregor's enemy.

A figure reached out from the gloom near the stairs, grabbed her and drew her towards a chamber entrance. Iain. He held a finger to his lips and tapped softly on the door. There was no response. Carefully, he opened the door and, finding the room empty, he drew them inside. It was a small, containing a fair size writing table, chair and shelves lines with rolled up parchments and a few bound ledgers. A map of the estate and a hunting painting hung on the walls, marking its function as the Steward's office.

She shook his hand off of her. "Where have you been?"

"What is it? What's wrong?" he asked.

"Nothing. I'm fine. It's just that I'd looked for you in the courtyard this morning. I needed to speak to you. But it doesn't matter now."

His expression became concerned. "Tell me anyway."

"'Tis only that Lady Elizabeth has arranged a marriage for me with Sir Robert. But it's of no consequence, really, since I have no intention of going through with it. It's just that she's pressing ahead with it sooner than I thought."

"Of course, ye dinna intend to. We'll be well away from here by then. I mean that, *Francach*. I've found what I needed and more. And I can tell ye wi' certainty that Damville is working for the Guise family and he intends to take you into captivity by any means possible."

"Well the note saying there was a spy from the Guise family was right. But we'd suspected that all along."

"Aye. So we must leave as soon as possible. We dinna want ye tae fall into Damville's hands."

"What purpose would kidnapping serve them, though, except to convince my father to do something?"

"Or say things he would prefer not to."

"Reveal secrets, you mean? About your activities?" Abby bit her lip. "That would endanger you and all the others who work with him."

"Perhaps, but dinna underestimate your father. He is nae fool. He will have ensured there would be some protections in place."

"Well, it goes some way to explain why my father wanted me to be married as soon as possible to someone who he felt would protect me." Abby looked at Iain. "Clearly, he felt you wouldn't serve that purpose.

"I believe it's self-evident. Since I've known you, your life has nearly ended more than once."

"Aye," he said, wryly. "And some of those occasions have been on your behalf."

"True," she said, her tone grudging. "But I believe the incidents were caused by this life both you and my father lead. And that's not a life I would choose, either to sit safely tucked away awaiting your return from who knows what peril, wondering if you would indeed return." She lifted her chin slightly, trying to convey her conviction.

"And I wouldna ask ye tae to do that, lass."

"I wouldn't languish at the Scottish court either, while you carry on in your spying."

He gave her a helpless look and rested a hand on her shoulder. "Aye, I ken that well."

"I see," she said, suddenly sad. She shrugged him off and left, keeping her mind as blank as possible, while he stood unmoving and silent, watching her go.

ABBY SCANNED the groups inside the main drawing room. Most of the Gordon children were there, along with Cameron, the tutor, and Lady Elizabeth, her attendants and some of the courtiers in the Earl's retinue. Surveying the scene, Abby suddenly realised why Lady Elizabeth didn't remain at the Scottish court serving the Dowager Queen. At first glance, waiting on the Dowager Queen would seem to be a position of some influence, but Abby now understood that here, where a large bulk of the Scottish court followed the Earl, Lady Elizabeth had her own court, where she was the centre of attention, as well as power. She reigned in her husband's absence and when he was in residence, she was his queen consort.

Her husband was present now, playing cards at a table with others, George included. Seeing Abby enter, George gave her an easy smile. Lady Elizabeth caught the exchange and frowned. Abby nodded to George and headed in another, quieter corner where she spied Claudine already seated.

"Ah, *ma cherie*, you've come to indulge an old woman and I thank you. Here, I saved a little cushion for you in hopes that it would be so." She indicated the seat beside her.

Abby took it gratefully, glad to be out of Lady Elizabeth's view. From her vantage point though, she could see most of the other inhabitants and was relieved to note that Iain wasn't present. She pulled the lute out of its sack and, after a spot of tuning, began to pick out a tune.

"Was there something in particular you would have me play?" asked Abby.

"If you have a favourite, it would please me to hear that. If not, perhaps something your father composed."

Abby thought a moment. "Yes, one of my father's pieces. I know the very one. He taught it to me some while ago."

She began to hum the tune a little, then began playing it on the lute. It was a simple piece at first hearing, but haunting enough so that it lingered in the mind, phrases within phrases, rendered somewhat different soon after, so that it echoed what came before, but not quite. With some clever plucking it overlapped slightly, each string's note blending just for a brief moment. The middle section was lilting and light, suggesting a bird in flight. The third section was similar to the first, but rendered even more heart breaking in its tone by the slowing pace and the supporting chords.

Abby hadn't played it since leaving France and wasn't certain why it seemed so fitting now, except it suited her own mood and her own emphasis and playing reflected it. Heart breaking. She closed her eyes at the piece's conclusion. It was some time before she looked up at Claudine and saw tears running down her cheeks.

Abby frowned. "I'm sorry. I didn't mean to send you into such a low mood. I think perhaps I made the choice based on my own frame of mind. Let me play something else more lively.

"But *non*, it was lovely. I am glad you played it. And played it so well, if I may say so. Your father would be very pleased at what you made of it. Did he play it often to you?"

"Over the years. It was a special piece of his. One that he said was drawn from deep within him, composed for himself and for no other."

"No other?"

"Well, no commission from a nobleman, or the Queen."

"Ah, I see. You mean the Scots Queen at the French court? I hear she has made such a lovely addition to the court there since she arrived there when she was five, what, nine years ago or more?"

Abby nodded. "Yes. My father respects musicianship greatly."

"Did he play for the Queen very often?"

Abby blinked, and quickly covered her slip. "Well it's expected of any composer of note to create pieces in honour of his Queen." Did it matter that Claudine knew she'd spent some time at the French court? Perhaps not as much as it did with the rest of this household. Until she was fully aware of each person's true motivations and interests, something that would never happen, she was sure, it required vigilance against revealing too much.

"*Bien sur*," said Claudine. "And now, you will play something else, one of your own favourites perhaps?"

Abby nodded and launched into a piece that came to her. Anything to change the subject. She put as much liveliness into it as she could, smiling and watching Claudine's expression lighten as she played. Soon it was finished. Claudine nodded and before she could say anything Abby handed her the lute.

"No quill?" said Claudine.

Abby shook her head and explained about the different tone it gave.

"*Bien, sur*. I have heard something of that reasoning." She gave a reassuring smile. "You play beautifully, so clearly it is a good approach."

"Would you play a piece for me?" asked Abby.

Claudine took the lute and with the ease of a person well used to playing she positioned her hands and began a tune.

Abby watched her play, noting the grace and nimbleness she displayed. It was a nuanced performance and the style reminiscent of her father's and Abby's. She hadn't noticed that when Claudine played the first time. Abby gave her a broad smile, nodding her own approval and when Claudine had finished she clapped softly.

"Beautiful," she said, laughing. "The tune, I know well. It's French, isn't it? But the style, though, it's so very like mine. Where did you learn?"

Claudine's eyes twinkled. "Ah, from a little fairy. One with great skill, like your own teacher."

"But the style is a blend of Scots and French, like my Father's."

Claudine shrugged. "Your father is a man of note, I would say, because his style seems to have travelled to others. As a style so remarkable should."

"Perhaps we might attempt a duet sometime. I'll see if John will lend me his lute."

"That would be very agreeable," said Claudine.

The door opened and Abby paled when she saw Damville enter, his expression full of outrage. He headed straight for the Earl, without a glance in Abby's direction and for that, Abby felt a small measure of relief.

The Earl laid down his cards when Damville arrived at his side. "What's to do?"

"Seigneur, I am most saddened to have to say this to you, but it is a duty I cannot avoid. There is a person in your midst who has no honour, a man who will stop at nothing to get information he desires. Information that may be used in a manner that is most uncourtly, a manner to which no man of the higher orders would stoop. I am afraid I must denounce a man in your household as a spy."

The Earl frowned and stood. "What is this? A spy in my own household? I am loath to question your word, Monsieur le Comte, but it is a serious accusation so I am compelled to ask by what right do you bring it? Have you evidence?"

"I have evidence of the strongest kind. I have caught the man in the very act."

"Caught him doing what, exactly?"

"Rifling through my papers. My private papers. I am a diplomat, seigneur. One entrusted with letters and papers of the most sensitive type. This man was searching them, in my own chamber. An outrage, is what it is, seigneur. An outrage. His majesty the King will be very unhappy to hear of this." Damville paused to calm himself. "I know you would not willingly allow such a man in your household so I am certain you will grant my request to seize this person and take him away for questioning and punishment."

"I understand your distress, but I find it difficult to believe that someone in my household would be guilty of that," said the Earl. "Who is it you found in your chamber?"

"One of your soldiers. He calls himself Duncan Kerr, but I know him as Iain MacGregor."

Abby had watched the exchange with growing horror. She forced herself to remain on her stool. Claudine slipped her hand over Abby's and squeezed hard.

The Earl looked at George. "Fetch Mister Kerr here, if you please."

George nodded, rose and without a word left the room. There were some murmurings and whispered exchanges but for the most part the group in the drawing room remained subdued. The Earl, trying to restore some sense of order, offered Damville a seat. Damville took it with a curt bow.

"Do you have an idea who is it is this man is spying for?" asked the Earl. "The English perhaps? They are likely enough to try and place someone among my household to discover what information could be found about France and its royal family."

"I have my suspicions, seigneur, but I cannot be certain until I question the man. Until then, I would not presume to suggest who it is he is working for."

"You say you know this man to have a different identity. How is that?"

"I've have seen him before, in France. And it was in circumstances that would lead me to think him involved in underhanded dealings."

"I see," said the Earl. "And are the papers you say he examined of great significance? Do you need to be concerned about any element of your nation's security?"

"Naturally, I can give you no details, seigneur, but suffice it to say that I am deeply concerned."

The door opened and George entered with a puzzled Iain in tow. George led Iain to the Earl and Damville. Iain gave each a brief bow, adopting a mildly curious expression.

"You wanted to see me, Monsieur le Comte?"

"Yes," said Damville curtly. "As I'm sure you expected it after I discovered you in my chamber."

Iain gave him a surprised look. "In your chamber, my lord? Why, when was this?" There was an edge to his voice.

"You are taking the role of the innocent, I see. I assure you, monsieur, it will not work. I saw you there as you came from my room just a little while ago. When I went inside I could see my papers were disturbed."

"I am sorry to say this, monsieur, but you have perhaps mistaken me for someone else. I haven't been near your room this afternoon."

"Can anyone support your assumption, Mister Kerr?" asked the Earl.

Iain frowned. "I'm afraid I was in my quarters. I cannot say if anyone saw me enter them and confirm I remained there."

The Earl glanced at Damville and then back at Iain. "We only have your word, then."

Iain nodded. "You do. My word is truth, but there is nothing I can do but ask you to trust it."

The Earl was silent for a moment and then glanced around the room. "Is there anyone here who can vouch for this man, or saw him enter his own quarters, or knows of someone who can?"

Margaret moved forward, and for a brief moment Abby had hope that she might have witnessed something that would help Iain. She'd watched him often enough, so it wasn't an unreasonable hope.

"Margaret," her mother said sharply. "Return to your seat. I'm certain you have nothing to say that can be of any help."

"On the contrary, mother, it is my duty to tell what I know." Margaret's chin was lifted, her eyes glittering.

"Very well, child," said the Earl. "Speak your piece."

"I come to support Lord Damville's accusations."

"How do you support them?" asked the Earl. "Did you see this young man enter Lord Damville's chamber?"

"No, I'm sorry to say," said Margaret. "But I can confirm that he is a man without honour. A man who takes advantage of a lady can only be described thus."

The Earl rose and took his daughter's hand. He looked at Iain. "This man has hurt you?" The threat in his tone was clear.

"He hasn't hurt me, but he made improper advances, Father," she said looking straight into his eyes. "And I must add my own request that this man be punished for it."

The Earl rubbed his daughter's hand in a placating manner. "I assure you daughter, that any man who takes liberties with any of my daughters will suffer dire consequences." He glanced at Iain. "Have you anything to say?"

Iain gave the Earl a direct look. "Though I can offer no witness to deny either charges, I do deny them both."

The Earl's mouth hardened. "I'm afraid your word in this case isn't good enough." He turned and addressed Damville. "You have a course of action in mind?"

"I do indeed, seigneur. With your permission, I would remove this man from your household to a place that a fellow countryman holds near here. There I will question him thoroughly and if it seems needful, remove him to France where he would be dealt with in an appropriate manner."

The Earl stared at Damville a moment, considering. "He is a Scots and so I must remind you of that and say only that if, after your own questioning, you decide to take him to France, you must consult me and the Council of Regents for permission. Is that agreed?"

Damville nodded. "It is, seigneur."

"George," said the Earl, "see that Mister Kerr is confined to his quarters with a guard posted until Lord Damville is ready to leave."

"Aye, Father," said George.

He gripped Iain's arm and led him away. Abby stared after them in disbelief. She looked up at Claudine, trying to keep the alarm out of her face.

CHAPTER 15

*A*bby got up again and went to the window, the unread book still in her hand. The view from the great hall was a grey mist, as grey as her mood. She pressed her face against the window pane, its coldness a welcome sting. Anything to distract her from the real dilemma that faced her since Damville had denounced Iain. She had to help, there was no question in her mind. All the enmity and anger were forgotten in the light of his current situation. But how could she help? At the moment it seemed all she could do, she realised, staring out this window, was wait. And what was there to wait for, she asked herself? Her father's return? She couldn't send word to him and it would be too late, even if he was able to do anything. And in the meantime it meant that Iain was increasingly in danger of being subjected to unimaginable things.

She was certain Damville wouldn't hesitate to use torture, if he needed to. Torture that even Iain wouldn't be able to withstand, and the information he would no doubt reveal would condemn him most likely in Damville's eyes and with an inevitable trip to Paris for imprisonment or worse, no matter what the Earl instructed. Damville, whatever pretence he might adopt, cared nothing for honour. Iain, damn him, was too concerned with honour and now he must pay the price.

She must find some way to help him, then, but her mind had come up with no solution. With a guard at his door, what chance had she to enable him to escape? The window in his quarters overlooked the earthworks of the moat and the drop was dangerous, and the opening, she thought, was too small. That left the guarded door.

"You've heard the news?"

Abby turned to find John standing behind her. He placed a hand on her shoulder.

"News?" asked Abby. She tried not to shrug off his hand. "There is news about Mister Kerr?"

John frowned. "Mister Kerr? No, he is safely locked up in his quarters with two guards posted. He should be gone by tonight with the Comte de Damville, so there's no need to concern yourself with him."

"Tonight, you say? They are leaving that soon? And at this time of the night? They must be going somewhere nearby."

John shrugged. "Damville is anxious to get the prisoner away so he can question him."

"Why can't he question him here?"

"That would be unseemly, of course. My father would never permit it. It would compromise his position should there be any question of Kerr's identity and activities. But why are you so concerned?"

"I'm not. I just wondered. It's not often a spy is captured. If that's what he is."

"I can't see any reason why Damville would lie. He has no reason to."

Abby cocked her head. "Perhaps he has an interest in Margaret, saw them flirting and dancing, and decided to remove Mister Kerr."

John gave this some consideration. "It's possible, but it seems an extreme measure for something that could easily be resolved with just a word in my father's ear."

"Well, it might not be that exact reason. Monsieur le Comte is a man given to dramatic gestures, at least it appears so to me, so it might follow he would personally remove the man if he had a vendetta against him."

John narrowed his eyes. "You defend the man admirably."

"It's only my desire for fair treatment."

His face eased. "You've a soft heart, and that's only natural."

"Perhaps you're right. I am too soft." Abby forced a smile. "But I would hate to see an innocent man taken to be tortured and..." she left the thought incomplete.

John rubbed his hand along her arm. "You mustn't worry yourself over it. It's not a matter for your concern. There are more serious matters at hand, though, that are your concern. Did you know that Sir Robert has asked for your hand? I heard my father discussing it with my mother."

She sighed. That seemed a trivial matter now. "Yes, your mother mentioned it."

"But it can't be. You cannot accept it." He took her hands and kissed them. "I'll speak to them, my heart. Tell them that we would wed instead. I'm sure they'll see reason when I explain everything."

Abby pulled away from him. "John, you know they would never approve. Did we not discuss that? And though I am fond of you John, it's as a brother. I could never be your wife. I'm sorry."

"Please, Abby I'm sure you'll care for me in time," said John.

Abby pressed a finger to his lips and shook her head. "Nay, John, it cannot be."

"Is there something I have not been told?"

Startled, Abby stepped back from John and looked across to see Sir Robert entering the room. He gave them each a severe look. "I was given to understand that ye had no attachments, Mistress Gordon. That ye were free to marry."

"That is the truth, Sir Robert," said Abby, her voice firm. She glanced at John. "John is as a brother to me, no more."

"No, Abby, please tell him you cannot marry him. I promise I will make it right with my parents." John straightened and looked Sir Robert in the eye. "I'm afraid you're mistaken about things, Sir Robert."

Sir Robert stiffened. "Is that the case?" He said to John. "Do you mean to tell me your lady mother brought me here under false pretences? This is no way to treat someone of my standing, and I shall tell your mother, and your father, if it comes to that."

"No, Sir Robert, I assure you, it is not the case," said Abby. Perhaps it would be better to let him draw his conclusions, she thought, and withdraw from the match from pique, but eventually, she knew it would create an even bigger mess. Lady Elizabeth would see to that.

Sir Robert gave her a hostile look. "I'll speak with Lady Elizabeth and the Earl about this. Though, at this point, I'm uncertain if their word can be trusted." After a curt bow he took his leave.

"Ah, John, you must go and mend this quickly," said Abby. "Tell your mother that it's all a misunderstanding."

"But why? Can't you see that now is the time to convince her?"

Abby gave an exasperated sigh. "Your mother has made it clear that she disapproves and I fear what steps she'll take now, if Sir Robert threatens to withdraw his proposal."

"Do you mean to tell me that you intend to marry that man?" John's voice was incredulous.

"John," she said, forcing patience. "My choices aren't your concern. But can you not see that your mother may now take an interest in your future bride and begin seeking someone on your behalf? And with your father's agreement, once she tells him I am a danger to those plans. The Lord knows what she will plan for me, then. So you must convince her that I'm no longer a threat in any manner."

John considered her words, frowning intently. In some ways she found his earnestness endearing, and in another situation his determination and singlemindedness would be admirable. But at the moment she only found them frustrating. She forced herself to remain silent and hoped he would finally see sense.

"Very well," he said. "I'll say no more on the subject."

She opened her mouth to protest that she didn't want his silence, she wanted him to convince his mother that he had no interest in her.

As if he'd read her thoughts he held up his hand. "Don't worry. I'll have a word with my mother."

She nodded, but his tone and emphasis left her with a distinctly uneasy feeling.

THE FEELING of unease strengthened when a short while later, a servant found her in her room and imparted Lady Elizabeth's summons. She took her time making her way to the drawing room, gathering her strength and courage. One look at Lady Elizabeth's face and she knew her misgivings were justified. She was seated surrounded by her attendants, her expression severe. The Earl stood at a far window, detached from the immediate proceedings, but nonetheless giving the meeting his weight. Standing just to the right was Sir Robert, his expression pleased, perhaps even triumphant.

Lady Elizabeth wasted no time. "I'm given to understand that you haven't heeded my instructions. In fact, I think I could be justified in stating that you have disobeyed them. Wilfully."

"My lady it's a misunderstanding, I assure you. John—"

"Enough." Lady Elizabeth held up her hand. "The time for excuses has gone. You've been a guest in this house and you have abused our hospitality with your conduct."

Lady Elizabeth continued on the theme of abused hospitality and Abby listened meekly, foregoing any interruption or further explanation in the hope that, having vented her spleen, the countess would be satisfied.

"Have you anything to say for yourself?" Lady Elizabeth asked sharply when she'd finished.

Abby was tempted to point out that a moment ago she'd wanted no explanations, but stifled the urge.

"I can only say that I've never intentionally said or acted in a manner that would give John, or any of your sons, cause to believe I had anything but the most vague sisterly feelings for them. In truth, I've done my best to discourage any such imaginings. John, I think, wouldn't accept these statements, but he does now and I'm certain he would say as much if you were to ask him."

"Is that so?" said Lady Elizabeth. "That's not my impression. But it changes nothing. The decision is made and everyone concurs. You will leave with Sir Robert first thing tomorrow and he'll take you to his home. In the light of the present situation, he feels that his home is the only place he can ensure your honour and purity are untouched until the wedding. It pains me to say I must agree with him. As soon as the contracts are completed he'll ride over with you and the ceremony will take place on that occasion. Until your departure in the morning you'll be confined to your room."

Abby stared at them, stunned. She opened her mouth to reject the decision, then shut it. She must think. She must find a way to leave or secure some aid before she reached the confines of Sir Robert's home. Once there, she'd no doubt he would place her under close observation until she was safely wed to him. In the meantime it would be best to appear to comply.

"My maid?" she asked. "You will at least allow my maidservant to attend me in my chamber and then on the journey."

Lady Elizabeth gave a curt nod. "Of course. She is in your employ and your responsibility. She'll bring you some food later and stay with you for the night."

"Thank you," Abby said. She kept her tone cool. "Have you anything further to say, or may I go now?"

Lady Elizabeth gave Abby a suspicious look, uncertain if her words were an insinuation or intended as rude. Abby kept her face deliberately neutral. Make it what you will, madam, Abby thought.

"There's nothing more to be said on this matter. We consider it closed." She glanced at her husband in a tacit acknowledgement of his support on her words. "You're dismissed."

Abby gave a brief curtsey and directed a nod to Sir Robert. Without any further word, she left.

ABBY SAT on the chair by the table in her room, presuming to read the book in her hand. She saw none of the words on the page, aware only of the fading light. In the hours she'd been there she'd come no closer to a solution to her situation. Enlisting John's help, though obvious, was fraught with too many dangers and success was far from guaranteed. She had no real confidence in his abilities to achieve her release, by fair means or foul, and if he did, she would only trade one problem for another, since he doubtless would want to spirit her away for marriage. The ridiculous alternative, was to leave through the window, but the window was too small and it overlooked the busy courtyard. It was only when Jeannette tapped on the door, waited for the man at her door to turn the key and entered bearing a plate filled with a meat pie and a mug of ale that a vague idea formed in her head.

"My *pauvre madame*," said Jeannette. "That they should treat you in this manner. It is awful. These Scots have no sense of decorum. Barbarians, all of them."

Abby smiled at her. "Dear Jeannette, I thank you for your sympathy. I must confess it tries me sorely how my affairs have been conducted. You know I'm to leave tomorrow with Sir Robert, to be confined at his home until the marriage contracts are signed."

"*Oui*, madame. I heard. A terrible thing it is."

"Oh, Jeannette," Abby said plaintively. "A terrible thing."

"Is there nothing you can do? Can you not write to your papa and have him stop this wretched turn of events?"

Abby shook her head. "My father cannot be reached. So I must act myself."

Jeannette eyed her keenly. "What will you do, madame?" she whispered. "Whatever it is, I will help you, for it is an insult to be so treated. This would never be permitted in Calais, *mais non*, it would not be permitted in the whole of the kingdom."

Abby gave her a weak smile and refrained from contradicting what she knew to be a naive statement. "You're a loyal servant, Jeannette, and I appreciate that, because I must indeed ask you for your help. I need you to take a message to Claudine, Madame d'Eauville and give it to no one but her, in secret, if possible."

"Of course, madame. You are right to trust her, a fellow Frenchwoman. But what help could she provide?"

"She may be able to find a way to secure my release tonight, perhaps with your help. A little something to make the guard sleep?"

It seemed so simple and certain in her head, but now she spoke the words the chances of success seemed remote. The castle was simply too full. They would see her go. The alarm would be raised too easily.

She frowned. "Well it might not work, but at least we can try."

Jeanette's sturdy hands gripped her shoulder. "Madame, it will work. And at the very least we will do our best."

CHAPTER 16

*A*bby sat on her bed in the darkness, staring at the door. She hadn't moved from the position since the lights from the other windows had been quenched, and the sounds of a settling household had ceased. The darkness then had been so absolute that she barely distinguish the shape of the door. That had been some time ago, but she wasn't certain how long. It seemed now that she might be staring at the door all night to no avail, that her hopes and half formed plan that Jeannette would find a way to give the guard at her door a sleeping draught and free Abby wouldn't succeed, and come the morning, she would be riding away with Sir Robert.

A faint tap sounded. Startled out of her reverie, Abby rose quickly and went to the door.

"Madame, it's me," said Jeannette, in French.

Abby waited for the key to turn in the lock anxiously. The door opened and two figures glided into the room.

"I am so sorry, madame," said Jeannette, "but that *canard* at your door has the constitution of an ox. It has taken an age for the sleeping draught to take effect."

"Who's that with you?" Abby demanded in a sharp whisper.

"It is I," said Claudine in a low voice.

"Claudine? Why are you here? I instructed Jeannette to tell no one."

"I'm sorry, madame," said Jeannette. "But she came upon me just now and threatened to raise the alarm unless I allowed her to accompany me. She has assumed you would plan something."

"You mustn't blame her," said Claudine. "I insisted only because I knew you would need help after I heard about Sir Robert and your confinement to your room."

"Thank you, though your help isn't necessary," said Abby.

"But of course I would help you," said Claudine. "But there, we waste time. You must change quickly."

"I have dressed in the servant boy's clothes I obtained some days ago."

"Oho," said Claudine. "So you planned to leave before this."

"Yes." She left it at that. There was little enough time and no real point in explaining.

"*Bon*, I expected as much," said Claudine. She fingered Abby's doublet. "I see you are experienced in this, *non?*" She handed Abby something dark and curly. A wig. "Your hair though lovely, is perhaps too remarkable?" said Claudine.

Jeannette gathered Abby's hair and pinned it securely to her head, then fitted the wig over it. She picked up the cap from the bed and pulled it down low over Abby's head.

"*Bon*," said Claudine. "We are ready, now. Come."

Claudine opened the door softly and led the pair of them quietly past the guard, now sitting slumped against a stool beside the entrance. The darkness was such that Abby felt the need to place her hand against the wall to assist her progress. Ahead, Claudine moved quickly to the stairs and, without hesitation, made her way down the winding steps. Abby forced herself to keep up, placing her hand once again, along the wall to steady herself. Behind her, Jeannette lumbered less quickly.

Once they were on the ground floor, they passed through the small corridor to the door to the courtyard, where Claudine stopped. "Now, we will go across to the stables and if anyone challenges us you will say that you are my servant and I am called away urgently to be with a dying relative."

"You're coming with me?" Abby hadn't planned on this.

"*Oui*. Of course. With me there is no doubt of success." Her tone was clipped. "Jeannette will go to the servants quarters and remain there so when the alarm is raised no one will think she had a part in it. You and I will go south, to Leith and from there, take a ship to France. I have friends there who will help us."

Abby couldn't make out Claudine's face to read her expression, but she heard the tone that brooked no resistance. Still, these were not her plans.

"No, there's no need for you to come. I'll be fine. I have a plan."

"It is decided, *ma cherie*, we are going together. I will hear no objections."

"But I must help Mister Kerr."

"You must not concern yourself with him. Besides, he is gone."

"Gone? When?"

"Some hours since with Damville. There is nothing you can do for him." Claudine put a hand on Jeannette's arm. "Now it is time for us to take our leave of you. You've been very helpful and I'm grateful."

Abby took up Jeannette's hand. "You have my eternal thanks as well. I appreciate how good you've been. I promise I will make it up to you."

"Just see that your papa arranges for me to leave this place and return to your employ, madame. I will be content then."

Abby gave a wry smile. The ambition was still there. "Of course," she said.

Jeannette gave them a brief curtsey and left.

"Now," said Claudine. "We must go to the stables and get two horses."

Claudine opened the door and made her way across the courtyard, Abby following. A faint light from a room on the second floor gave some bit of assistance to their progress in the misty darkness. They reached the stable without encountering anyone and Abby entered, the sounds of rustling hooves and an occasional snuffle were the only noises that greeted her.

In one of the stalls she found a stable boy. She shook him awake and in a voice as deep as she could make it, instructed him to saddle two horses. Once saddled, she led them back into the courtyard, and to the mounting block. Abby and Claudine both made quick work of it and were seated and heading for the gate moments later. A lone guard was posted and as they approached he stirred and greeted them.

"Ye're late abroad on such an evening," he said. "Is there something amiss, my lady?"

"Alas, yes," said Claudine in English, all trace of any French accent gone. "I am sorry to say that I have a close relative who is dying and I'm required to attend. I must make as much progress as possible as quickly as I can."

The soldier gave her a nod. "Have a care mistress, for though it is safe enough on Gordon lands I canna vouch for beyond."

"Thank you for the warning," said Claudine.

Abby and Claudine rode on in silence, breaking into a trot that eventually became a gallop. Intent on escape, she pushed back the growing unease she felt about Claudine. The wig that had adorned Claudine's head was obviously on Abby's head now. The marked limp seemed to have disappeared, along with her French accent. Who was this woman and where was she leading Abby?

They slowed after a while at Claudine's signal. The mist had lifted somewhat, but it was still difficult in places and as they moved further from the well-worn track by the castle it required more careful watch for ruts and holes that could cause a horse to stumble. At present there was no sign of pursuit. Abby could only pray it would continue and her decision to leave with Claudine would prove the correct one.

THE MIST HUNG in patches and through them stars began to shine. Abby glanced at her companion, trotting carefully ahead and in the starlight Abby could see that Claudine was in fact fair-haired and her vast size had been trimmed down considerably.

"Claudine," said Abby in a low voice.

Claudine turned and placed a finger to her lips. "Shhh. We don't know who is around and voices can carry."

Abby frowned. The white makeup paste, rouged cheeks and lips were gone to reveal a woman who was younger than Abby expected. A woman of great beauty, with clear, startling blue eyes that needed no glasses.

"Who are you?" she asked. The urge to know, to hold this woman to account seemed more important than a chance they might be overheard. "Why do you adopt a disguise? Are you a spy?" It made sense to her now. The warning in the note—perhaps it was this woman? "Who do you work for?"

Claudine gave a soft laugh. "Child, your imagination runs away with you," she said in a low voice. The accent was back, but only slightly. "I am flattered that you think me clever enough to be a spy who managed to find a welcome in the Earl's household, but *non*, I am not so glamorous as that, I assure you. I am merely a woman who has fled her husband, a husband of great influence I must add, and has come to Scotland to hide. Forgive me that I was not honest with you, but you see I felt I could trust no one."

"What is your real name, then?"

"Ah, tut, I am most sorry but I am afraid I cannot tell you that. For your own safety. Suffice it to say that I am called Claudine, though."

"So where do you propose we go now then? Two women running away?"

"You mustn't worry, *ma cherie*, we will be safe. First, we will head south, to Leith and take ship there to France, as I said. In France I have many friends with whom we can take refuge until we can contact your father."

"Will you be able to contact my father?"

"Do not worry yourself over that. I will find a way. I have friends who will be able to discover where he is. And then we will send word and have him come."

She thought of Iain and her frustration was great. What could she do for him in her current situation? "Would you know where Mister Kerr is being kept? Did you perhaps hear the Comte de Damville say where he was heading?"

Claudine gave a small sigh. "Mister Kerr again. You must not trouble yourself about him. You have your own safety to think about."

"I owe Mister Kerr a debt," Abby said. "A great debt. So I feel I must do what I can for him. Would you have any friends or contacts here that might act on his behalf? He is innocent, after all."

"Are you so sure?"

"Yes," she said.

"How can you be so certain? You hardly know Master Kerr well enough to judge that."

"I know him to be a loyal and honourable man," she said and added, muttering under her breath, "too honourable."

"You have met before?" Claudine's tone was sharp.

Abby hesitated a moment. "Yes."

"It is more than friendship, then."

"Yes."

"Oh, *ma cherie,* did I not warn you to avoid such a man as Master Kerr?" She shook her head. "This is not good, no, not good at all."

"You mean you will not help him?" Abby said curtly.

"Not *will not*, ma cherie, but cannot. And I will not endanger you for his sake. We must leave this country as soon as possible and get you to safety."

"And just why are you helping me, madame?" said Abby stiffly. "Perhaps it's best if you leave me go and I will find my own way to safety."

She thought of Iain's father. This distance was long, but perhaps she could reach Glen Strae in time for MacGregor to use his influence to get Iain released before he was taken to France, something she was certain would happen. Once in France, she knew there was little to be done.

"I have no cause to doubt this man's honour, but he is a man clearly involved in matters that you should not be." She studied Abby. "You are not entangled in them, are you?"

Abby stiffened. "It's more the case that he is involved with my matters," she said quietly. "This man Damville, he has intended me harm for some months now. Mister Kerr came to my aid a few times. Without his help I have no doubt Damville would have succeeded."

"Are you saying that it was his desire to assist you that led to his capture?"

"Yes," Abby said.

In part it was true. She was certain that Damville would have had no interest in Iain had it not been for his assistance in helping her escape in France. But it made her face the fact that by detaining Iain, Damville had recognised him, even with his disguise. Why then hadn't he challenged her or accused her to

Huntly? This thought which had niggled at the back of her mind since Damville had taken Iain, now made her uneasy.

"You care for this man, Kerr. I can see that plainly." Claudine sighed. "Well, we must make the best of it. I will do what I can, but I have little influence, whatever you may think."

"I appreciate any help you can offer, madame." Abby hoped that the level of trust she'd placed in Claudine was warranted.

Hooves crashed through the underbrush to their left. A rider emerged and drew up in front of them, causing Abby's horse to rear. She fought for control, as beside her Claudine worked to keep her own horse in check. The figure grabbed her reins and the horse bucked against it. The force of it jerked Abby off the horse and she fell to the ground, losing consciousness.

CHAPTER 17

The stars yawned overhead, and for a moment Abby thought she was still unconscious. She blinked again and realised she was flat on her back, and only a brief time had passed since she'd been knocked from her horse. Before she could sit up, she was grabbed roughly by the arm and dragged to her feet. She blinked again and looked into her captor's face. Damville.

She tried to twist her arm out of his grasp but he held a dagger to her throat and she stopped.

"I would advise against any kind of struggle," he said. "Lest your pretty little throat be cut."

Claudine, no longer mounted, moved towards them. "Unhand her. You have no business with her."

"I do indeed, madame."

"I say you do not." Claudine withdrew a small dagger from the inside of her coat.

Damville laughed and pressed his dagger tighter against Abby's throat. She felt a small prick and a trickle of blood.

"I say you will both come with me. One to ensure the other's cooperation."

"Go Claudine," Abby choked out. The knife pressed harder and she could say no more.

Claudine looked at Damville, narrowing her eyes. "Very well. I will follow you."

Damville studied her for a moment and smiled slowly. "Do not think to try any of your tricks on me, madame. It may have worked with my aide, but I assure you it will not work with me. I wouldn't hesitate with this knife. Do you understand?"

"I understand," said Claudine.

Damville replaced his dagger, took Abby to his horse, withdrew a small rope from his pack and tied Abby's hands.

"Have a care also," he told Abby. "You are merely a tool of limited use. I have no qualms about killing you, should it become necessary."

He looked over to Claudine who stood beside her horse, watchful. He turned when an arrow hissed through the air, hitting him in the arm. A figure emerged from the trees. It was Master Cameron, the tutor, his dark hair plastered with sweat. In his hands he clutched a bow with an arrow cocked, ready to fly at Damville again.

"Oh, Monsieur Cameron," said Claudine. "Have you come to help us?"

Cameron, dressed in dark clothes, his face wary, moved closer to Claudine. He lowered the bow, slung it on his back and with his free hand withdrew a dagger from its sheath at his side. Quickly he grabbed Claudine and put the dagger to her throat.

Damville held his arm, wincing with pain. "You have me at a disadvantage, monsieur. I'm not certain I understand." He pointed to Abby. "You wish this lady here returned?"

"I've no interest in the lady, or the youth, though. I want your other prisoner. The one called Kerr."

"*Vraiment*? I think we are both in luck, then, for I have no real interest in him. My reason for his capture was to draw these fine ladies out of the castle. Now that this has been accomplished I would happily relieve you of them in return for your man."

"Ladies?" Cameron looked at Abby.

Damville laughed, reached over and swooped off her hat and wig. *"Voila."* He threw the wig across to Claudine. It fell to her feet, unheeded. "I believe that's yours."

Abby stared at Damville. "What do you want with Claudine? I thought it was me you were so desperate to capture?"

Damville ignored her. "Can we come to an arrangement, monsieur? Kerr in exchange for the lady."

"Where's Kerr?"

"He is not here, unfortunately, but that is easily remedied."

"Aye, it is indeed. Ye'll take me to him and I'll bring the lady. If he's there and ye hand him over in good form, I'll give ye the lady."

"Of course, if you so wish it settled in that manner, though I'd advise bringing the younger lady along too, if only to ensure that one behaves."

"I'll behave," said Claudine, a hard edge in her voice. "If you promise to let this young woman go when the exchange is made."

Cameron grunted. "We'll see." He flicked Abby a glance. "You'll make sure she keeps her word, or you'll not see this woman alive." He nodded to the horse. "Mount up."

Damville looked down at his arm. With a grimace he took hold of the arrow in his hand and broke off the shaft, so that only a small section protruded from his arm. He removed his dagger and, holding it at Abby, ordered her to mount his horse. When she was seated, he gingerly mounted the horse behind her, taking the reins with a grunt. Cameron handed him the reins of Abby's horse.

"Wait here," said Cameron.

Cameron dragged a protesting Claudine into the woods, reappearing a short while later with a horse in tow. He gave her a boost to mount the horse and swung up beside her. After a nod to Damville the two rode on, eventually breaking into a slow canter.

THE STARS HAD long since disappeared under thick cloud. The air was sharp, still and Abby's breath hung in the air from the cold, as well as the fear that was a constant presence. Eventually, a large building loomed in the distance. The trees had long since disappeared, replaced by hilly scrub. They had taken a small track and it was to this house it led them. As they neared Abby could see that it was a small manor house of stone, probably built earlier in the century.

Damville halted outside the house, and with a stifled moan dismounted. He'd emitted an occasional hiss against the jolting of the ride since he'd mounted up on Cameron's orders. Now Abby could just about make out the beads of sweat on his face as he dragged her off of the horse and shoved her in front of him. Behind her, the other two dismounted. The door opened and a figure stood in the entrance.

"What is this?" It was Damville's aide, speaking in French. "You go out for the woman and bring back this young man as well?"

"Quiet," said Damville sharply. "It is not for you to question me. All is well with the prisoner?"

"*Oui*. He is still tied up and locked in the room."

"Good. That is all that matters." Damville turned to Cameron and spoke in English. "Come inside and we will get warm and discuss matters in more comfort."

"Aye, but not for long. I need to be on my way."

"And what way would that be, if I may ask?"

"Never you mind."

Damville shrugged and pushed Abby across the threshold. Claudine followed them, Cameron just behind. The entrance opened out into a small hall, sparsely furnished with a scarred table, a few chairs and a chest. Two large tallow candles on the table provided enough light, along with the feeble fire that burned in the hearth. Damville walked towards it and held the hand of his good arm briefly in front of it. The stump of the arrow shaft was just visible in the leather sleeve of his jerkin.

"You have good aim, monsieur," said Damville. He touched his arm lightly and winced.

Cameron only nodded and took hold of Claudine, the dagger pressed once more against her throat.

"Not so innocent as you appear, my friend."

"Enough. To business. I'd be obliged if you could bring the prisoner here."

"Let her go, please," said Abby, trying to keep her tone firm.

Both Damville and Cameron gave her disdainful looks.

"Quiet, madame, before I lose my patience."

Damville looked over at his aide and gave a nod. The aide disappeared, and when he returned he had Iain in tow. Iain's eye patch was gone, along with his leather jerkin and boots, leaving only a badly torn shirt, hose and breeches. A mottled bruise was evident on his left cheek and his lower lip was swollen. He blinked against the light of the fire and cast Damville an insolent look until he saw Abby. He frowned.

"What's this? Have ye taken tae preying on innocent women, now too, ye wee gowked man?"

"So, you still prefer to pretend that you have no knowledge of these women, especially the young lady? Bah. You disappoint me. You would think me such a fool?"

"Based on my past experience, is it?" said Iain. "If that be the measure, then I can hardly think otherwise."

Damville stiffened, but eventually forced a smile. "You may try all you will to bait me, monsieur, but I assure you it will not change the fact that I have the upper hand."

"If that is the case, then why does the gentleman with ye, Master Cameron, I believe, hold a knife tae the fair lady's throat?" said Iain. "Does he not trust you? Or is it me he hopes to coerce? Forbye, if that is the case, then he's sadly mistaken, for I know nothing of this woman."

"The plans have changed direction slightly," said Damville. "Master Cameron has a great interest in you, as it happens, while I have a great interest in the lady. We are here to make an exchange."

Iain appeared amused. "Ye have an interest in me, Master Cameron? I am flattered, but I canna imagine why."

"You can imagine all you desire," said Cameron. "But I'll be taking you with me."

"May I ask where?" said Iain.

"Aye, you can ask, but I'll not tell you."

"Can I guess that ye have a friend...." he glanced at Damville. "An English friend who has promised ye riches? Riches that ye'd never see in your lifetime."

Cameron flushed. "That's none of your concern."

"Ah, but it is. Ye have it wrong, ye see. For I have nae information for your friends, whatever ye may ha' told them. I dinna have anything tae do wi' *Sasenachs*."

"Do you think I'd believe your word?"

Iain shrugged. "I'm just trying tae warn ye that your English friends may not take kindly tae being duped."

"Enough," said Damville. He gave Iain a rough slap. "We will have no more words from you." He gestured to Claudine. "You have your prisoner here. Now make the exchange. Pass the lady over."

"No!" said Abby. She clutched Claudine's arm. "What can you possibly want with her? She's not involved in this."

Damville laughed. "Is that what she told you? Well, my little madame, she has lied to you."

Abby looked at Claudine but she was staring at Damville, her face expressionless.

"Now, Monsieur Cameron, if you would be so kind." Damville nodded at Claudine.

Cameron wrenched Claudine from Abby's grasp and shoved her towards Damville. Damville took hold of Claudine, nodded to his aide who grabbed Iain and handed him over to Cameron. The exchange was complete.

"You'll let the girl go?" said Claudine.

"Why would I do that?" said Damville. "She will guarantee your cooperation."

"Let her go," said Claudine. "I will do whatever you want, just let her go."

"And why would I trust you?" asked Damville.

"Please, I beg of you, let her go. I give you my word I will tell you what you want to know. If you do not let her go and you hurt her, I will tell you nothing."

Damville narrowed his eyes. He nodded towards Cameron. "She can go with you, Cameron. I take it you will be on the road south, to your…English associates?" He looked at Claudine. "And if you do not cooperate, Madame Claudine, I will send word to have her killed. Is that clear?"

Claudine nodded. "Agreed."

"Now, if that is all, I will leave you be," said Cameron.

Cameron took Abby by the arm and with Iain in tow, his hands still bound behind his back, headed towards the door and out into the cold night air. Damville's aide followed them and assisted Iain on to his horse. Cameron put Abby on his own horse and swung up behind her, took the reins and Iain's reins. He urged the horses down the track. Abby glanced over at Iain, but his face gave her no hint of what he was thinking. She'd no doubt there was some plan in his mind, but couldn't tell what it might be. All she knew is that she must be ready for it.

CHAPTER 18

The track ahead curved and disappeared into the woodland. They'd been travelling on it for some time now and Abby felt weary and bedraggled. The weather had long ago settled into an earnest mizzle that eventually penetrated her jerkin and her shirt underneath. She tried to brush a wet lock of hair from her face, but a grunt from Cameron stopped her. She shifted on the horse. Her boot was pinching and the pain, though a minor irritant, gave her an idea.

"Be still," said Cameron sharply.

"I'm sorry. It's the boot. I think there is something in it."

"I don't care. Be still, or I'll ensure your stillness with a blow and strap you to the saddle."

Abby sighed and tried to comply, but the pain made it difficult. Perhaps she might convince him to stop. An idea occurred to her. Her hopes that Iain would make some kind of move had disappeared a while ago and she realised, with some disappointment and exasperation, she would have to take it upon herself if they were to manage any kind of escape. And now, as they approached the curve in the road, it seemed an ideal time to attempt something.

She shifted again slightly. Cameron hissed his disapproval in her ear.

"I'm sorry, but it can't be ignored. The pain in my foot is too much."

He brought the horses to a halt. With a glance back at Iain, he dismounted. "Which foot?"

Abby pointed to the opposite side from where he stood. "This one."

Cameron grunted and went around the horse. Abby heard, rather than saw Iain's horse move closer. She smiled inwardly. This was it. She held her foot ready and when he came close enough she thrust it forward in a good kick, aiming for his head. Her boot connected with his chin and the force shoved him back and off balance.

¶Iain seized the opportunity and threw himself from his horse on top of Cameron. The two struggled, Iain limited by his bound hands, but the press of his weight and Cameron's stunned state gave him the advantage. Abby dismounted quickly and ran to the two men. With one quick movement she managed to unsheathe Cameron's dagger. Iain, clearly noting her action tried to hold out his bound hands while still pinning Cameron down. Cameron freed an arm and swung wildly at Iain, the blow catching him on the side of the head. It wasn't hard and Iain recovered quickly, using both hands to block further swings from Cameron.

Abby tried to cut Iain's bindings again, this time stepping on Cameron's hand. She managed to get the knife on the bindings for a few moments and she sawed away madly. Underneath her boot Cameron's arm twisted and turned as he struggled to free himself, causing Abby to lose her balance. She fell back and the knife clattered from her hand. Cameron prepared to swing again, his hand closed into a fist. At that moment Iain's bindings broke under his added efforts to free them. He blocked Cameron's blow and landed one of his own, knocking Cameron to the ground. Cameron remained still.

Iain scrambled up and kissed Abby quickly on the mouth. "Well done, lass."

Before Abby could react he moved away and untied her bindings. He knelt down, took Cameron's hands, tying them behind Cameron's back.

"Well, what have we here? Seems you don't need my help, after all."

Abby turned to see Calum coming up to them, mounted on a horse.

"Calum," said Iain, relief in his voice.

Abby stood up, dagger finally in hand. "Father! What are you doing here?"

"Rescuing the pair of ye."

"Ye left it a while, didn't ye?" said Iain. "Ye've been following us this last hour, if I'm not mistaken."

"Aye, well, ye could have moved your horse over a bit, ye gowked fool, so I could have a clear shot."

"What about Cameron? Ye ken he's a spy for the *Sasenach*."

"Is he now? Aye, perhaps. Well, we'll take him back tae the castle where he can make an account of himself."

"We canna do that yet. We need tae rescue Claudine."

Calum looked at Iain. "Damville has Abby's mother?"

Iain nodded slowly, his expression puzzled. "Aye. She agreed to cooperate if Abby was let go. Are ye saying Claudine is Abby's mother?"

Calum sighed. "Aye, that's what I'm saying. But we have no time for this discussion, we must hurry. Her life is in danger."

"Wait," said Abby. "Claudine is my mother? But my mother's name was Marie."

"Your mother's name *is* Marie Claudine."

"Claudine?" Abby shook her head, trying to grasp what her

father was telling her. All at once an unreasonable rage flared up. "You're going to put your life in danger for that woman? No, you can't."

"That woman is your mother," said Calum.

"She's been no mother. She's a spy. She deserves what she gets," said Abby flatly.

"That woman is your father's wife," said Iain quietly. He moved to Cameron's horse and removed the sword strapped there, adding to the dagger already in his possession.

Abby looked at Iain and frowned. "You will stay out of this."

"This is not your decision, Abby," said Calum. "Ye'll stay here with Cameron while Iain and I get your mother."

Abby frowned again and fought to subdue the anger that still filled her. She took a deep breath. "If you insist on doing this, then I'm coming with you," said Abby. "Cameron will live or die whether I'm here or not. You might be glad to have a third person."

Calum glanced at Iain, who shrugged. "She'll only try tae follow us."

Calum sighed. "Very well. But ye must do as I tell ye." He glanced at Cameron, bound and still unconscious. "I imagine he'll be fine, apart from a headache and swollen jaw."

Without any further word, Iain moved Cameron to the side of the track and covered him with his cloak. Cameron groaned at the movement, but did nothing more. He was pale and sweating and Abby wondered if he would last until their return. She pushed the thought away and tried to focus on the task at hand. But her thoughts were a confused jumble.

She found it difficult to accept that Claudine was in fact her mother. Deep down she'd suspected Claudine to be more than she'd pretended to be all along and when Claudine had admitted to being a spy Abby had thought she'd pinpointed what her instinct had been telling her. But now, she realised the clues had been there even before her father had told her the truth of Claudine's identity. Her protectiveness had exceeded what was expected. But that gave Abby little comfort or clarity now. Now all she wanted was to rescue Claudine, like her father wished. But only so she could finally confront the woman who had abandoned her and her father all those years ago. She wouldn't allow this woman to escape that.

THEY PUT their horses to the test as they covered the ground to the manor house where Damville held Claudine. The drenching drizzle had eased and promised to cease with the coming dawn and Abby was glad for that. She'd managed to stuff her wet hair into her jerkin so that it at least didn't flap about in her face as she rode. Ahead of her was Iain, his back straight, head high, but giving no other clue to his mood, or his thinking. Her father, riding next to her, was grim, his face set, his limbs taut with contained energy. There was no trace of the devil-may-care manner that had been so familiar to her over the years.

The manor house finally came into sight and they slowed their horses to a stop. At Calum's signal they dismounted.

"Surprise is our best weapon," Calum said to Iain. "Circle the house and report back."

Iain nodded, and with a quick glance at Abby, he left, his sword and dagger drawn. Abby watched him melt into the surrounding scrub, a dark shadow, and then nothing. She bit her lip. Her anxiety had arisen from out of the blue and it was now filling her at an alarming rate. She definitely didn't want anything to happen to Iain or her father.

"What will you do?" she asked, the worry clear in her voice. She tried again. "You have a sound plan, I take it?"

Calum finished hobbling the horses and took her hand. "Shh,

my little one. It will be fine. Nae harm will come tae any of us. Now take your horse away tae the side there."

He guided his own horse out of the line of sight to the side of the track. In what seemed like an age, Iain returned, emerging out of the darkness towards them.

"They're in a small chamber at the back, next to the kitchen," he said. "Damville's assistant as well."

"Marie? Is she conscious?" asked Calum.

Iain shook his head. "I couldna tell. Her head was down. She's tied to a chair."

"But she said she would cooperate. Why have they done that?" said Abby.

Iain glanced at Abby. "Nae need to worry, it's probably just a precaution."

Abby tried to take comfort from his words, though she knew that it was only for her benefit. She was angry at this woman who was supposed to be her mother, but she had no wish to see her hurt.

"There appears to be a rear entrance, but that's too near them and they may hear us if we try to gain entry there," said Iain. "But there is a window that willna shut all the way on the front corner room. I ken we'd get in there, nae bother. We have surprise on our side, so it shouldna be a problem for us. Especially wi' Damville's injury."

"Damville's injured?" said Calum.

"Aye, he took an arrow in the arm from Cameron."

"I suppose it's too much to hope that it's his sword arm that's hurt."

"Ye'd be right there. Nay, it's his other arm."

Calum drew his sword and dagger. "Are ye ready, then, Iain?"

"Aye."

"If you give me a dagger, I'll be able to free Claudine, while you both keep the other two occupied."

Calum opened his mouth to object, but then shut it. He glanced at Iain. They frowned at each other and Calum reluctantly surrendered his dagger.

"I want ye tae stay back, do ye hear? Until we are well in and engaged in a fight with the other two. Remain well away from them, ye dinna want tae be used as bait again. Promise me?"

"I promise, Father," said Abby.

With a nod the three set off, creeping as quietly as possible towards the house. The rosy light of the coming dawn peeked through the trees and reflected off the glass of the windows. They halted by the faulty window and with a little persuasion from Iain's dagger he prised it open wide enough for them to climb through. The width was barely able to allow the men's passage, but Abby slipped through with little trouble.

Once inside, they made their way quietly to the corridor and along to the back, Iain leading. He halted outside the designated room and gave a little nod. Calum turned to Abby and motioned her to remain where she was. She gave a nod and stepped back, allowing them space to rush at the door. At an unspoken signal the two of them thrust their full weight against the door and burst in.

Cries of alarm and the hiss of steel greeted Abby's ears. She dared to peer in. Iain was attempting to disarm Damville's aide who only had a hastily grabbed sword, and Damville was attacking her father with both sword and dagger, his wounded arm now bandaged but beginning to bleed. Claudine sat slumped on a stool, her hands bound behind her, blood trickling from her mouth. Both Damville and her father, fighting very close to Claudine, prevented Abby from a clear view.

She watched helplessly as Damville's aide began to give as good as he got, a better swordsman than his appearance had suggested. Iain's full concentration was engaged and Abby couldn't judge when he might safely dispatch the aide, so that he might help her father. Her father, she could see, was moving backwards, and for a moment she thought she might slip into the room and free Claudine, but they shifted and she held back.

A moment later Damville feinted and then rushed and feinted again, throwing Calum back toward Iain and the aide. The aide was jolted and swung his arm, catching Calum in the rear. Damville used the advantage and thrust with his sword, finding purchase in her father's side. Blood bloomed instantly on the doublet and her father sucked in his breath at the pain. A moment later he collapsed to his knees and fell.

Abby could wait no longer. She ran into the room, startling both Damville and his aide, and threw herself against Damville, heedless of her father's warning, dagger in hand. She would kill the bastard if it was the last thing she did. The pair fell to the floor and Abby thrust the dagger, home, sticking it upward in his chest. Damville, a look of surprise on his face, stopped his struggle and released his grip on her. He opened his mouth to speak and his eyes went dead.

Abby's actions had given the aide a moment's hesitation that Iain quickly seized to his advantage. Iain thrust the aide's sword aside with a strong sweep, knocking it from his grasp. The aide switched his dagger to his other hand and began to circle Iain, glancing at the advancing Calum. The aide feinted, thrusting forward, then a moment later, took off towards the door and disappeared down the corridor. Iain ran after the man, the sound of the outside door slamming shut once and then again, telling Abby the pursuit would continue outside.

Abby finished slashing Claudine's bindings with the dagger and Claudine's arms dropped to her sides limply. Abby went round to face her. Claudine opened her eyes slowly and attempted to focus on Abby.

"Are you well enough to ride?" asked Abby. "Did they hurt you badly?"

"No, not badly," Claudine managed to get out. Her lip was swelling and there was some blood in her mouth which she spat out on the floor. She glanced behind Abby. "See to your father, first."

Abby followed Claudine's gaze and saw that her father had slumped to the floor, his wound bleeding freely.

"Father!" She ran to his side.

He lay there, his eyes closed, his pallid skin deathlike. She leaned her ear near his mouth and thought she heard a faint breath. She noticed a faint rise in his chest. Tears came to her eyes.

"You'll be fine, Dada. Just hold on."

She tore at the laces on his leather jerkin, opening it just wide enough that she could see the large gash that bled freely at his side. Without hesitation she lifted her own jerkin and took her dagger and ripped a section of her shirt. She bundled it quickly against the wound, pressing hard and then pulled the jerkin back in place so that it held the compress in place.

"Here, give me the dagger," said Claudine.

She knelt beside Abby and took the braided sash that had been around her waist, a small looking-glass dangling at its end, and cut the object off. With the sash free of the object, Claudine tied it around Calum's waist, securing the compress tighter. When she was finished she placed a hand on his cheek, murmured softly to him, and leaned over and kissed his lips briefly.

Abby watched and was surprised that Claudine's action raised only a livid anger inside her. This woman was the cause of her father's state. It was an unreasonable rationale and she knew it, but her heart would not be told. She forced herself to rise and go over to Damville. One look at him told her he was dead. Finally, she was free of him. Would she be free of his employer? She glanced at Claudine. There was much to be discussed, but she had no time for that now.

"Help me get him to his horse," Abby said.

"It would be best to treat him here," said Claudine. "It's not safe to move him. He could die." Her voice broke on the last phrase and Abby gave her a scathing look.

"What right have you to say what will be done with him? If indeed you are his wife, you have not been so in fact in years. We'll move him now and take him back to Huntly Castle where he will receive better care than he could get here."

Claudine pressed her lips together, her expressive eyes full of misery. "No. I cannot agree."

Iain appeared in the doorway, his sword and dagger sheathed. He halted when he saw Calum lying on the floor. "How is he?" he asked.

"He's very badly hurt," said Abby. "I was saying to Claudine we need to get him back to Huntly Castle, quickly."

"*Non*," said Claudine, her voice firm. "We must nurse him here. I told her that. Send for a physician. Moving him now could kill him."

Iain looked from Abby to Claudine, assessing the situation. He made his way over to Calum and knelt beside Abby, giving her a brief reassuring squeeze on her shoulder. He checked the wound, which had stopped bleeding for the moment, and put a hand on Calum's head. He called his name softly. Calum's eyelids fluttered for a moment and then stilled. Iain sighed.

"I think it's best we take him to Huntly, as ye say, Abby. The bleeding has stopped and there will be medicaments and such at the castle."

"The bleeding may have stopped now, but it will start at the slightest jolt. *Non*, you cannot do it."

Calum rose and faced Claudine. "I understand your concerns

and I canna deny they are valid, but his best chance, ye ken, is at the castle."

Claudine bit her lip and nodded. "We must make a litter then, to carry him. It will be too rough on a horse."

"Aye, good thinking." He glanced over at Damville. "Is he dead?"

Abby nodded and Claudine muttered something under her breath. "And the other one? His aide?"

"Dead also," said Iain flatly. "We'll leave them here for now and inform the Earl when we're back at the castle and discuss whatever steps are necessary"

Abby tried to smile at his words, but failed. Iain saw and knelt beside her, taking her hand.

"Dinna fash yourself, quean, he'll be fine. We'll get your father tae the castle and they'll look after him there."

The words were really empty promises, Abby knew, but she took comfort nonetheless, managing a smile this time. Beside her, her father stirred and she took up his hand, taking heart from that as well.

"I'll be back in a moment," said Iain. "I'll just fashion a litter for him and we can be on our way."

He gave her a light kiss on the head and rose. She heard him leave. Claudine moved towards her and knelt down on Calum's other side. She took the remaining hand and kissed it.

"*Mon amour, s'il te plait*, you must live," said Claudine. "Now that we are both here together." She continued murmuring endearments in French, kissing Calum's hand.

Abby watched her, the anger burning strongly, but she held her tongue. All the accusations and recriminations that were building inside of her could wait. She would hold her peace while her father lay before her, on the edge of death.

CHAPTER 19

The sun was well on its way by the time the small party drew in sight of Huntly Castle. When Abby finally saw it rising up in front, she breathed a sigh of relief. She'd watched her father carefully as they slowly retraced their steps back to Huntly, noting his response to each jolt and the growing pallor of his skin, her fear rising. The road seemed never to end and now, as they made their way to the castle gate, Abby's fear increased as a new jolt elicited no response at all.

By the time they reached the courtyard several servants were assembled, ready to assist, the small party's approach and situation long since spotted from the castle. On Iain's orders the servants untied the litter he had fashioned from two tree limbs and a coverlet from Calum's horse. Once the litter was freed they carried it carefully into the castle and up to Calum's chamber.

The three had dismounted quickly and followed the servants into the castle. The door to the hall was open and there the Earl stood waiting, along with Lady Elizabeth and George. There was little welcome on their faces when they saw the bedraggled threesome and Abby stepped forward to greet them and explain. Iain put his arm out, stopping her, and she halted at his side.

"You were under our protection and guidance by your father's direction and yet you chose to flee your obligations under cover of darkness like a coward, a person with no honour," said the Earl, icily. "This is not the behaviour of a Gordon, I assure you and I am afraid I can only divest myself of any further connection with you, or your father."

"My father is wounded, possibly fatally while protecting me, and may I say in a more successful manner than you were ever able to manage," said Abby in a hard tone. Her anger gave her courage and she allowed all her fear and frustration to vent itself in her words. "You would deny my father aid? My father who has served his queen and his country in a manner you could never attempt?"

"Of course I wouldn't deny your father aid," said Huntly sharply. "Have I not sent for a physician to tend him? And our servant, Fenella, who has knowledge of such things, is on her way to him this very moment."

Iain laid a hand on Abby's arm to calm her. "I think what she means to say is that her father ran into some difficulties from Lord Damville, a person who not a few hours before had been given every welcome here. Lord Damville was employed by the Guises."

Huntly drew himself up and gave Iain a haughty stare. "The Guises and the French government. I knew that of course. He was here on a diplomatic errand. There is nothing in that to find fault with, indeed he had every endorsement from the Dowager Queen." He narrowed his eyes. "And just who are you to question my decisions and the conduct of my guests, Mister...Kerr, is it? Or didn't Lord Damville mention you had a different identity. I demand you make yourself known immediately."

Iain bowed gracefully. "I am Iain MacGregor, of Glen Strae, eldest son of the MacGregor and directed to protect the Queen."

Huntly's tone was sceptical. "And just who directs you?"

"Certain noblemen."

"And why don't I know of this?"

"It is direction of long-standing, my lord. Verra informal, ye ken. A few like-minded people who, when the Queen went tae France sought tae ensure that her throne and her person was secure."

"Tell me the names," said Huntly.

"I canna tell ye anything, I'm afraid, because I ken nought about them. I receive anonymous instructions. As does Calum Gordon."

"And what was your business here, was it to observe Lord Damville?" Huntly's tone was curt, but Iain had his attention.

"Aye, my lord. I'd been keeping track of him for some time. He has a small group of people who spy for him. He does his own share too, ye ken. Forbye, I'm certain he and his aide have found ways to discover many things here that ye might have wanted kept secret."

Abby, who knew that Iain's arrival at Huntly had nothing to do with Damville's presence, but rather to observe Huntly himself, was impressed by the calm manner with which he handled Huntly's question. Still, she felt a distraction was needed both for herself and Iain. She wanted to discuss with Iain what they would tell the Earl privately before they offered any explanation to him.

"Can we talk about this later, my lord?" said Abby. "In light of this night's events and my father's condition would you allow us all to refresh ourselves and have something to eat before we get into more detail?"

The Earl frowned, his obligations as host clearly struggling with his desire to have possession of all the facts quickly. He nodded and looked at his wife. "See to it, will you, Elizabeth?"

Lady Elizabeth curtseyed. "Of course, my lord."

With a few sharp words the orders were given and before

Abby was led away to her chamber she glanced at Iain, suddenly fearful now that he would leave her side. Without his reassuring presence she would feel adrift, uncertain about her father and her future. As if sensing her unease, he took her hand and squeezed it. She tried to take that comfort as she and Claudine made their way out of the room and up the winding stairs to their chambers.

Outside Abby's door, Claudine rested a hand tentatively on Abby's arm. "We will talk later, *non?*"

Abby looked at Claudine and refrained from saying the biting words that came to her. "I can't possibly think about anything but my father, now," she said eventually.

"But will you let me at least go to your father and nurse him? I have some experience."

Abby's first instinct was to reject Claudine's offer out of hand, but she forced herself to put her father's well-being first and managed to nod tightly. "If they will permit it, I have no objection."

"*Merci, ma cherie, merci.* I promise I will do my best."

Abby turned her back and entered her chamber. She could say no more to this woman who professed emotions and care that were years too late.

ABBY SAT ON A STOOL, not caring that its hard surface had numbed her nearly from her rear to her toes after hours sitting at Calum's bedside holding his hand. All her attention was fixed on the slight rise and fall of his chest and the lips that seemed paler than his skin. Fenella, the servant who had some knowledge of herbs and healing had already dressed his wound, noticing that the bleeding had appeared to stop. Abby had recognised Fenella as the woman George had been fondling the first morning after Abby's arrival.

Fenella's ministrations had given Abby some degree of hope and for a while she had taken heart that things would turn out well. But now, beads of sweat had begun to gather on her father's brow, and she knew that fever was setting in. The wound was in danger of putrefying.

Calum stirred and murmured something, the sweating increasing. "Shhh, *mon amour*," said Claudine. "Rest now. You are with those that you love."

Abby glanced at Claudine, who had taken up her own vigil soon after Abby had arrived, tapping gently on the door and opening it with an inquiring expression on her face. Abby had just nodded and Claudine had entered, carrying a bowl of water and cloth. She took a seat on the other side of the bed and began to sponge Calum's forehead. She'd done that on occasion in the few hours since and now, with Calum's sweating and restlessness increasing, it never left her hand.

Claudine murmured further words of comfort, stroking his head tenderly with the cloth, tears forming in her eyes. Abby couldn't fault her nursing, or the obvious love she poured out to Calum as she did it, but Abby felt the need to reserve judgement. There was no denying that Claudine was a consummate actress, and this might be just another one of her performances to ensure her own safety and escape from any type of recrimination for the incidents that had brought Calum to this pass. Or perhaps it was to impress Abby and try to win her over to use Abby in some other manner.

A tap came at the door. She waited for Claudine, but there was no reaction. With a sigh Abby rose and opened it. Iain stood on the threshold.

"How is he?"

She glanced over her shoulder. "As you can see, not well."

Her tone was curt. For some reason she was annoyed at him,

but she was too tired, too bone weary to work out why. Slowly she moved back and allowed him inside.

He moved over to the bed and looked down at Calum "He's feverish?"

She could only nod. He moved closer, looked at Claudine bathing Calum's forehead. Claudine gave him a brief nod and returned to her ministrations.

"The physician, has he been?"

There was silence for a moment until Claudine gave a soft, "*non*." She paused and turned to Iain. "And what would he do? Tut a bit and explain the humours and the need to bring down the fever by bleeding him, which would only weaken him further. Thank you, but no."

"The servant has put on some herbs and told us to ask her for a tisane if he became feverish," said Abby. She frowned at Claudine. "I was just going to do that."

She made for the door and Iain followed her. "I'll come with ye," said Iain. "I wanted to have a few words with ye if I could."

"You're welcome to come, but there's nothing to say at the moment." She opened the door and stepped into the corridor, Iain right behind her.

"It's about Huntly."

She closed the door softly and turned to him. "Can it not wait?"

"I must talk to him soon, give him an account of what happened. He willna trouble ye, lass, I'll see tae that, but I do want to discuss a few things wi' ye first."

"There's no need. Just tell him what occurred." She tilted her head. "Or do you want to tell him some other story that hides the fact that you were spying on him?"

He gave her a puzzled look. "Is that what's bothering ye? That I was spying on him? Because he's...what is he, your cousin?"

"My cousin, yes. My father is his uncle. But I know nothing of him, knew nothing of him, so I have no particular care for him and what he does."

"Then what is it, *Francach,* for as certain as I am standing here ye're angry at me for something."

"I'm not angry at you. On the contrary, I have no emotion attached to you at all, at present. My concern is solely for my father."

His eyes darkened and he placed his hands on her arms. She flinched.

"Ye feel nae emotion, is it?"

He pulled her into an embrace and lowered his mouth onto hers. Carefully and slowly, he kissed her, until her own mouth softened. She fought the feeling, the caress of his tongue and the pressure of his hands along her back. It was tears that came finally, rising up inside and giving her the strength to pull away in a deep sob.

"No," she said.

She raised a hand when he tried to pull her close into him again. She shook her head. "No. Leave me be. I've had enough of you and your ways. You talk about honour and duty and where does it bring you?" She pointed to the door to her father's chamber. "Lying on a bed near to death. A woman who is a wife and is a stranger. I will not be that woman. It's bad enough that I am that daughter. A daughter with a father I thought I knew and don't, and a mother….well who is that woman who claims to be my mother? Perhaps you can tell me, for I don't know. I know nothing."

The tirade finished. She stared a moment at Iain, clamping her mouth shut. She brushed the tears away and stalked off down the corridor. It wasn't long before she felt a hand on her arm, halting her in her steps.

"Ye've every right tae be angry, lass. Those that ye love have put ye through so much, and now they're asking more of ye."

She tried to shrug him off, but he wouldn't let her. He pulled her firmly into his arms and held her there. She stiffened.

"Let me go," she said.

"Nay, lass. I willna let ye go like this." He leaned down and kissed her hard. "I love ye, quean. Do ye no ken that?"

"Hah. So you say. But what does that mean? I must take you as you are, always wandering off on some dangerous purpose, at my father's bidding, to serve your queen? Didn't I just tell you that I will not be that woman?"

"But do you no ken that it's finished? I willna be wandering off, as ye put it."

She gave him a sceptical look. "And why should I believe that?"

"Because, ye ninny, I am known, now. By Huntly and others here from France. I am nae longer useful." He took a deep breath. "And I love ye more than anything else. If I learned anything since I've arrived here, it's that.

"But your disguises? They would take you some places."

Iain shrugged. "Nay, there is little use in that. To reach those high circles, these very people need tae ken ye well. I had trouble enough to get a place at Huntly. As it is, I found little of interest to anyone except to conclude that Huntly is a man who is loyal to whomever promises the biggest rewards. For the present, it seems, the Dowager Queen's favour has been enough for him."

"Truly? You are finished with all of that?" She couldn't bring herself to believe his words yet.

Iain nodded. "I'm afraid all I am now is a hieland barbarian."

"But now, can you prove who sent you and why?"

Iain shook his head. "I only received a letter. It was encrypted and it directed me to come here tae observe Huntly for any sign of betrayal. I had a letter of introduction by an unfamiliar hand and signed by a nobleman I'd never before had contact with."

"Which nobleman?"

"One of the Hamiltons."

"Not Sir Robert?" she asked in disbelief.

"What? Och, nay, not him. Have ye seen him since ye were back?"

"No. I have only been to my own room to change. The rest of the time I've been with my father." She blinked at him.

"How is your mother faring in all this?"

"My mother?"

Iain shrugged. "Did ye ever stop tae think why she was here, with ye?"

"I'm certain it had more to do with Damville and Huntly than with me."

"Are ye sure of that, lass? I see how much she cares for ye."

"Cares for me? Why would she care for me now, after all these years? Years when we heard not one word. Years when I just found it easier to think she was dead, than face that she had no thought for me or for my father."

"Have ye asked her?"

Abby folded her lips tightly and shook her head. "Why should I bother? She'd only lie."

He cupped her chin and looked into her eyes. "Ye should talk wi' her. Ye owe her that at least."

She pulled away. "I owe her nothing."

"She helped ye, as best she could when ye needed her. She did try to assist your escape from Huntly when he was determined tae send ye off with Sir Robert, after all.

"How do you know that?"

He grinned. "Do ye no ken that ye're the talk of the castle? Sir Robert has been bellowing about how ye were spirited off with that 'harlot widow' to whomever will hear him."

She allowed herself a small smile. "I can imagine. Hasn't Lady Elizabeth or the Earl said anything in response?"

"Nay, the earl has just put him off and said he must wait now until your father has recovered before the matter can be addressed. I fear Sir Robert sees his bride slipping out of his hands."

"This bride was never in his hands," she said flatly. "And never will be."

"Aye, there's no hope of that. For ye're already a bride. My bride."

She glanced at him and sighed. "I can't think about any of that now. Not until my father is well."

He nodded. "I ken that well, quean. For now, we'll just get that tisane and take one moment at a time."

He took her hand and led her along the corridor and down the stairs. The pair were just passing the hall when a voice called out Abby's name. She turned to see the Earl coming towards them.

"Where might you be going?" said the Earl.

"To get my father a tisane Fenella made up. He's feverish now, and she said it would help."

"Feverish?" The Earl frowned. "Aye, well. We'll do what we can for him for him. I'll send a servant along with the tisane. For now, I want you and your companion to present yourself in my library and explain yourselves."

"I'll do it," said Iain. "Let Mistress Gordon attend her father. I'm certain I'll be able to answer whatever questions ye may have."

Huntly gave Iain a disdainful look. "Nay...whatever your name is. You will not serve. I want the two of you, and that woman who calls herself Madame d'Eauville, to give your account at the same time, so I might measure well the truth of what you say."

"You'll have to wait then, my lord," said Abby. "Until my father is better, for there is nothing you can threaten me with that will persuade me otherwise. You may try Claudine, but I cannot imagine her answer would be any different from mine.

The Earl's face reddened visibly. "I will allow that you're distressed and unable to fully comprehend the situation in which you find yourself, or its consequences to your future. But suffice it to say that you have been warned. I expect you all there as soon as possible."

"As soon as possible, my lord," said Iain. "Aye. We will be there as soon as it is possible."

Iain gave a quick bow and Abby followed with a short curtsey. The pair resumed their journey to the kitchen, Iain grabbing her hand. "It will only be possible when we are good and ready," he said under his breath.

Abby squeezed his hand in appreciation and left it there, content for the moment that he should support her.

CHAPTER 20

The draught pulled at Abby's skirts as she passed along the corridor towards the earl's library. The chilly morning air created clouds from her breath and stung her nose. She rubbed her eyes which felt red and tired after another night spent by her father's side. This morning he was still restless and his fever held, but at least it hadn't worsened, she told herself. His wound, when she'd removed the dressing earlier this morning, was red and angry around the stitching and a small amount of pus seeped at the edge. She'd wiped it away and applied the poultice Fenella had given her and her father had groaned when she'd done so.

It was these concerns that filled her now as she followed Claudine reluctantly, Iain by her side. The three had put off the Earl for two days now, but he would wait no longer for them to give their account. Iain placed a reassuring hand on her shoulder and she smiled wanly at him. He'd been attending her these past two days, just as she'd attended her father. He'd brought her tempting soups and cups of warm ale, coaxing her away for a short time to eat, or take some exercise, all the while talking of nothing more than amusing tales of his childhood or old court gossip. She had to admit the attention had proved a distraction for her for a short while when she wasn't consumed with worry for her father, or angry at him and her mother for the years of deceit that had brought them to this pass.

They arrived at the library and Claudine knocked. She too showed the signs of little sleep in the dark marks that shadowed her eyes and the drawn look of her face. Her fair hair was bundled under one of the dark hoods of her former disguise, but her slender figure was clearly evident in the same burgundy gown she'd worn the night of their escape, now soiled and crumpled. Abby had offered her one of her own, but Claudine had refused with a simple shake of her head. Despite the initial dishevelled appearance there was an air of quiet dignity about her.

The summons came to enter and the three slipped inside and made their way to the Earl who was seated at a large table, near an array of mullioned windows, a cup of warm ale at his side. Iain gave a small bow and the two women curtseyed briefly.

The Earl leaned forward. "I feel I have been patient enough, given the situation, but there are several pressing matters connected to your accounts and they must be attended to speedily. I must give an account to the French ambassador, the Dowager Queen and the Council of Regents, since this appears to involve matters of state." He frowned at Abby. "This is not to mention the presence of Sir Robert and his demands."

"That is a minor matter and easily resolved," said Iain.

Huntly pulled his fur lined cloak closer around him and glared at Iain. "I'll be the judge of that young man."

Iain shrugged and nodded. "As ye wish, my lord."

Huntly took a deep breath and directed his glance at Iain. "Now, we took you into this household on good faith as Duncan Kerr, soldier, yet now you inform me that you are...?"

"Iain MacGregor, my lord, first son of the MacGregor."

Huntly paused a moment to contemplate Iain's words. "Was that clan not outlawed not so long ago?"

"Nay, my lord, the clan wasna put to the horn, I was. But only briefly. I was issued a pardon."

Huntly seemed unimpressed by Iain's last statement. "So, an outlaw, welcomed into my house under a false name to spy on me and my guests under some dubious authority, and now I am meant to take your word that the men you have killed are traitors?"

Iain gave him a wry smile. "Aye, put in such a manner it hardly looks well for me, I grant ye. But I assure ye, my lord, I was under instructions tae look after the lass and keep my eyes open. I've had dealings with the Comte de Damville in the past and then he was acting on occasions against the best interests of our queen and our country. I believe he was doing so in this instance as well." Iain scanned the contents of the Earl's desk. "Ye might find something among his papers that would prove my words."

The Earl followed Iain's eyes. "Letters from the French ambassador is what I found, containing legitimate business."

Iain raised a brow. "Is that all? Nothing that may appear innocent but perhaps would be encrypted in some subtle manner? Or it might be that documents of that type would be secreted among his baggage, or in the room."

"But wouldn't you know? Didn't he discover you searching his papers?"

Iain gave an amused grin. "Och, that was his own ruse to get me out of the way. He didna discover me in his rooms at all."

"But you did search his room."

"I found letters that were encrypted that stated he was working for the Guise family and was here under their instructions to gather information about you and the Scottish government, as well as abduct Mistress Gordon.

"Abduct Mistress Gordon? Why? Because she's my cousin and they would hold her hostage for my cooperation?"

Iain glanced at Abby and shrugged, his face neutral.

"Perhaps, my lord. They have many irons in the fire and wish to keep their position secure."

"But the Dowager Queen is a Guise. Why would they concern themselves so much?"

"They are ever eager to be the first to scent a shifting wind," said Iain. "Perhaps they felt the wind was shifting here."

Huntly reddened but remained silent for a moment. "And now he lies dead. I had someone collect his body and the aide's. They also collected their belongings. We'll see if there are any encrypted letters that you claim were in his possession."

He gestured to Abby. "As for you, there is still Sir Robert to deal with. What do you suggest I say to him to explain these incidents?"

"You may tell him that there is no reason for him to delay here any longer. There is no contract."

"I will tell him no such thing. You are still placed under my care and your father's last instructions regarding you were to arrange for your marriage. Sir Robert was the person nominated. He is suitable and from all his bellowing, I gather, still willing. We will settle this matter as soon as possible."

"I will settle nothing while my father lies ill unto death," said Abby firmly.

"Nay, if things are as thon man says, then we will have you safely married and away from here as soon as possible."

Abby opened her mouth to speak but Iain laid a hand on her arm. "I'm afraid she canna marry Sir Robert, because she's wed tae me."

"To you?" Huntly said in disbelief.

Iain withdrew a folded parchment from his jerkin and handed

it over to the Earl. The earl took it, opened it and read the contents quickly.

"But this is a contract for a handfasting. That's a Highland custom, and besides, it states that it becomes indissoluble only if the two of you have bedded."

"A highland custom it may be, but it's still legal," said Iain. "And we have bedded."

Huntly snorted. "And you would have me take your word for it? Nay, Sir Robert will be willing to disregard this document and anything you may try to say to the contrary. Something as trivial as this won't halt his desire for a connection to this family."

"*Non*, I will not allow this marriage to Sir Robert," said Claudine.

"And you, madame. I also welcomed you into the household as someone you are evidently not?"

"I am her mother."

"Her mother? If you are her mother, what need was there for subterfuge?" demanded Huntly.

"I came to protect my daughter from the Comte de Damville. It was necessary to adopt a disguise because Damville and I know each other of old. I had foiled one of his little endeavours in France years ago. He never could forget it and seemed determined to prove me a spy in revenge for it. To that end he has been trying to abduct my daughter and use her to make me confess. "

"So why did you spirit your daughter away after Damville had left the castle? Surely the two of you were safe at that point."

"How could I be certain? You were keeping her captive and held Damville in high esteem as an emissary from the French government. It was better to take her away to a safe place until her father could come."

"You haven't convinced me, madame, I'm afraid. I have it on my wife's authority that your husband made no mention of you.

Sir Robert's offer still seems the best solution for Mistress Gordon."

"Can't you delay your decision until my father's health improves?"

"I am being asked to take the word of three people who have practised deception in my household. I must also still give an account of two dead men and one injured man. One, a foreign noble will require a detailed explanation and reckoning to avoid an unpleasant situation with the French. As for the third person, Master Cameron, I have still to hear the account for his injury."

"He's recovering?" asked Abby, concern in her voice.

"He is concussed, apparently, but recovering. It could have been fatal. What in God's name made you leave an innocent man on the road in that manner? " Huntly looked at Iain. "I suppose he has you to thank for that."

"There is nothing innocent about Cameron. He was holding us captive and taking us to be traded to the English. Calum tracked us down on the road, later."

"You would have me believe that Master Cameron, who has been in my employ as a tutor for a number of years, is actually working for the English? That's preposterous. I know the man well."

"I dinna think he has done this much in the past, though he is skilled well enough with the sword and the bow. Nay, I believe the English enticed him with promises of wealth. I can show ye the note."

"But I have only your word that any of this is true, and that the note you possess came from Cameron, when it could just as easily have come from you."

"You have my word, as well," said Abby.

"And mine, of course," added Claudine.

Huntly lifted a brow. "This is hardly reassuring, given both your actions since your arrival." He frowned at Iain. "Nay, I think

I must confine you again to your quarters, until such time as I have further proof of your innocence. When Cameron recovers sufficiently I will question him and Calum should he be able for it at any time." He paused. "Unless you can produce a letter now that supports your reason for being here, signed by a person of noble repute."

Iain smiled wryly. "Alas, my lord I'm afraid I dinna have the letter with me. Only the note. But perhaps if ye question the lady that tends your wife ye might discover something of Cameron's activities. I believe he may have attempted to pay court tae her in an effort to garner information."

"And which lady is this?"

Iain looked at Abby. "I believe she is called Jane...."

"This is a serious accusation. My wife ensures that all her ladies are carefully supervised. No misbehaviour is allowed. Nevertheless, I will discuss this with my wife and see what she may make of it. In the meantime, I would be obliged if you would confine yourself to your quarters." He looked at Abby. "Regardless of whether there is a contract between you two or not. This takes precedence."

Iain bowed. "Very well, my lord. As ye see fit."

Huntly regarded the two women. "Given the circumstances surrounding Calum, I will concur that you both need to be at his bedside and on errands regarding his welfare, but I must insist that you restrict yourselves to these activities, until such time as we can clear up these issues to my satisfaction."

Abby and Claudine acknowledged his instructions with brief curtsies. There was nothing more to be said.

ABBY WATCHED the physician lay out his materials on the table in the bed chamber. Among the various items were the knife and bowl for letting blood. She looked across at Claudine and saw her frown.

The physician examined Calum carefully, studying his eyes, his tongue, listening to his breathing, as well as asking Claudine questions about his bodily functions and their colour. He looked at the wound, sniffing and poking it, all the while making little disapproving noises. He was thorough, there was no doubt. When he was finished, he moved over to the items on the table.

"What do you think, doctor?" said Claudine.

The physician glanced at Claudine, his brow furrowed. "When I have finished I will make a full report to the Earl, madam."

"*Mais non*, you will tell me now, monsieur, what you intend to do. As his wife, I have every right to know."

The physician straightened and smoothed his long dark robe. Grey wisps poked out of his black cap giving a somewhat comical air to his attempt at wounded dignity.

"Madam, this is a most complicated case and I'm certain it would be best if I spoke first with the Earl. He will would let you know what is necessary, I'm sure."

"I am fully capable of understanding whatever you have to say concerning my husband," said Claudine, sharply.

The physician gave a sigh and pursed his lips. "The news is not good, I am afraid. Your husband is gravely ill. The humours are sorely unbalanced and the wound is starting to putrefy. I will do what I can to alter the humours, but I have little hope it will work."

His tone had been clipped, impatient almost. Abby paled at his final words and started to speak, but Claudine held up her hand.

"What is it you are proposing to try to alter the humours?"

"I will bleed him, madam. I can make no promises that it will be enough to halt the course of his illness, though. I have seen such cases before, and they usually do not end well."

"You will not bleed my husband," said Claudine. "If you can offer no other help I suggest you collect your materials and leave."

The physician reddened. "I beg your pardon, but I answer to the Earl. Only he can dismiss me."

"Well go to him, if you must, monsieur, but be assured that you are no longer welcome in this room."

Claudine went over to the table and began to pack up the items there and place them in the bag.

He moved over to Claudine and grabbed the knife from her hand. "I demand you leave off my instruments. They are precious and not to be handled ill advisedly."

Claudine stepped back and allowed him to finish putting away the rest of his things.

"And I will inform the Earl that whoever has been tending his wound used methods verging on witchcraft." He turned to face Claudine. "And that, madam, is a very serious charge."

He gave a curt bow and left the room, the threat of his words hanging in the room after him.

Claudine waved a hand in dismissal. "Bah, empty words from a bag of wind."

"I don't know, he sounded serious," said Abby.

"Would you have your father dead? For that's what would have happened if this man tended him with his humour balance and poking and prodding. I have more faith in that wise woman, Fenella."

"I know and I agree, but I still worry he will make good his threat. There is no telling then what might happen."

"Surely nothing. She is only a serving woman with knowledge of herbs. What harm is she?"

Abby shook her head. She knew of nothing first hand, but she remembered a story or two from other Scots. And in these times of growing religious contention who knows what some innocent treatment might be twisted into something evil by a more powerful person who feels offended by their ministrations?

Claudine moved to her and placed a hand on her shoulder. It was the first time she had touched Abby since they'd returned. Abby flinched involuntarily, but allowed the hand to remain.

"*Ma cherie*, we must do all we can for your father. First and foremost we have to believe that he will get well. And he will."

Abby looked into Claudine's eyes and saw the pleading there. She was unmoved by it, still unable to shake off the anger at her, at both of them.

"Of course I want my father to get well. But you, why do you care? You've not cared for all these years, why now?"

Claudine paled and removed her hand. "Be assured I care. I have always cared. I have cared so much for you, and your father."

Abby snorted. "I find that difficult to believe. Either that or I have no understanding for what you mean by caring. Does caring mean having no contact with your daughter for fifteen years? Does it mean leaving my father to care for me without benefit of a mother's love? For that's what I've experienced, madame, in the years since you left us. It has been so long that I am surprised you found the need to adopt any disguise, because I must confess, I don't recognise you at all."

Claudine stepped back, her eyes filled with tears. "I am more sorry than I can say, *ma petite,* that you have had to suffer for my absence. But I must tell you that there is much you do not understand or know about from the past that made this necessary. I thought it best...well, for your safety and your father's safety that you would know nothing about me, or where I went."

"Did my father know?"

Claudine sighed and nodded. "I think he guessed some of it. He's been trying to find me this past year."

"So you were a spy as well? I should have known. The pair of you lying to everyone including each other, I'll be bound."

"What? No. You mustn't blame your father. I left without explaining anything to him. It was too dangerous for him to know the truth. That's why I never contacted him."

"And you can't say now? Why have you decided to reveal yourself at this point, if you cannot explain yourself?"

Claudine looked down at her hands, twisting her fingers among themselves. "I-I didn't intend that I should be revealed. I wanted to protect you, though. I was desperate to make sure you were safe." She glanced at Calum. "He no longer could, that was clear, and I was worried."

"How did you know that I wasn't safe?"

Claudine gave a wan smile. "I have my friends, my contacts. Don't think I haven't followed your progress all these years?" She looked at Abby with longing. "You have become such a beautiful young woman, Gabrielle. I am so proud of you. If only Henri had lived. You would be safe now, ensconced in the French country-side, under the protection of an influential family."

"Some things don't go to plan, do they Claudine?" said Abby tartly.

"Gabrielle, I ask you not to forgive me, but to give me a chance. I love you and your father beyond all reason."

"But why would you leave us, if that's the case? How am I to believe what you say when your actions over the years infer the opposite?"

Claudine took Abby's hands and squeezed them tightly. "I see nothing but the truth will satisfy you, but you must understand that I haven't said anything up to now for your own protection. Events appear to have changed this somewhat."

"Damville's death?"

Claudine nodded. "As I said to the Earl, I thwarted one of Damville's little schemes some years ago. It was when you were a young baby. He, with the support and power of the Guises behind him, was intent that I be exposed as a spy and executed as a traitor."

"But you served the Dowager Queen when she first came to Scotland from France, didn't you? Couldn't you get her to protect you?"

Claudine smiled ruefully. "If only it was that simple. The Dowager Queen had no real liking for me and her family were continually suspicious of me because, although my father was born in the Guise's home territory of Lorraine, my father's family and my mother were not. They were from the south, a place near Florence, the seat of the Medici family. We are mixed blood, you could say. So, our loyalty was always in question. Especially when the French King married a Medici and made her his queen. She has now set herself up as a rival power to the Guises."

"Is it enough to be from the Florence area to cause suspicion among the Guises?" Abby knew the answer before it was said. But something else struck her. "Are you connected to the Medici family?" asked Abby, studying Claudine's face. It was difficult to trust Claudine's words.

Claudine hesitated, biting her lip. "Yes, in a way." She glanced over at Calum. "He discovered that. My mother has no love for the Guises and Lorraine. The people of Lorraine were hardly welcoming when she married my father. Knowing that, the Medici found a way to persuade me to work for them." She sighed. "My father borrowed heavily from them to fund an enterprise. One that did not go well. They said I might work off that debt if I was to gather information for them. I was still at court then, just married to your father. My father pleaded that I help him. I could hardly refuse.

"Soon after, I foiled one of Damville's schemes to put the

Medici Queen Catherine completely out of favour. Damville, so intent to avenge my interference, was determined to prove me a spy. He took me once and threatened to harm you and your father unless I confessed, but I escaped. It was then I left the pair of you without letting you know where I was or why. If I'd told Calum he would have gone after Damville and I couldn't risk that danger. I missed you both so, and I found it very difficult not to reach out to you."

Abby studied Claudine, saw the sorrow laid bare and the resignation that the passing years had brought. "What has changed that you decided to come to me?" Abby asked finally.

The tears came again to Claudine's eyes. "You were in danger, as I told you. I couldn't let you be at Damville's mercy. Your father had tried to protect you before, but it wasn't enough. And he was becoming too distracted in his efforts to find me."

"He made efforts to find you?"

Claudine nodded slowly. "Yes, he was close at one point, so I sent him a note to draw him to a manor house in the south of France. The men I hired were to hold him until I could make my way back to Florence. They were also to make it clear that I was not to be contacted. But they were fools."

"That was you at the manor house?" Abby thought back to the manor house from where she and Iain had rescued her father.

"Yes." She smiled wryly. "You outwitted my carefully laid plans and in the process you were nearly captured by Damville. I couldn't have that. So I used my contacts to find where you were going and came myself to watch over you. I knew by then Calum wouldn't rest until he could find me. And if he did, it would lead him back to here, to you."

"Is that why he was on the road when Iain and I were in Cameron's hands?"

"*Non.* I confess I grew worried soon after I arrived. I sent a message to your father to come at once to Huntly Castle. It was by a stroke of luck that he came that quickly."

"It was fortunate," said Abby.

Abby's tone had been non-committal. At this point she didn't know what she felt. She could neither condemn nor welcome Claudine as a friend, let alone a mother. She glanced at her father. What would he feel? She could only hope that he would be allowed to recover and express his own thoughts on the matter.

$\mathcal{T}$he steam from the posset rose up and created swirls around Abby's face. She paused in the corridor and took a deep breath. The heady, slightly sweet aroma calmed her mind and gave her a tiny thread of comfort for which she was grateful.

"You're taking that to your father?"

Abby turned to see George ambling towards her. There was a smile, but little conviction behind it.

"I am," she said cautiously.

"He is recovering then?" He indicated the posset. "He's well enough to be able to take nourishment?"

"He's the same really. I hope that I might get this posset down him that Fenella made. She says it will help him fight the poison."

George frowned. "Have a care. Thanks to your lady mother, Master Fiske has complained about Fenella."

"He has? Is it serious?"

"I don't know. Father must be seen to give Doctor Fiske's complaints every consideration and try to appease him. Fiske is well connected." He laid a hand on Abby's arm. "Please try to rein in your mother. Fenella is a valued servant. Trusted. We wouldn't take it kindly here if we were forced to surrender her for questioning."

"Questioning?"

"For witchcraft," he said, an impatient edge to his voice. "Didn't you realise that when you and your mother decided to challenge the treatment of a respected physician?"

"Witchcraft." Abby repeated the statement, too dumfounded to do more. "But surely not," she said eventually. "It was only that Claudine felt it would weaken him if he were bled. It had nothing to do with Fenella."

"Nevertheless, her name was mentioned and Master Fiske understood that she'd attended to Calum."

"It was nothing much really, just a poultice put on the wound. To help the healing and fight the fever."

"Well, let's hope my father can persuade Fiske and others that it was harmless, or that there is no case for taking her to the church authorities for interrogation." He glanced down at the posset. "And this is Fenella's also, you say?" He said softly.

Abby nodded.

"Make haste, and if possible ensure no one sees you on your way to the room."

She gave another nod. "Have you heard anything of Iain MacGregor's situation?"

The faint curl of his lip left Abby in no doubt of his opinion of Iain and his situation. "You mean the man who claims to be innocent of all actions, as well as being wed to you?"

"Has there been any word to verify his statements?"

"Alas, I'm afraid I must disappoint you and tell you that your lover, for I presume he is that, given that you both claim you are bedded, still remains confined to his room. We have, however, heard from the French ambassador and he demands that Father hand him over immediately."

Abby paled. "What has your father decided?"

"Nothing, as yet. But I would say your Highlander should pray for a miracle. My father's patience can be stretched only so far."

George bowed curtly and left, leaving Abby to stare after him. She had thought Iain safe enough confined to his chamber, leaving her to concentrate on nursing her father back to health. But it was clear that she had miscalculated the French ambassador's indignation. She could only pray that the fever would abate and her father would recover, not only for her own sake, but for Iain's too. His word would certainly be enough to clear Iain.

SHE COULD HEAR Claudine's voice as she opened the door. For a brief moment Abby thought that her father had awakened and was listening to Claudine, but then she realised it was singing. For a moment Abby paused on the threshold and looked at the scene before her. Claudine sat stroking her father's head, her rich, warm voice singing the words of a French song. A memory stirred inside Abby as the familiar notes and words threaded their way back to her from the past. The voice was the same and Abby realised her mother had sung this to her when she was young. For a moment she allowed the warmth of long ago emotions to wrap itself around her and give her the comfort it had provided so long ago. But with great force of will she pushed the feeling aside and entered the room.

She placed the posset on the table. "How is he? Do you think he will be able to take any of this posset? Fenella says it should help fight the poison."

Claudine looked up and smiled. "He may be a little better. His brow is perhaps a little cooler and he isn't quite as restless. Shall we try the posset then?"

Abby studied her father and was pleased to see that she could confirm Claudine's words. With some effort she helped lift her father so that Claudine might try spooning a few mouthfuls at a time to Calum's mouth. It was a painstaking and awkward procedure, but Claudine had managed at other times to get Calum to swallow most of any tisane Fenella had brewed as well as an occasional bowl of broth. The posset was thickened with honey and proved more difficult to get Calum to manage. Some dribbled down his chin. He opened his glazed eyes during the process and seemed to know that it was important that he take all that was given, but after a few mouthfuls it was clear that it was all he could manage.

Claudine put the cup on the table while Abby settled her father back down on the bed. She pulled the coverlet back up, tucking it carefully around him and brushed his cheek with her hand, in part as a caress, but also to assess his fever.

"Please, Dada, you must get well, quickly," she said. "For the love you bear me."

Claudine returned to the bedside and looked across at Abby. "Quickly? Is something amiss?"

Abby sighed. "It's Iain. I just spoke with George and he says that the French ambassador has demanded that Iain be handed over to him."

"But so soon? This is very strange."

Abby shrugged. "Bruised dignity. Or perhaps something more. Who knows exactly what Damville was sent to do, that now cannot be done? Or perhaps he feels Iain is a potential threat because of information the ambassador suspects he might know?"

"This is too much. I will speak with the Earl and convince him not to hand Iain to the ambassador."

"I'm not certain that's a good idea. I have reason to believe Huntly doesn't hold you in a favourable light at present."

"What do you mean?"

Abby sighed. "The physician has protested about the use of Fenella's poultice to Huntly. He accused her of practising witch-craft and threatens to take his concerns further."

Claudine paled. "*Mon Dieu*, but that is wrong. My refusal of his services had nothing to do with Fenella's ministrations."

"Whatever the intentions, the result will be that Fenella could very well be charged with witchcraft unless Huntly can persuade the physician otherwise. I believe he will try. He wouldn't want his household tainted with that, as well as harbouring traitors and spies."

Claudine shook her head. "It is all wrong. Iain should be here, beside you, comforting you."

Abby smiled wryly. "I thought he was too dangerous."

Claudine waved her hand. "That is past. He is your husband, as you say, and it is too late to steer you away from him." She took Abby's hand. "I can see that there is a strong love between you two."

Abby glanced over at her father. "I hope he will agree with you when he recovers. If he recovers."

Claudine squeezed her hand. "He will recover, *ma coeur*, he will. And when he does I will make certain that he puts no obstacle in the way of your marriage."

SHE WAS DESCENDING the stairs and out into the courtyard before she knew her purpose. It was raining heavily and her loose curls were soon plastered to her head. She hadn't worn a cloak and the bodice of her gown was soon as wet at its hem. She hurried past the stables and by the time she reached the Tower House she was wet through. Her hands trembled slightly, but she knew it wasn't the chill from her wetting.

She took a deep breath and ascended the stairs, passing soldiers who gave her questioning looks and servant boys who stood back against the corridor to allow her to pass. She supposed they knew her well enough now to refrain from unseemly remarks and for that she was grateful.

When she arrived at Iain's chamber she halted before the guard who leaned against the wall beside the door. When he saw her he straightened and frowned.

"Mistress, this is nae place for ye," he said. "What cause have ye tae come here?"

"I must speak with Iain MacGregor, the man you hold inside there."

The man shook his head. "Nay, I'm afraid I canna do that. My orders are tae let no one pass."

"But you can make an exception for me. He's my husband."

The man gave her a dubious look and shook his head sadly. "As much as I might have a mind tae, mistress I'm afraid I canna do that."

"But it isn't much that I ask. Just a little time alone with my husband. Just so I can say goodbye before they take him away."

The guard glanced behind her and then gave a small nod. "Just for a few moments, only. I canna afford for the Earl tae discover that I've let ye in."

Abby smiled brightly and thanked him, promising her visit would be short. He withdrew the ring bearing the key from his belt and opened the door. It swung back and Abby stepped through hurriedly, careful to shut it behind her. She glanced around and saw Iain rising from one of the small pallets that filled the room.

"Abby. What brings ye here, lass? Is something amiss? And look at ye, you're wet through." He strode across the room to her, put his hands on her shoulders and studied her face.

She bit her lip. "Oh, Iain. Iain. You must find a way to leave, now. We'll hit the guard over the head and I'll get a horse for you, so you can escape...."

"Hush, quean, hush. Ye're going tae fast for me tae make sense of your words. What is the sudden urgency that I must leave?"

"It's the French ambassador. He's ordered for you to be sent to him under guard. The earl feels he cannot refuse the request."

"Can't he wait until I can gather the evidence to prove my statement?"

Abby shook her head. "No, the ambassador will not wait. But, quick, there's no time. We must get you out of here, before they take you. Once the ambassador has you, who knows where they'll take you and what they'll do with you?"

Tears that she'd held at bay for so long suddenly took hold of her and she emitted a sob. She turned around so that Iain wouldn't see it but his hands pulled her back to him and into an embrace.

"Sshh now. Dinna fash yourself. This clishmaclaver will blow over, ye'll see." He kissed her head. "Ye're all of a piece for worry over your father. Does he fare any better?"

Abby shook her head, unable to speak at first. "That's it. If only he would recover enough to vouch for you so the Earl would think twice before giving you over to the French."

Iain smoothed her hair away from her face. "There's nought ye can change about that, I'm sure ye've done all in your power to help him. It's in the hands of God now."

Whether it was his tone, or his words but she felt some reassurance and she relaxed, looking at him, her eyes filled with gratitude.

"Ah, quean, I hate tae see ye so distressed."

He leaned down and kissed her, drawing her tighter into his arms. She gave way to him, responding to the pressure of his lips and for a moment there was nothing but the feel of his mouth, the feel of his arms, and the need she knew would never leave. Eventually, Abby pulled away and forced herself back to reality.

"We mustn't waste time. We have to capture the guard, tie him up and gag him. Then I'll get you a horse while you wait behind the barn…"

Iain placed a finger on her mouth and shook his head. "Nay, it willna work. There are too many about. I would be captured before I made it to the gate."

"You're wrong. We can try it. There is a chance."

"I'm verra sorry lass, but can ye no see that it does my cause harm if I were tae try and escape?"

She paused and looked at him. "But can't you see that once the French have you there is little hope they will surrender you, whether or not there is evidence to contradict their assumptions?"

"It's a long way to the French ambassador's residence," said Iain wryly. "Much can happen in that time."

A loud knock sounded on the door and the guard opened it. "Ye must leave now, mistress. I think they are close by."

"Who is close by?" said Abby.

The guard glanced at Iain. "The men who are tae take MacGregor here tae the French ambassador. All is ready, it remains only tae collect the prisoner.

Abby clutched Iain's hand and lifted it to her mouth, kissing it. "Be safe," she whispered. "And promise me you'll do nothing foolhardy on the road? I will try what I can to get the Earl to release you."

Iain pulled her to him for a brief moment and planted a kiss on her mouth. "Take care, *mo cridh*. You have my heart and soul," he said in Gaelic and then in English.

Abby heard the heavy footfall of boots on the stairs and their progress down the corridor until, they stopped at the entrance. A group of armed liveried men stood there, George at their head.

He frowned when he saw Abby, but said nothing. He gestured quickly to the men behind them and they stepped forward. One of the men tied Iain's hands behind his back and moved him forward, past Abby. He nodded to George and proceeded out of the room and along the corridor. Abby watched him leave, the feeling of helplessness so overwhelming it was all she could do not to sink to the floor.

ABBY KNOCKED on the library door and waited only a moment before opening it. Huntly was sitting at his table, George bending over his shoulder. They both looked up in surprise when they saw her.

"I don't believe I gave permission for you to enter," said Huntly. "But since you are here, you may tell me the purpose of your visit, but be quick about it. George and I have important matters to discuss."

Abby glanced at the documents spread out before them. She wasn't able to tell if they concerned Iain, or the French ambassador, but she did observe seals attached to some of the documents. Government matters of some kind, most certainly.

Abby drew herself up. "I've come to ask you, no plead with you, to send out a messenger to get the men to bring Iain back to Huntly Castle."

"Why would I do that?" said the Earl. His tone was almost amused.

George sighed and shook his head. "You seem to be a bit addled, cousin. There is no change in the situation since his departure. We are under obligation to the French ambassador, you seem to forget."

"This is no longer a matter for your concern," said the Earl.

"But it is my concern, I tell you, he's my husband."

"So you keep stating. But the only document I saw was a contract for a handfasting. And if there were such a marriage, it doesn't alter anything. I have no cause to believe that you are bedded, as you state."

"But my father will support Iain's words. If you will only wait until he recovers."

"How is your father?" asked George. "Last I recall he was still feverish and it was doubtful he would live."

"I'm afraid I cannot wait on the off chance of a statement, when his very life is on a thread, my dear," said the Earl.

His tone had become a little more kindly, but there was an underlying firmness to it. Abby glanced from one to the other and noted the resolve. These were men who put state affairs above personal concerns. They were ambitious, desiring power and opportunities. She would have to find another way to help Iain. That much was clear.

She pressed her lips together, gave a short curtsey and left the room without replying. Slowly she made her way back to her father's chamber, her mind sorting through possibilities. They all seemed desperate and unworkable. There was no Angus to assist her, no one trusted man that could help her fight the guards that were escorting Iain. Where was Angus? She'd hardly thought of him, until now. He was Iain's trusted man. Why hadn't he accompanied him to Huntly Castle? It was too far to send word to Glen Strae for help, even if she was able to. No, she would have to do without Angus and the other MacGregors.

CHAPTER 22

*a*bby entered her father's bedchamber and looked over at him. There seemed no real change, though perhaps his breathing had eased into a more comfortable rhythm. Claudine gave her a questioning look and Abby shook her head. The tears were just too close.

She straightened and moved over to the far end of the chamber where the leather bag that held his things was placed. The servants hadn't bothered to unpack since his arrival, so it lay there, untouched. She knelt down beside it, untied the laces and opened it. There was only a change of shirt and hose, a pair of shoes, a doublet and a few other items in a pouch. She dug around deeper, pulling each item out, until they were scattered around her.

"What are you looking for?" asked Claudine quietly.

Abby stared up at her silently for a moment. What was she looking for, really? "Something, anything that can prove Iain's innocence. A letter, a note, or...I don't know."

Claudine sighed. "I am so sorry. I wish there was something I could do to help."

Abby shook her head and went back to her search, until she

had examined every single item carefully and found nothing. She frowned and then looked over to the kist at the end of the bed and smiled wryly. The clothes he'd worn when he'd arrived. Would they be in there? She went over to the kist, opened the lid and looked inside. Laying on top was a carefully folded coverlet. With a sinking heart she moved the coverlet aside and found an old blanket. Nothing more. She threw the coverlet back into the kist in disgust and shut it.

Without further word she went to the door and opened it.

"Where are you going?" asked Claudine.

"To find his clothes," said Abby and she left, shutting the door firmly behind her.

She walked purposefully down the corridor, past her own room just as Jeannette was emerging. Seeing Abby she halted, confused. Jeannette bobbed a curtsey but she wouldn't meet Abby's eyes.

"What are you doing in my room?" asked Abby.

"Oh, please excuse me, madame. I am so sorry. They asked me to pack your things. I wanted to tell you but they gave me strict instructions you were not to be disturbed in your father's chamber."

"What? Who are they? I have no intention of going anywhere?"

"Of course, madame, and didn't I tell them the very same thing? But they would not listen to me. Oh know. I am just a lowly French woman. But they are wrong. They are the barbarians forcing you to leave with that man, and your father on his deathbed. It is not decent I tell you."

Abby blinked at this tirade. "They plan to have Sir Robert take me away?"

Jeannette nodded. "They say it is for your protection."

"Who is they?" repeated Abby.

"Monsieur the Earl and his lady wife."

"Well they can try all they may, but I am not leaving my father's side."

Jeannette puffed out her chest. "Of course you will not, madame. I will go and unpack at once."

"No, that can wait. I want you to retrieve my father's clothes. The ones he arrived in when he was hurt."

Jeanette frowned. "I will do my best, madame. I just hope they haven't burned them. They were full of blood."

Abby bit her lip. She hadn't considered that such steps might be taken. She could only hope it wasn't so.

ABBY RETURNED to her father's chamber and slipped inside. Claudine rose and came over to her.

"What is it. You look pale. Have you discovered something?"

"What? No, no. They took Father's clothes and Jeannette thought they may have burnt them. Anything he might have had hidden in them would have gone too, if they did burn them."

"What? No, they wouldn't have burnt them. He wore a leather jerkin. That would easily be cleaned. And well, the breeches surely were not so badly stained. Perhaps his shirt, yes, but… well there would have been nothing there."

Abby nodded, comforted by her words. She was hanging on to threads, she knew that. There was likely nothing in his clothes. It was just a desperate act from a desperate woman. And that's how she felt. Short of riding out after the two who accompanied Iain and trying to take them by surprise, she could think of no other solution. It was a foolish step to take, but she was prepared to try if she couldn't find anything among her father's possessions.

"Jeannette was told to pack my things," said Abby, forcing

herself to change the subject. "It seems they will try and make me go with Sir Robert to his estate."

Claudine gave her a surprised look. "What? No. Well that is impossible. I will see that such plans are put aside." She patted Abby's shoulder and moved to the door. "Wait here with your father. I will speak with the Earl and explain to him that he neither has my permission, or your father's to do such a thing."

Abby grimaced. "He may not see it that way. As the head of the Gordons, as the Earl of Huntly, he may feel that he has every right to dispose of me as he sees fit."

Claudine gave a little Gallic moue. "He may think what he likes but he will not dispose of my daughter's future to suit him." With those words lingering in the air she left the room.

Abby allowed herself a smile. There was something about this Claudine that brooked no argument and she wondered if she might make some headway with Huntly. In any case, it mattered not, because Abby wouldn't be going anywhere with Sir Robert.

THE KNOCK on the door was soft when it finally came. Abby looked at Claudine, caught by the promise and fear of the moment. Claudine gave the words to allow entry and Abby watched as it swung open. Jeannette stood there, the bundle of clothes in her arms, frowning.

"Well, madame," she said, stepping across the threshold. "I have retrieved them, filthy as they are. They were still in a heap in the corner of the laundry shed. These people here care nothing for cleanliness, I tell you."

Abby held out her hands for the garments. "Thank you, Jeannette you have been very good."

Jeannette placed the bundle in Abby's arms with a sniff. She curtseyed. "Is that all madame?"

"Yes, Jeannette. You may go. I shan't need you any more for the present."

Abby had the bundle of clothes on the floor and was crouching down beside them as soon as Jeannette had closed the door behind her. She took up the cloak, crusted with blood and examined it carefully, feeling every inch of the lining. Nothing. She tossed it aside and examined the leather breeches, still soft and pliable despite the wear and small stains of blood. There was no secret pocket that she could find, no extra padding where there shouldn't be. She shoved it aside and took up the last item, his jerkin. The laces had been cut and one side of it sliced open in a section to allow easier removal. She had little hope that anything would be there, but she wanted to be thorough. She put aside the sleeves that had come loose from their lacing and felt along the side of the jerkin. The leather was stained on the outside but it was the lining that had taken the bulk of the blood. The red bloomed darkly against the blue fabric lining, making it stiff and unyielding. She pressed carefully, willing her fingers to read what her eyes couldn't see. And then she had it. A change in the texture beneath.

Abby cast around for a knife. Across the room was her father's bag. He always carried an eating knife. She was certain it had been there when she'd looked earlier. She rose and went to the bag, digging around until she found it at the bottom. She knelt beside the jerkin again and, taking the knife, slit the stitching of the lining until it was big enough for her to insert her hand. She slid her hand inside and felt around the space provided, stretching her fingers as much as possible around the suspicious area. It took a little more stretching but her fingers hit home. A piece of paper. Small and thin, it was bound in the middle of the lining by a single stitch so it would remain as smooth as possible within the jerkin's lining.

She withdrew the paper carefully and stared at it. It was one sentence only.

A commission to a loyal subject and queen's protector. M

Abby stared at it. It was more than she hoped for, but was it enough? This referred to no one in particular. But surely Huntly would recognise the handwriting?

In the bed her father stirred, mumbling something. She stood up, paper in hand, and peered across at him. His eyes were open. They were clear, with no trace of a fever.

"What are ye doing?" he asked in a hoarse whisper.

She hastened over to the bed and sat beside him, laying a hand on his forehead. It felt cool and dry. She sighed in relief.

"Dada," she said softly. "Oh, thank God. How do you feel? Can I get you something to drink?"

She glanced over at the table and saw there was some remains of the honeyed posset. She grabbed the cup quickly from the table and sat down again, offering it to him.

"Just a little," he said, his voice cracking.

She held it to his lips and, after he took a few sips, he laid his head back on the pillow, exhausted.

"We'll try more later," she said.

He lay quiet for a moment. "What have ye been doing?"

Abby gave him a sharp look, but decided to say nothing on the subject of her mother.

"I was trying to find a way to save Iain."

"Iain?"

"Yes. They've taken him. The French ambassador has demanded that the Earl present Iain to his residence and the Earl has commissioned two of soldiers to escort him there. They've gone this hour."

Calum frowned. "But that's ridiculous? Why would they do that?"

"Because they want to question him in regard to the deaths of

Damville and his aide. And also, of course, because Damville had reported him as a spy. "

"Damville. What made him accuse Iain of spying in the first place?"

"He claimed he found Iain searching through his papers, but of course that was a lie. Iain was nowhere near his room at the time. Earlier though, Iain had discovered that Damville was intent on kidnapping me. He also came here to try and discover any evidence that Huntly's loyalty was shifting away from the Dowager Queen. But Damville didn't know Iain had uncovered that information. I think Damville recognised Iain under his disguise and wanted to prevent him from interfering with his plan to kidnap me."

Calum listened to Abby's words, his frown growing. "Iain didna explain this tae the Earl?"

"He did, but Huntly didn't believe him. He said there was no evidence to support Iain's word and there was no one to vouch for Iain. Huntly said he couldn't accept the word of a man who was welcomed into the household on good faith and was only deceitful in return." She held up the piece of paper. "I found this in your jerkin. What would happen if I showed this to Huntly?"

Calum's face darkened. "I shouldn't do that."

"Then you must tell Huntly that Iain's innocent and he's to be brought back immediately."

"Is that where your mother's gone?"

Abby frowned. "No. Claudine has gone to address something else. The Earl has seen fit to insist that I be shuffled off with Sir Robert to his estate near Stirling, until the marriage contracts between us are finalised."

"What? Sir Robert? Who's he? I never mentioned a Sir Robert as any possibility."

"It matters not because I have no intention of marrying him."

She took her father's hand. "And besides I'm already married, as I keep telling you, and I shall have no other."

Her words echoed in her head and she knew them to be true. So true that anything else she might have tried to convince herself of seemed preposterous now.

"Iain MacGregor."

"Yes, we are bedded in truth, so there is no going back on it now," she said firmly. She leaned forward. "So you must, you have to help him."

"And I am to take your word for that?" he said.

She could see that she'd tired him out, but something in her kept driving onwards. "Yes. And Iain's. He will tell you the same. Please."

"I will, on one condition. That ye agree to have the marriage set aside."

She suppressed the angry retort that came to her and tried to face him calmly. "Why would you request such a thing? Would you let one of your own men suffer torture and more at the hands of the French for something that you are directly responsible for? He didn't kill Damville, in any case. He wasn't caught searching Damville's papers. He was there, looking after me." She gave him a direct look.

Calum turned his head. "This is not for argument." He glanced at the document in her hand and frowned.

The door opened and Claudine entered. "What is not for argument? Abby, your father is just awake and all the two of you can do is fight? But this is not good. Calum you must rest. Recover your strength."

"He refuses to help Iain unless I agree to set aside our marriage."

Claudine raised her brows and frowned at Calum. "But *non*, how could you do such a thing? It is too late for separation.

These two are beyond that. They are as one, Calum. If anyone understands how that is, it must be you."

Calum's expression darkened. "And it's because of that I have tried to keep them apart. It hasna ended well for us and will most probably end badly for them. I canna have that for my daughter."

"Our daughter. And our life together, Calum, it is not finished, and their life together is a different matter."

There were beads of sweat breaking out on his face. He closed his eyes for a moment. Abby took a cloth and started to pat his forehead. He batted the cloth away.

"We have nae life togther, Marie," said Calum. "You made that clear long ago."

"*Non, mon amour,* I left because of my love for you and our daughter, and no other reason."

"A strange way to show love."

"It is a long and complicated story, and one that I suspect you know something about."

"Please," said Abby. "Rest a moment, but I beg you to consider speaking with Huntly about Iain. I have my own life to live, my own mistakes to make. It's not for you to protect me now, I'm not a child."

Calum stared at Abby, his eyes searching hers. His glance dropped to the paper in her hand. Finally he sighed and nodded. "Very well, ask Huntly if he will please wait upon me here, as soon as he's able."

Abby smiled back at him, gratitude filling her. She leaned over and kissed him. "Thank you," she whispered.

HUNTLY STOOD over the bed while Calum, pale and still weak, laboured to sit up. Abby, who'd entered with Huntly, stood near the bed, watching her father carefully, filled with concern.

Though she was desperate for him to clear Iain, she didn't want it at the cost of his life.

Claudine laid a restraining hand on Calum's chest.

"Don't tire yourself, *mon amour*. The seigneiur can hear you just as well lying down."

Huntly nodded. "I would not have you suffering a relapse, Calum. And I will not keep you long. I understand you can support young MacGregor's story?"

"Aye, nephew," said Calum, with a trace of humour at the mode of address. "He was here at my behest. To give aid to my daughter should she need it."

"But why not inform me? What point was the disguise?" Huntly darkened. "Did you not trust me?"

"It wasna that. It was essential tae be discreet because it was possible that a situation might arise that would compromise your position. I wouldna permit that. A disguise seemed best for all parties concerned. I didna anticipate Damville appearing in that manner and being so direct."

"So you think that Damville's visit to discuss French matters with me was a sham? That his sole intention was to kidnap your daughter?" asked Huntly.

"Nay, I feel he did have some legitimate cause to visit, but it was given to him so that he could make the visit openly and contrive a way to get my daughter away from the castle, out from your protection. He managed in the end."

"And you feel this was done because of her connection to me?"

Calum glanced at Claudine. "Aye, to some degree. And as we said, because of the past conflict with Claudine and also myself."

"Can you gather support for this charge?"

"I can, my lord. You have my word."

Huntly sighed. "Very well, on that basis, I'll send a message to recall the men who have taken Iain. With any luck they will not have gone too far."

Abby breathed a sigh of relief that Calum's lie about Iain's purpose had been received as truth. She gave her heartfelt thanks to Huntly and he departed. She moved over to Calum and hugged and kissed him. When she rose from the bed she looked at Claudine.

"I have you to thank as well, I think, Claudine," Abby said. Shyly, she leaned over and kissed Claudine on the cheek.

"Do you think you could find your way to calling me *Maman*, someday?" asked Claudine softly.

Abby looked down at Calum and he smiled weakly and gave a little nod.

"Someday, perhaps," she said.

Claudine nodded. "Thank you. That hope is enough."

Abby nodded, fighting the confusing emotions that warred within her. In the days that she'd spent with this woman since her arrival at Huntly Castle, Claudine had been nothing but kind and supportive. Abby had liked her very much, had been drawn to her in ways she hadn't been drawn to any other woman, yet she found it difficult to match this woman with the hurt and pain she'd caused Abby and her father over all those years. It wasn't something she could snap her fingers and have disappear. It would take time.

She gazed at her father, who was looking at Claudine, a similar mixture of feelings evident on his face. It was for him to decide whether he would be able to understand and forgive her actions. Her explanation to Abby had resonated with truth, but it would take a while to accept it in her heart.

~

ABBY HAD PERFECTED the angle that she must stand at the window in order to see the road leading to the castle. She was in the far end of the hall of the castle's main section and she could just about manage to see the bend of the road as it emerged from the distant woodland. She'd been staring for hours, and in that time there had only been one arrival, a lone carter, bringing stores to the castle. A day had passed since the messenger had been dispatched and as each hour ticked by the niggling concern had grown. Now, as darkness fell on yet another day, the anxiety was becoming fear.

A hand rested on her shoulder and she jumped. Turning, she saw it was Claudine, her eyes full of compassion.

"You must not worry," said Claudine. "He will be here. Come away now, and have something to eat."

"I don't think I could."

"But you have hardly eaten a thing all day. Come *ma petite*, just a quick morsel of food."

Abby forced a smile and shook her head.

"Your father is worried about you, you know. Just eat a bit for his sake?"

Abby sighed and allowed herself to be drawn away. "Is he still abed?"

"Non, he insisted on rising this afternoon and he is sitting in a chair. I tried to make him go back to bed, but he will not listen. Always so stubborn."

Abby smiled wanly. "Little has changed in that regard."

"*Oui.* When he and I were married first...." she gave a quick glance at Abby. "But that's for another time. For now, we must get food into you."

"Has his manner eased with you?" asked Abby.

Though she was hesitant in her own acceptance of Claudine as more than just a friend, she found herself hoping that Claudine could repair things with her father. Marie, not Claudine, she reminded herself, for that was what her father called her.

Claudine's eyes lit up at the question. "It is a little better, I think. But it will require patience."

She asked the question that had been simmering in her mind for some while now. "Will you stay then, to give him some time?"

An instant smile gave Abby her answer. "Oh yes, if he will allow it," said Claudine. "And if you would like me to," she added softly.

Abby paused. The answer surprised her. "Yes, I would like that."

Claudine blinked back the tears that suddenly filled her eyes. Impulsively, Abby rested a hand on her arm and smiled. Claudine put her own hand on top of Abby's and the two regarded each other silently.

The Earl entered. He looked at both of them sternly. "I've spoken with your father," he said to Abby. "And though he has vouched for your young man, I wonder if I must reconsider. I've also had Margaret pouring tales into my ear."

"Margaret?" said Abby, slightly alarmed. "What has she to say?"

"Well, on top of the accusation that he behaved in an inappropriate manner towards her, she says that he spent the night with you. She saw him coming out of your room early one morning."

Abby suppressed a snort. She shouldn't be surprised the Margaret had watched Iain's movements so carefully that she knew when he'd arrived and left Abby's room that night he'd spent with her. And that Margaret would try to link it to her tale of Iain's misconduct to herself.

"While it's true that Iain spent the night with me, there is nothing untoward about it since, as I have stated before, he is my husband. As for Margaret's other accusation, in my view, I think she might have read more into his gallantry than was there. As I'm certain your sons will confirm."

She'd added the last bit with some emphasis, hoping it was enough to convince the Earl not to pursue it further.

He frowned at her again but nodded slowly. "Yes, I fear you may be right in this case. And your father says he has some proof to verify Iain's statement, and he will provide it as soon as he can obtain it. So, I imagine there is nothing further needed. I shan't hold MacGregor. He'll be free to go." He glanced out of the window. "If the message should reach him in time."

Abby laid a hand on his arm. "I give you my most ardent thanks, my lord."

He sighed, nodded and with only a nod to Claudine, left the room. Claudine squeezed Abby's arm.

"All will be well and your father will give his blessing to your marriage," said Claudine.

Abby sighed and nodded. "I hope so. But while I would wish for his blessing, my father's refusal won't make any difference to the outcome. Iain and I will be together." If he survives this, she added to herself silently.

"I know, *ma cherie*, I know. But be patient with your father. He is lamenting the loss of his child and all that is past. In time he will realise that there is much promise in the future."

Abby closed her eyes and let the words resonate inside her. There was a truth to them and they gave Abby comfort. She would do as Claudine suggested, if she could. She opened her eyes and a movement in the distance caught her eye. A small group of riders emerged. She studied them carefully, not daring to breathe until the familiar beloved form became more distinct. Iain. He had returned.

She turned to Claudine, her face alight and Claudine took her into her arms. "Oh, *ma cherie*, I am so happy for you." She pulled back and looked at Abby, tucking in a stray lock, straightening her gown. "Now go, greet your *amour.*"

Abby nodded briefly and hurried away, through the castle and into the courtyard. By the time she arrived, the horses were just coming in through the gate. She ran to Iain and he dismounted, sweeping her up into his arms, kissing her deeply.

She pulled back, touching his face. "Oh, Iain, Iain. Thank God you're safe."

"I owe my release to ye, quean, And I willna ever forget that."

"I'll be by your side to remind you every day of the rest of your life."

"Aye, I'll hold ye tae that."

He leaned down and kissed her again and she tasted the salt and dirt of his journey and underneath, the pure essence that made him Iain. She knew his word to be truth, that he would never be the Iain of the ballad, but the real Iain, the Iain who was a proud MacGregor, forever tied to Glen Strae and forever tied to her.

CHAPTER 23

The spring air was fresh against her skin. Abby inhaled deeply, gazing up at the mountains that rose so bold and imposing before her. It was a welcome sight and one that at times she thought she'd never see again. And now this moment, this peace and happiness she felt was so much more precious to her. She had realised her dream at last.

They had arrived last night. Her father, still weak enough but determined to be present on this important occasion, had insisted on riding his horse, so their progress had been slow. Claudine had been very attentive on the journey, easing his discomfort with salves to his slow healing wound. Fenella had accompanied them, the threat of witchcraft still hanging over her. They had waited until the end of winter before travelling here to Glen Strae, so that Calum might come in person to give his support to the marriage in person. Iain had gone ahead to prepare his family and his home for the return of his bride.

It had taken only a little persuasion for her father to give his blessing on the marriage, especially after she made it clear that taking up her role as wife to Iain wasn't dependent on his permission and that the proof they had wedded might very well be already growing inside her.

"Are ye anxious tae start the day, quean?" asked Iain, his hands sliding around her waist.

She leaned back against him, savouring the warmth and luxury of his embrace. She had missed him terribly in the time she'd been parted from him and last night, at everyone's insistence she had shared a bed with Claudine. Today would be the first day of their official wedded life. A day of celebration. Anything for an excuse to feast, Iain had told her.

She turned to face him and put her arms around him, pulling him in for a kiss. "I am anxious for something to begin," she said eventually.

His eyes twinkled and he caressed her cheek. "It willna be long. We'll away tae bed early, I think."

"Oh, yes. After the first toast or two, I doubt they'll notice where we are."

"Och, but they will witness the bedding lass. Tae make it official."

She laughed. "But that's ridiculous."

"Nay, it's only a bit of fun."

"But there's nothing virginal about me." She placed his hand on her stomach. "Most definitely not."

He gave her a questioning look and she nodded. "There's no escaping me now, Highland man."

A broad smile broke out on his face and he swept her up into a tight embrace. "Aye but that's marvellous news. Ye couldna have pleased me more." He kissed her hard, his arms holding her tightly.

She pulled back, eventually, panting a little and laughing. "If you're not careful you'll crush both me and the baby."

He gave a wry smile. "Not you, *Francach*. There's no holding you down, if ye want something."

She gave him a light slap on his arm. "I'd say there's just as much wanting on your side, Highlander, as on mine."

"Aye, and dinna forget it."

THE MUSIC, though not as sophisticated as that played at the court, or Huntly Castle, was certainly enthusiastic. MacGregor had managed to unearth something resembling a tambour which was now being tipped away at with great energy by one of the sons of a MacAlpin chief. Alasdair, Iain's brother, was doing the honours on the recorder and another MacGregor had somehow located a hurdy gurdy and was earnestly attempting to master it. The dancers paid little attention to the skill level of the musicians, their own movements and steps finding an uninhibited rhythm and measure made even looser by the flow of drink.

Abby saw Iain's sister, Morag, dancing among the others, a graceful beauty moving almost like a sylph among the earthbound. Abby didn't recognise the partner, but she saw the handsome face and the broad back and thought them an elegant pair. Morag had been difficult at the first meeting, the unruly but loyal sister who was suspicious of any newcomer. This time she'd thawed a little and seemed to accept the idea that Abby was Iain's wife. It would be a journey of patience with her, though, Abby knew.

Abby heard her father laugh heartily at something the MacGregor had said and, leaning over, she saw a look of pure enjoyment on his face. She hadn't expected that. Her father, who had inhabited the French court and played music for some of the most cultured dignitaries of Europe, at home in a Highland dwelling, speaking Gaelic, albeit brokenly, but nonetheless communicating in a language she knew little of at the moment.

Claudine sat beside Calum, her face beaming as she looked at her husband, his hand enclosed in hers. In the past few months since his injury Claudine's patience had won out. Calum had gradually allowed her back into his life, his mind and eventually his bed. And Abby was happy for them. She wasn't certain she could ever call Claudine "Maman", but she was increasingly regarding her as something more than a friend.

Another plate of food was laid on the table in front of her. Abby groaned inwardly. She was still only just recovering her appetite for food after the past few months, but today had taxed her abilities. A small piece of fowl and plenty of bread had been as much as she could manage. But Iain, sitting next to her, seemed more than happy to manage her portion as well as his own. The drink flowed just as heavily as the food was piled high, but at least Iain was more restrained in that area.

She nibbled a little more on the food and watched as the dance ended and another struck up. It was a Scots branle, and ordinarily she'd have been eager to dance, but she was tired and was content to only watch it. She sat there for a while longer enjoying the various dances, picking a little more at the food, half dozing, until she felt Iain grasp her hand and kiss it.

"Soon, it will be the last toast and away to bed."

"Can't we slip away now? Perhaps they'll let us alone. Forget about the bedding."

"Nay, I'm afraid we canna do that."

She sighed. "I know. Just let me get a breath of air a moment, so I can wake up."

"I'll come with ye." He started to rise.

"No, no. It's not necessary. And if you come they'll all think that we're escaping to bed and they'll follow us."

He hesitated and then nodded. "Aye, ye may be right. Dinna linger, though." He pulled her down for a quick kiss. "I'd have ye by my side as much as possible, now."

She pulled away, and gave him one last lingering look before leaving. She weaved her way through the back of the hall as discreetly as possible, making for the door and then outside to the back of the castle, near the stables. She could still hear some of the music drifting out of the hall and it made her smile. Such a place. Such a people. They were her people now and here was her home. There were no regrets. Except perhaps that her father and Claudine would leave soon. To go…well somewhere, just the two of them. He'd hinted that it wouldn't be far, that this somewhere was in the Highlands. Perhaps it was his childhood home and there the two of them would be safe. They'd promised they would visit Abby frequently. She must be content with that.

A horse neighed and then was quickly silenced. In the dusk she could just make out a figure quietly leading a highland pony towards the gatehouse. Abby strained to see who it was. The trews, the padded leather jerkin and the short swathe of plaid were all too familiar.

She walked out from the shadow of the stone wall and strode over to the figure. "Morag," she hissed. "What are you doing?"

Iain's sister halted and turned, frowning. "Leave me be. It's nae concern of yours."

"It is my concern. And Iain's. You promised you wouldn't go reiving and fighting Campbells again."

"I canna help it. I have nae choice in the matter. This celebration, it's too tempting for the Campbells. They're bound tae try a cattle raid tonight, at the very least."

"Surely someone else is keeping watch?"

"Aye, but they dinna ken the best places as I do."

"But on your own? Are you daft?"

She drew herself up. "I'm more than capable. Besides, I'm no on my own. I'm meeting the others at the end of the road. We left one by one. I'm the last."

"Well, ride down there and tell them you won't be joining

them tonight. And if you don't return within a quarter of an hour, I'll tell Iain. And I'm certain you don't want him chasing after you."

Morag's face darkened and remained silent, considering. "Aye, all right," she said eventually. "I ken that it's your wedding night and ye hardly want Iain clambering around in the bog." She gave a saucy smile. "Consider it my wedding present."

With a nod she mounted the horse and galloped off. Abby stood there waiting. After a while she felt a presence beside her. "Is something amiss?"

Abby turned and smiled at him. "No, nothing's amiss. Your sister was talking with me. And now, you're here, we can go in, have the toast and head for bed. With company, or without, I want you lying next to me within the hour."

He put his arm around her and squeezed her tight. "Naked, ye dinna say, naked."

"We have to be naked when they witness us in bed?" she asked, alarmed.

"Aye, lass, of course. And examine us both tae make sure there's no fault with either of us."

She stared at him. "Well they can go whistle for that. I will not."

"But it's the Highland way. And ye're married tae a Highlander, so ye maun do as we do."

She folder her arms. "Again, I tell you, I will not. They may come into the bedroom and watch us lying there *clothed*, but that's all. I'll tell your father that this minute."

She took his hand and walked with great purpose across the courtyard to the entrance, Iain laughing behind her. Once inside, the noise and heat took her aback for a moment, but she resumed her stride and made her way to the MacGregor.

He looked up at her, smiled and nodded. "Daughter."

Standing before him she curtseyed. "My lord, I understand the bedding involves, uh, certain aspects which I find I am unable to comply with."

He gave her a puzzled look. "Such as?"

She glanced over at her father who regarded her curiously. She took a deep breath, struggling how to phrase the words.

"Iain explained that, well that the company follows us to the bedroom and …."

A hand was slipped through her arm. "Ye mustna mind the song," said Morag. "It's just a song. We'll sing it in Gaelic so not to embarrass ye."

Abby looked at Morag in surprise, her dress somewhat askew and her hair no longer artfully arranged, but still convincing as a woman who had perhaps danced and drunk a little too much. She smiled, happy that Morag had chosen to obey Abby.

Morag leaned over and whispered, "Dinna mind Iain's words, he was only codding ye."

Abby blinked and looked around at Iain who stood a little back, his eyes full of amusement. She gave him a threatening look and turned to the MacGregor.

"Well if it is as Morag says and it's sung in Gaelic, then I'm certain it will be fine, my lord."

"Aye," said the MacGregor. "That's all right then." His expression was still a little puzzled but a hint of laughter lurked in his eyes.

Morag led Abby away linking her arm tightly in Abby's. "Ye owe me a favour now. Two if I have a mind to be strict."

The tone had been light, but Abby wondered if it was meant in kindness. She looked at Morag.

"Nay, I dinna think badly of ye for doing what ye did. In truth, I am glad ye're my sister-in-law. I like ye. Ye have fire. And Iain needs a strong woman. Not some wilting flower who can exist only in court. Ye'll make a fine Highland woman, one day."

Abby felt tears come to her eyes at the compliment. "Thank you Morag. I can't tell you how much those words mean to me."

"And dinna be too hard on Iain. He would have never let ye say it all tae Father. He likes tae tease, that one, but he doesna let it go too far. Not usually," she added.

"You heard him, out in the courtyard?"

Morag nodded. "He loves you, I can see that. He'll do anything for you."

Abby nodded. "And I love him the same."

Morag squeezed her hand. Iain came up beside Morag.

"What have ye been saying tae my wife, sister?"

"Nothing ye need concern yourself with." Morag smiled at Abby and left them.

Iain shook his head. "She needs some watching now. Time she was married."

"Well I'd say she would have something to say about that. She won't be 'arranged', that much is clear."

"Aye. But that's for another day." He looked down at Abby and took her hand. "Now it's time for us to go to bed."

"So they can examine us naked to see if we have faults?"

He grinned. "I'm the only one who will be examining you naked. Ever."

She laughed. "I might do my own examination of your naked body as well."

He pulled her into his arms and kissed her soundly and deeply, amid growing roars of approval from the guests. Stomping feet and loud toasts and orders to go abed soon drove Abby and Iain up the stairs to their chamber to begin their new life.

THIS VOLUME CONCLUDES ABBY'S STORY.

Try the next one in The Highland Ballad Series, *Highland Lioness.* Read the excerpt that follows.

HISTORICAL NOTE

The Earls of Huntly were prominent figures in Scottish History beginning with the first Earl, Alexander Gordon, who was created Earl of Huntly in 1445. His son was Chancellor of Scotland for many years.

This novel takes place during the time of the fourth Earl of Huntly, George. He was the son of John Gordon, and Margaret Stewart, the illegitimate daughter of James IV. John's father, the third Earl (John died before he could become Earl), had married twice and the second marriage was in his later years. There are no recorded children from that marriage, so I took advantage of that and put Calum as a product of the second marriage, born just before the Earl's death, thereby making Calum the uncle to George, the 4th Earl of Huntly.

George had inherited his title in 1524 at the age of ten and was virtually raised at court. He was great friends with his uncle, James V who was his contemporary and was a natural choice as advisor to the Dowager Queen after her husband died in 1542. As commander of the King's Army, he defeated the English at the Battle of Haddon Rig in 1542 and after the King's death, was a member of the Council of Regency under James Hamilton, 2nd

Earl of Arran and Cardinal Beaton. In 1546, after the murder of Cardinal Beaton he was appointed Chancellor. He was captured at the Battle of Pinkie Cleugh against the English in 1547 and held prisoner. Three months later he made a daring escape at Christmas time, worthy of Errol Flynn. In 1550 he accompanied the Dowager Queen, Mary of Guise, to France when she went to visit her daughter, the Mary, Queen of Scots.

The Dowager Queen's influence and power grew and she employed a policy directing various regional lords to settle dispute in their areas, rather than interfere personally. That directed blame away from the crown, but it wasn't always successful. That proved to be the case in 1554 when the Dowager Queen directed Huntly to take action against some miscreants in the north and he returned without accomplishing anything. He claimed that he was unable to raise enough men to carry out her commands. The Dowager Queen was furious. She thought his actions flouted her authority and she imprisoned him in Edinburgh Castle until the following May. At that point she considered banishing him to France, but settled for a hefty fine instead.

His loyalty, which is called into question in the novel, was to the Queen and the Dowager Queen up to this point, though it wouldn't be surprising that it was shaky at best. The lords were growing restless and factions were springing up. The Protestant faction seized key places in Edinburgh and other important cities in 1559. The Dowager Queen ordered Huntly and others to march on Edinburgh and seize it back. The group opened negotiations instead and an agreement was reached in late summer. In March of 1560 Huntly joined the Lords of the Congregation. A few months later the Dowager Queen died. Huntly was prepared to continue to accept Mary (who was still in France) as Queen, until she transferred the Earldom of Moray, which had been given to the Earl of Huntly in 1549, to her half-brother Lord

James Stewart. Following that action, Huntly withdrew to his estates.

Mary Queen of Scots, newly returned to Scotland, toured the north-east in August 1562, and was refused entry to Inverness Castle on Gordon's orders. The Queen's forces captured the Castle before moving to Aberdeen where she issued a summons for Gordon. He refused to answer and was outlawed . He subsequently marched on Aberdeen but was defeated by James Stewart, 1st Earl of Moray at the Battle of Corrichie in October 1562. He died of apoplexy after his capture, and his son, Sir John was executed in Aberdeen. Huntly was posthumously forfeited by the Scottish Parliament in May 1563.

AUTHOR'S NOTE

Originally from Philadelphia, Kristin Gleeson lives in Ireland, in the West Cork Gaeltacht, where she works as a librarian. She holds a Masters in Library Science and a Ph.D. in history and for a time was an administrator of a large archives, library and museum in America. She also served as a public librarian in America and was a professional harper and storyteller for a time.

Kristin Gleeson has also published *The Celtic Knot Series* and *The Renaissance Sojourner Series*, as well as *In Praise of the Bees*, a novel of 6th century Ireland. A free novelette prequel, *A Trick of Fate* is available free on e retailers. In addition to her novels, a biography on a First Nations Canadian woman, *Anahareo, A Wilderness Spirit*, is also available.

If you have enjoyed this book please post a review. It helps so much towards getting the book noticed.

If you go to the author website and join the mailing list to receive news of forthcoming releases, special offers and events you'll receive *Along the Far Shores,* and *A Treasure Beyond Worth* a **FREE prequel e-novelette** and the ebook *Along the Far Shores.*

www.kristingleeson.com

Music is a big part of Kristin's life and many of the books have music connected to them. Listen to the music while you read- go to www.kristingleeson/music and download the files. Keep checking back as more pieces will be added to the library in the course of time.

HIGHLAND LIONESS
Book Four of the Highland Ballad Series

KRISTIN GLEESON

An Tig Beag Press

EXCERPT

CHAPTER 1

*M*orag tugged at the wet neck of Iain's old leather jerkin that draped loose on her, and peered through the mist that hung heavy around her. She'd managed to adjust his old trews at least, so that she could move with ease in them. She peered again. Nothing. She shifted her highland pony cautiously for a better vantage, wincing at the sound of the hooves. Hopefully the mist would muffle the noise.

She called softly to her ghilly, "Rob."

A figure came up beside her. "Here, *cailín dhu*," he murmured.

"Are they there?"

"Aye. In the field below."

"Is there anyone attending?"

"At the far end."

"Davey and Calum, are they in place?"

"Aye."

She nodded. "How many can we manage in this mist? Five, six?"

"Less I'd say in this mist."

Morag gave a little snort. "Och, no. We'll go for six."

She heard the soft sigh. "Aye. Six it is." He moved away, swallowed by the mist.

She bit off a remark and wished yet again that it was Davey at her side and not Rob. Davey would have agreed with her sudden impulse to take six. Still, it was the point they were making and not the number. The Campbells would be furious that their prize cattle had once again been taken from under their very noses.

Morag started to urge her highland pony forward but a hand took her bridle. A familiar figure appeared out of the mist. Iain. She frowned and started to speak but he cut her off

"Signal them all to leave," he said in a low voice that left no room for anything but obedience.

She shook her head. She wouldn't obey him, no matter that he was her older brother and she had solemnly sworn to him three years ago she wouldn't go reiving again. That he hadn't caught her until now, she must count herself lucky and owe to the fact that he'd been living somewhere else for the most part, until events had allowed him and his wife to return to Glen Strae.

"I won't repeat myself," he said, tone razor edge sharp now.

Morag bit her lip, weighing the consequences against the beauty of this coup. To take the Campbells' prize cattle right under their noses. Who could resist such a challenge? And to the Campbells, who deserved every last humiliation that could be heaped upon them and more.

Iain clasped her wrist in a vice-like grip. "Will I have to take you away, lass?"

She knew what that meant and the mortification she would feel in front of the men who looked to her, whose respect she'd won over the years, was something he knew she wouldn't bear. She suppressed a fierce surge of rage and jerked her wrist from his hold.

"You no longer understand these matters, Iain. You've been gone too long."

He gave a snort. "I understand well enough and I'll not be moved. Will ye give the call or will I?"

His accent came thick and strong and she knew that he was very angry. She pulled in a frustrated breath and gave the faint bird call they used. Iain's posture eased and she glared at him.

"There. You can go now. It's done."

Iain frowned down at her. "We'll go. Together. Now. The rest can follow when they can." He reached over to take her reins but she pulled the pony aside before he could.

"No need for that. I'll come on my own."

Iain studied her and then relented. "Lead on."

She pursed her lips, and with a toss of her head and a few muttered words started the journey back to the castle.

THE MACGREGOR STOOD tall and imposing in the castle hall, despite the stick supporting him and the fur draped on his shoulders for extra warmth, as the fire was only embers at this time of the night. His grey hair hung loose around him, almost obscuring the deep scar to one side of his face. But his eyes were clear and full of fury.

Morag stood before her father and knew that this time there would be no softening, no words that would make him proud of her and her defence of the clan and its proud heritage that traced back to the first ruler of the Scots, MacAlpin. Beside her, Iain shifted his weight slightly, causing her father's attention to turn to him for a moment. But it was a moment only. His piercing eyes focused on her once again.

"So, you went against your pledge that Iain made you give." His tone was cold, a knife edge. He spoke in Gaelic, the language common here in the glen. He would want all in the household to know she was being reprimanded.

"I got to her before any harm was done, though," said Iain.

She glared at Iain, furious at him for betraying her to her father. How long had her father known about the pledge she gave to Iain three years ago? She straightened, determined not to let her father see her anxiety.

"It would have been six cattle at least, Father. Right under their noses." She made a disdainful noise. "They deserve it for the little care they take."

MacGregor brushed her comment aside with a wave of his hand. "I don't care for them, or what they do with their cattle. The point is you broke your pledge. And a MacGregor doesn't break his pledge. In all your eighteen years, did you not understand that much?"

She blanched under his stare, his words hitting home. "Nineteen years," she muttered and Iain gave a soft 'wheest' to hold her tongue.

"What did you say?" her father demanded.

She lifted her chin. "I said nineteen years. I am nineteen."

"Is it no wonder I mistake your age when you behave as though you're a babe?" He struck the heavy stick on the stone floor, the noise resounding in the hall. "You're my daughter and I expect you to behave like a MacGregor."

She bit her lip, fighting the tears. She wouldn't show him her distress. "I am sorry, Father, I did what I thought was best. The pledge to Iain I gave under duress." She gave her brother a dark look. "He didn't think I would hold to it, I'm sure."

Iain gave a nearly imperceptible shake of his head. She sniffed.

"It is clear you didn't understand my full meaning, daughter." He frowned and gave Iain a brief nod. "I've no choice, it seems. You're right, Iain. She must leave here and go to the court."

"What? No!" Morag said, shocked into the protest. "There's no need for that."

"There's every need," said MacGregor. "Since you clearly don't know how to behave as a lady of this castle, a daughter of MacGregor, we'll see if court can make a lady of you."

She couldn't leave her home, her Davey. Leave everything that meant anything to her. Morag cast her glance around the hall, noticing Abby, Iain's wife, seated in a chair by the table, her belly, swollen with child, only partially hidden by the large shawl she clasped around her shoulders. Next to her was crouched, Cú, the dog that had been Iain's but was clearly Abby's these days, loyal and protective, especially now. She'd been pregnant once before, but she'd lost that child before it was born, making this one even more special.

"Abby, please. Dinna let them send me away. Tell them I will mind them now. That I didn't mean to flout Iain. I will honour my pledge now. I promise."

Abby's eyes filled with sympathy. "Och, Morag, I know you couldn't help it."

Morag couldn't resist giving a small inward smile, despite the fact that she knew her cause was lost. After three years in Iain's company the faint trace of French accent that hinted Abby's years at the French court and her mother's heritage had disappeared, leaving a decided Scottish burr that gave her hesitant Gaelic a throaty sound that Iain loved. She'd grown to love and admire Iain's wife and was glad to have her as a sister, though her support was missing now. Morag turned back to her father and frowned.

She lifted her chin further. She wouldn't flinch or make any further fuss. "I am to go to court, then. When am I to go?"

"As soon as may be," said her father.

"And will Iain and Abby accompany me?"

She saw the unspoken communication between her father and Iain. Her heart sank further, knowing what was to come.

"Nay," said Iain. "Abby is too close to her time. It's not safe. And I won't leave her."

"Some of the ghillies will accompany you," said her father. "And a woman from the household."

Morag nodded, her face grim but taking care not to show the anxiety that sprang up. She knew no one at court. She'd never had any desire to go there and practise all the courtly manners and skills to negotiate the turbulent waters of the Scottish court. Especially now with John Knox landed on the Scottish shores, stirring up unrest among the troublesome Protestant earls who sought to overthrow the Dowager Queen's authority as regent.

"What of Mister Knox and his ilk?" asked Morag. "Will it be safe for me there among such people?"

Her father frowned. "Don't think that using some clever angles will get you out of going, lassie."

"It will be safe enough," said Iain. "Better this than have you wreak havoc across the countryside and rouse the Campbells' ire further. Things are bad enough."

"Don't fret," said Abby. "I'll write to the Dowager Queen and ensure you a warm welcome."

Morag gave her curt nod. "That is kind of you, sister, but don't go to any trouble on my account."

Abby gave a wry smile. "It's no trouble, Morag. I'll do it."

Morag returned her smile with one that didn't reach her eyes. One letter would make no difference, she was certain. The time ahead would be something to endure. But first she must meet with Davey. Maybe he would have some idea to prevent this.

IAIN CAME up beside her and grabbed her arm just as she was about to enter her chamber. Though she had height enough, he loomed over her and his piercing blue eyes looked into hers, a hint of frustration and anger present.

"You were lucky tonight, *a cailín*. And I know you think being sent to court is the worst thing that could happen to you, but it's for the best. Father could have been harsher in his punishment."

She snorted angrily. "Well, I don't know any harsher one."

He frowned. "And do you understand that if you'd killed one of the Campbells, a punishment beyond what you could dream would come down on all of us? Campbell is not a man to be trifled with. Did you learn nothing from three years ago?" His voice had risen slightly, his words fierce and filled with anger.

She bit her lip, remembering when Iain was under the threatening shadow of banishment and the clan thrown into disgrace. It had only been by sheer luck and the wiles of Abby and Iain that they had managed to get his good name, and the clan's, restored.

"Yes, I did. And I'm sorry. But I've been careful. I would never kill any one of them. As much as they might deserve it."

Iain sighed and shook his head. "You could have had the clan put to the horn. We'd be disbanded and banished. Where would we be then? And our tenants?"

She shook herself from his hold, too ashamed, but unwilling to concede the point. "It wouldn't have happened," she muttered. "It didn't happen."

MORAG DREW up her pony outside the croft. The mountain was to her back and rose high behind her. The air was clear, but with a distinct bite from the late winter day. She drew her cloak around her as the wind caught it and lifted it from her skirts. After dismounting swiftly, she made her way through the gate to the door until she caught sight of a flash of colour in the stone shed to the right of the croft, across the small cobblestoned yard. It wasn't a large tenancy, but it provided enough for Davey and his widowed mother.

Morag turned away from the door and made her way to the

shed, the penned ewes bleating as she passed. It would soon be lambing time and Davey had brought the ones at risk here, ready for his trusty and capable assistance. He came out of the shed as she approached and his brow furrowed in concern when he saw her. She admired the glint off his auburn hair, hanging in locks about his face. It was a face some might call pretty, with his long lashes, but she only could call it dear.

"Is something amiss, Mor—Mistress?" he asked in Gaelic

She bit her lip at the correction. He'd began to insist on calling her 'mistress' this past year or more, since Iain had reminded him after he'd overheard Davey's banter with Morag. She had scoffed at Iain's remark, saying Davey was a loyal clansman, a playmate of years and now her closest friend. Iain had just given her a look that spoke volumes.

"Morag, Davey. I've told you to call me Morag. Especially when we're alone."

Davey shifted on his feet and looked down as she came up beside him. He was little taller than her, with a wiry strength she admired. Perfect for these highland moors and crags. She put her hand on his arm. He blushed.

"Of course, mistress – and we shouldn't be alone. Ye know that it's wrong."

"It isn't for us, Davey. Never for us." She squeezed his arm. "Besides, it's important that we speak." She took his hand. "They're sending me away. To court."

Davey released her hand and stood back, his face full of surprise. "Nay. Why is that?"

"Because of what happened two nights ago. My father is determined that I should be taught a lesson for breaking my pledge to Iain."

"Pledge? You broke a pledge?"

She nodded. "Yes, well, not really. I mean, Iain never could imagine I would keep to it. He wanted me to give up reiving and taking action against the Campbells." She emphasised the last phrase, though she was certain he would know how important it was.

"You broke a pledge, though." His voice was filled with scorn. "To your family."

She looked into his hazel eyes and frowned to see the disappointment there. "But it was for a higher honour. The honour of the clan! You understand that, Davey, you must."

He nodded slowly, his eyes clearing. "Yes, for the honour of the clan. Yes, you have it right. As you always do."

She leaned over and kissed his cheek, relieved. He blushed again and looked down. "Mistress, you mustn't do that. It isn't seemly."

She placed a hand on his cheek. "It's me, Davey. Your playmate of years. Your companion in arms. And now won't you pledge to me?"

He looked up, startled. "I'm pledged to you already."

She frowned. "To my family. Nay, I mean pledge to *me*." It was her turn to look down, a small blush forming on her face. "Pledge your heart, Davey," she added softly. "For you have mine."

She leaned over and kissed him, a soft kiss, full on the lips. It was her first and she'd been long dreaming of how it would be and was glad to find it pleasant and warm. He kissed her back, but only for a moment, then pulled away with a gasp.

"I can't do this. It's madness. You're my lady, Morag."

She tugged him forward again. "Nay, Davey. I'm Morag and you are Davey." She took his hand. "And I am pledging myself to you, Davey."

He shook his head. "You don't mean it."

She smiled at him, her eyes twinkling. "I do of course and you must do as I say, for am I not your Lady Morag?"

He groaned. "How can I refuse you anything? You know I'll do whatever you ask of me."

"And I request we plight our troth. Here. Now. Before they send me away. So you know that it will always be you. And nothing they do will change that."

He gave her a puzzled look and then nodded. "Aye, I'll do it. But if at any time you wish to be released from it, I will do so."

"Of course. But that will never happen." She beamed at him and took his hands. "For you are such a grand companion and have always been in all the times we've had together. Better than any brother of mine."

He gave her a rueful look. "Only because you can bully me better than your own brothers."

She laughed. "Nay. That may be true, but I do care for you, Davey." She pressed a kiss on his lips again, fierce and long. Davey put a tentative arm around her. She sighed. Two kisses in one day. Her heart gave a leap. She was becoming a woman indeed. No courtier could gainsay her as a backwards highland lass.

She pulled away. "Now, we must say the words to each other. I'll go first and then you can repeat them back."

He bit his lip and then nodded. She took up his right arm and clasped it hard, then pulled out the bit of ribbon she had tucked in her kirtle and wrapped it around their clasped wrists.

"I Morag Elizabeth, daughter of Gregor MacGregor, descendant of MacAlpin, do pledge my troth to you, Davey of Glen Strae of clan Gregor until such time as we decide to release each other. Or," her eyes twinkled, "we bed each other as husband and wife, as custom dictates, and become truly wed."

Davey opened his mouth in surprise but closed it after a moment. He cleared his throat and at her nod he repeated the words.

"There," she said when he had finished. "It's done. We're pledged to each other." She released the ribbon and reached up to hug him tightly. His arms went tentatively around her waist. "I shall keep this ribbon with me always, Davey. So I know that no matter where I am, I will always have a part of us with me."

He nodded. "Of course. As you like." He released her and stepped back, shifting uncomfortably. "What's to do now?"

"Now we must create a secret code and manner in which we communicate while I am at court. So we'll know how we go on. And in case I might need you. For I don't intend to let them stop me from discovering a way we might revenge upon the Campbells."

"You still intend tae go reiving?"

"No, of course not. At least I don't think it could be managed so far away." She looked at him, a hopeful expression on her face. "Unless you have devised a manner in which it may be done?"

"What? Nothing of the sort. It seems more than impossible."

She sighed. "Yes, just so. But I won't give up. There might be some way, as I said. And I will tell you when I find it, so you can help me. You will help me, Davey?"

He smiled at her. "Yes, you know I will. Have I ever done anything but do as you wish?"

She grinned broadly. "Never. Is it any wonder I care for you so much?"

She hugged him again. "Now, I will have some of the ghillies with me. Rob, probably and a few others. I can send him to you with a note or something of that nature to tell you what I discover, or if I need you. My family will doubtless send me word from time to time and I will endeavour to send them messages for you in my replies."

He nodded slowly taking in her words. "Fine. I'll await your word."

She squeezed his arm. "Good. Now I must away. Someone is bound to be looking for me by now."

She put her arms around him and drew him closer once again. "Now give me a kiss again Davey," she said softly. "Forbye I don't know when I'll see you next and I want something to remember you by."

She pressed her lips to his and he returned the kiss hesitantly. She pressed tighter, wanting to feel as much as possible before she let him go. She felt him gasp, his mouth opening slightly and she pulled away, grinning. "Have you ever been kissed so well, Davey?"

He flushed deeply. "Never."

She gave him a smug smile. "Yes, well, be sure you remember that."

Morag drew away and headed towards her pony. She grasped the reins and pulled herself up on its back, blew him a kiss and trotted away. She'd done what she could to make experience at court bearable. She had her pledge with Davey and thoughts of revenge on the Campbells to help bolster her among the cruel and ruthless courtiers she was certain she would encounter.